CLAIRE KANN

Swoon **READS**

Swoon Reads | New York

YA

A SWOON READS BOOK

An imprint of Feiwel and Friends and Macmillan Publishing Group LLC
175 Fifth Avenue, New York, NY 10010

Our books may be purchased in bulk for promotional, educational, or business use. Please contact your local bookseller or the Macmillan Corporate and Premium Sales Department at (800) 221-7945 ext. 5442 or by e-mail at MacmillanSpecialMarkets@macmillan.com.

Library of Congress Control Number: 2017944696
ISBN 978-1-250-13612-1 (hardcover) / ISBN 978-1-250-13882-8 (ebook)

Book design by Liz Dresner

First Edition—2018

10 9 8 7 6 5 4 3 2 1

swoonreads.com

LET'S TALK ABOUT LOVE

CHAPTER

1

Everything was perfect before Alice unlocked her dorm room door.

"I want to break up," Margot said.

Alice stood, stopping and starting whatever she had planned to say. Her mouth moved, forming shapes of words, but only tiny ticks of noise echoed in the back of her throat. A sharp, bruising ache crept upward from the pit of her stomach.

"I know this seems kind of sudden." Margot had begun to wring her hands. One of the things she and Alice had in common was their aversion to direct conflict. "I wanted to wait until I moved out but I've really been thinking about things and it's better to just get it out of the way now so I can focus on my finals. Instead of this."

"Why?" Alice asked. Unable to meet Margot's eyes, she stared at her arms crossed over her chest.

"Because you won't have sex with me," Margot answered.

Alice knew it before the words even left her mouth. Of course this was about sex—what else could it have possibly been about? She held her back straight, refusing to hunch her shoulders to hold the pain in. She allowed it to fill her, allowed that raging, anxious monster to spread. The tension in her legs kept telling her to *RUN*, but where would she go? They shared a room and still had a week to go before the semester ended. Eventually, she'd have to come back. Eventually, they'd have to have this conversation.

Couldn't Margot just send her a breakup text like a decent human being?

"We had sex this morning," Alice replied. Dread pumped through her veins, making her voice sound as skinned as she felt. "Twice."

"That's not the kind of sex I want to have," Margot said. She tucked one of her wild blond curls behind her ear.

That monster flared white-hot inside Alice. The only reason why Alice bothered to have sex was to make her girlfriend happy. If Margot didn't want it, what in the hell was the point?

"Sure fooled me. If I recall, which I do, there was a lot of happy screaming involved."

"Because you're good at it!" Margot stood, walking toward Alice, hands outstretched. "You know exactly what I like. I can't say the same about you." Margot sighed. "I want to touch you, Alice."

"You touch me all the time." Alice's limp hands dangled while Margot held her wrists. "You're touching me now."

"I want to lie in bed and kiss you everywhere for hours. I want to be able to show you how happy you make me."

"We do that, too. You *know* me: I need cuddles or I will die."

"And that's something I love about you, but when it's time to get serious, it's like you turn into a different person. I want to have passionate sex with you. It's weird that I can't reciprocate anything."

"It is not *weird*." Alice snatched herself away.

"It makes me feel weird," Margot clarified, her voice pleading. "It's like you don't like me as much as you say you do. When we have sex, it's because *I* want to. You never initiate it. I'm not allowed to do anything to you. On the rare times we do make out, I swear to God I can feel your mind wandering."

"But I like kissing you!"

"And the worst part is you don't trust me enough to tell me why."

Why, why, why? Why did Margot need to know about the *why*? As if she were a problem to be fixed, as if Margot's magic fingers could make it all better. She realized, before the concept of *Them* was even a blip in the universe, that Margot would never understand. Before they decided to be together, Margot had brought other girls to their room so often they had to create a Scarf on the Doorknob system so Alice could stop walking in on her frequent sexcapades.

Sex mattered to Margot.

And it didn't matter to Alice.

"I trust you," Alice said. Not a lie, but not the truth either. "It's just hard to talk about."

"I'm asking you to try. If you care about me, you will."

The words *I'm asexual* knocked around inside Alice's head. She knew she was, had known it for some time. She had also hoped she could wiggle her life around that truth like it didn't matter or would never come up. High school had been hell, but college was a whole new beast dimension. Everyone seemed to be trying to have sex with everyone else.

And Alice was caught dead in the center of bloodied, shark-infested waters. It had gotten so bad, she had begun to give the disasters names: *The Great Freshman Letdown: Robert Almanac Edition*, followed closely by its sequel, *Turns Out She Was Pansexual (And Totally Coming Onto Me)*, which then turned into an unexpected trilogy, *Boys Like Girls Who Like Girls*, and now it had become a quartet, *The Hazards of Sex and Other Unwanted Lessons*.

When it came to accepting that she was asexual, it was about an eighty-twenty split. That twenty part encompassed the fact that Alice could not call herself asexual in front of another person. So instead of telling the whole, hard truth, she danced with the definition.

Alice sat on her bed, finally allowing her body to fold in on itself. The time had come to hold that in, to feel that pain and keep it close to her heart. Brand it, press it down deep, right next to her old nickname, *The Corpse*. She stared at Margot's baby-pink ballet flats with the tiny rhinestones near the toes. Alice had bought those for her.

"I don't see the point," Alice said. "I don't need it. I don't think about it."

"Sex?" Margot laughed—a tiny giggle, as if Alice had told a mildly funny joke. "But you're Black."

"Oh Jesus, save me." Alice covered her mouth with her hands and stared at Margot.

"What? I can tell jokes, too." She looked confused for a moment before shame made her face turn red. "That was racist wasn't it? I'm sorry. I didn't mean it to sound like that. I swear it was a joke."

(The perks of having a soon-to-be ex-girlfriend from middle-of-nowhere Iowa were endless.)

"But I'm not joking. I meant exactly what I said. I don't care about sex. You're right. I did it because you wanted to do it."

Margot lowered herself down next to Alice, slowly, as if she were dealing with a scared animal. "Have you gone to a doctor?" she asked. She traced her delicate fingers over Alice's shoulder, curving toward her spine. It tickled, but Alice didn't show it.

"I don't need to." *Number one*, she thought.

"Were you abused? Is that it?"

"No." *Number two.*

"Are you saving yourself for marriage?"

"I hope that's a joke."

"It was," Margot admitted. Her sad smile burned in the corner of

Alice's eyes. "Then what? Tell me. People don't just not like sex without a reason. It's kind of not natural, don't you think?"

To that, she had *absolutely* nothing to say.

After a few minutes (Margot had never been into begging), she left Alice's side.

"I can't be with someone who can't talk to me," she said.

The finality of the moment punched her in her stomach. "Margot—"

"And I can't be with someone who doesn't desire me. You could never love me as much as I would love you. You understand that, don't you?"

CHAPTER

2

Margot had been gone exactly seventeen hours. After five days of awkwardly inching around each other in their room, she had told Alice she wanted a "clean break" right before she finished moving out. Didn't even want to be friends anymore because asexuality was *unnatural*.

(Okay, so maybe Margot didn't *say* that exactly, but that's how it felt.)

(Like her identity was contagious and had the ability to make Margot's above-average libido disappear.)

"Here you go," Moschoula said, setting down Alice's third cup of coffee on the table. Moschoula had tanned skin, the kind of color that implied she was most likely mixed rather than white, with kinky, natural burnt-orange hair pulled up into a bun on the top of her head.

Cutie Code: Yellow, no question about it.

An intense obsession with aesthetics had taken Alice by surprise in high school and she had begun to code her reactions. She had created Alice's Cutie Code™, complete with a color wheel for easy categorizations—from Green to Red, with all the colors in between.

"And a bear claw on the house," Moschoula said. "Try to have a better day?"

Even nestled in the back of Salty Sea Coffee & Co with its chalkboard walls, glorious wood paneling, and dimly lit ambience to spare during peak morning hours where no one should have been paying attention to her, sorrow radiated around Alice like a mushroom cloud. She had gone there to discourage herself from wallowing alone in her now half-empty dorm room. And also from crying.

(But *God*, did she feel like giving her tear ducts a solid workout.)

"I'm not having a bad day. I'm fine. Really."

"You've been watching baby animal videos since you got here and I have yet to hear a single giggle float out of this corner. You forget I know you. Something is definitely up."

"I've dubbed this the Misery Corner. I'm infected."

A girl who looked stressed to death sat two tables over from Alice. She stared at nothing, eyes open, watery, and bloodshot. Her fists pulled the sleeves on her jacket taut. The cuffs stretched across the back of her trembling hands.

Gloom flowed out of the girl in waves, dimming her shine. Goodness, did she look like she needed a hug. Several hugs and probably an hour of silent cuddling. Alice (a steadfast believer in the power of hugs) loved affection but knew it wasn't everyone's cup of tea.

Moschoula peeked at Alice's screen. "I mean, look at that! That at least deserves half a smile."

Presently, a baby badger rolled around in a pile of blankets, and the sight did make Alice's heart *squeeeeee* with mounting intensity.

Instead, she sighed. *Sighed* before biting on her lower lip. "I'm fine."

Moschoula smiled, kind and concerned. Alice loved that they were friends—and not just because Moschoula started making her to-go order as soon as she spotted her walking down the street and gave her free pastries. She had met Moschoula and her friends during a Pride rally at school. She was the only girl in that group who didn't snub Alice for being bi.

(And the only person she met who had an undying love for watching gymnastics.)

Glancing over her shoulder, Moschoula said, "I have to get back. Holler if you need anything." She grinned as she backed away. "Anything at all."

Alice nodded before sliding her headphones on. She switched from videos to a music playlist aptly titled *Nobody Knows* after a song by one of her favorite one-hit wonders and laid her head on the cool wood of the table.

If she was being honest, she wasn't in love with Margot, but they had had potential! She had even planned to tell her dad she had a girlfriend (with hopes he would break it very *gently* to her mom). Even her best friend, Feenie, had approved of Margot, which was rare as hell.

(Excluding her boyfriend, Ryan, and Alice, Feenie hated everyone, including her own biological family.)

A pool of tears collected in the space between Alice's eyes and the bridge of her nose. When she blinked, the first drop crested over and rolled down, splashing on the table. She wiped it away before anyone who cared enough to look would see.

It had all been Margot's idea. She had kissed Alice first. She had convinced her to date. She had wanted this, wanted her. And Alice had fallen for it and Margot and everything they were and could be. She had believed in Margot and their relationship. Had thought herself to death about it, and each night it resurrected itself in her dreams. Margot made her want this specific brand of happiness. Made her believe she could have it.

Feeling stupid didn't even cover it.

How could Margot say something like that?

What made sex so integral that people couldn't separate the emotional love they felt from one physical act?

Love shouldn't hinge solely on exposing your physical body to another person. Love was intangible. Universal. It was whatever someone wanted it to be and should be respected as such. For Alice, it was staying up late and talking about nothing and everything and anything because you didn't want to sleep—you'd miss them too much. It was catching yourself smiling at them because *wow, how does this person exist??* before they caught you. It was the intimacy of shared secrets. The comfort of unconditional acceptance. It was a confidence in knowing no matter what happened that person would always be there for you.

If Alice couldn't even tell Margot she was asexual, then no, she hadn't been in love. This moment, this unexpected ripple in her timeline, wouldn't kill her. But, universe help her, did she want to press that Fast-Forward button anyway.

(This shit hurt like a bitch.)

(A very persistent bitch that seemed to be trying to claw its way out of Alice's chest.)

A package of Kleenex landed on the table near her head. Startled, she sat up and uncovered one ear.

Moschoula slid into the seat across from her with her apron slung over her shoulder.

"I'm on break," she said. "You're crying. We should talk."

"Margot broke up with me," Alice blurted.

"That sucks. I'm sorry." She nudged the Kleenex toward her.

Alice nodded in acknowledgment of her sympathy while trying to blow her nose without honking like a goose.

"I thought things were good between you. Did she say why?"

By the grace of all things floofy, she managed not to start grinding her teeth.

"That bad, huh?" Moschoula asked, eyebrows raised. "Do you want to talk about it?"

"No. But thank you."

Moschoula was more of a *Hey, let's watch the first three seasons of* American Horror Story *in one weekend* than a *Hey, my heart hurts. Please listen to me and make me feel better* kind of friend.

"Are we still on for Friday morning?" They had lived two rooms apart in the same dorm, two semesters in a row. Moschoula had volunteered to help Alice load up her rented moving truck, but couldn't help unload. She had a plane to catch for a summer vacation on some wondrous island paradise.

"Yeah. Those boxes aren't going to move themselves. I appreciate you, your time, and your manpower in advance."

"You can appreciate me by ordering anchovies on the pizza you bribed me with."

Alice's face pinched in disgust. "But they're so salty and taste like ocean. Why?"

"It's what I want."

"Well, I want you to fit me into your suitcase, but you're not even willing to try."

Moschoula tapped the back of Alice's hand. "It's good to see you smile."

"Only for you."

"You know my girlfriend hates it when you say things like that to me."

"Adoration and continuous compliments are how I express my affections." Alice rolled her eyes. "And it's not like I say it in front of her. There's literally nothing to be jealous of."

Moschoula sighed. "I think she just wants you to, uh, compliment her, too."

"Oh." Alice pursed her lips. "I thought she didn't like me, but

I think I can arrange that." The alarm on her phone beeped: her ten-minute warning before her final class started. She lived (and thrived) by the constant alarms she set for herself throughout the day. If it weren't on her calendar to remind her, she would most likely forget to do the thing. "I feel like throwing up, to be honest. On top of everything else, I'm about to fail this math test. Finals are absolute murder on my digestive system," Alice said, packing up.

"You got this. I have full faith in your mathematical abilities. Walk you out?"

"No need. Hug me, please?"

"Always." Moschoula gave great hugs. Just the right amount of pressure, none of that awkward back patting, and she always smelled like lemons. "I'm going to miss you when I leave." She pulled back. "Cheer up, Charlie."

"Great. Now I want chocolate. And Fizzy Lifting Drink."

"Good luck on that last one."

"All those juice bars sell edible grass now, so it should be on the way. Some scientists somewhere will figure it out soon." Alice laughed for the first time in seventeen hours and twenty-nine minutes. It was small, barely more than an amused chuckle, but it was there all the same. Thank God for her friends. What would she ever do without them?

(God willing, she would never, ever have to find out.)

CHAPTER
3

I don't understand how you have so much stuff. You had half a room. Half!" Feenie complained, pulling her long blond hair into a ponytail. "You knew how small it was in here."

Alice had met Serafina (Feenie if you knew what was good for you) on the first day of kindergarten. She had walked right on up to Alice, offered half of her cherry Fruit Roll-Up, and kindly and without preamble declared herself Alice's best friend.

(Obviously, the title stuck.)

"It'll all fit," Alice said. "My dad got me these cool floating shelves and stackable storage bins."

Her new room wasn't so much a bedroom as it was a small den—the curious 0.5 in Feenie and Ryan's 1.5-bedroom apartment that they may have not-so-legally agreed to sublet to her. Truth be told, if she stood in the middle of the room and stretched her arms out, she could almost touch the walls. And the ceiling. But a tiny windowless hole in the wall wouldn't deter her from artfully designing this room within an inch of its life. There were pictures on Pinterest of rooms the same size, or smaller, where people had worked sheer decor magic.

Personally, Alice was obsessed with color and clutter, but she could separate herself from what the room needed. It spoke to her instantly—one single word: minimalist.

A monochromatic theme with the tiniest swaths of soft colors. Her twin mattress would line up nicely in the corner along the far wall with her easily paintable nightstand next to it. She could loan her TV to the living room, since it was bigger than Feenie and Ryan's, to reduce the overcrowded feel. Washed-out black-and-white posters and fan art from her favorite TV shows and movies would function as wallpaper. She would hang soft white Christmas lights and lanterns. And buy a pale, lilac-colored comforter.

(As much as it pained her, there wasn't much she could do about the ugly brown carpet.)

"It'll take some doing," she said, still semi-lost in her vision. The final result would be a soft Cutie Code: Pale Yellow—comforting as sunshine. "But I'll make it work."

"I'm sure." Feenie rolled her eyes. "I'm going back to the truck."

"Aye, aye, Captain, my Captain." An old joke of theirs that would never die. She eyed Feenie's bare shoulders. "Are you wearing sunscreen? You know your skin goes from snowy owl to boiled lobster in a matter of minutes."

"I love you." She laughed, heading for the door. "But you still have too much shit."

Feenie didn't walk—she stomped everywhere she went. Alice could never figure out if she genuinely walked hard or if she did it on purpose to make her seem more intimidating. The semipermanent scowl on her face certainly took care of that.

(Not to mention the few scars on her face she'd earned from fighting whenever she felt disrespected—which Alice learned meant just about any reason. Feenie's pride and joy was the one that cut straight through her top lip on the left.)

Alice began unpacking the first box, wincing at the contents. Instead of sorting through her desk, it seemed far more efficient to pull out the entire drawer and upend the contents. *Way to go, Past Alice*, she thought, sorting through the wreckage. Near the bottom, a photo of her and Margot stuck to a ticket for a concert they had attended during her first semester.

Freshman move-in day last year had been eventful to say the least.

She noticed Margo's giant mound of hair before anything else about her—it was that natural sunlit blond tempered with streaks of light and dark brown that sent customers in droves to hair salons. It complemented her beautiful olive skin, soft gray eyes, and that wickedly easy smile always up for a challenge.

She was Cutie Code: Orange-Red and then she was just Margot before becoming Alice's Margot, but now she wasn't anything.

Because Alice was a Corpse.

Because she was *unnatural* and *incapable* of loving someone.

(God, when in the hell was this going to stop hurting?)

Alice's shoulders began to shake as silent tears flowed out of her.

"Oh, Buttons," Ryan said. He set down a box in the last free cubic inch of space on the floor.

Alice and Feenie had met Ryan at the same time—sixth-grade social studies class. The majority of Ryan's baby fat had melted away in tenth grade when he joined the swim team, but she still saw him as the tan, chubby-cheeked boy with giant glasses, dark brown hair in a bowl cut, who didn't like talking because of his thick Tagalog accent (which had also seemed to melt away during high school). The thing she remembered most, though, was when she used to make him laugh so hard, he'd have a wheezing fit.

"It's fine." She swiped underneath her eyes. "I'm fine."

He plucked the picture from her fingers. "It's for your own good," he said when she protested. "I just can't believe she said that to you. I mean, I know you're not lying, but she seemed so nice."

"It's the nice ones you have to watch out for." She crossed her arms. "Or whatever that stupid saying is. Why can't I find someone who loves being with me, as is, as much as I love being with them? Romantically. Am I asking for too much?"

"I say this cautiously because it's not the only answer, but maybe try dating someone who's ace, too."

She scoffed. "Long-distance relationships are not my jam, and that's probably all I'd find. The Internet is great, a lot of my friends live there, but I want a partner who's here with me." She flicked a white speck off a black stuffed bear before setting it down on her sliver of a desk. The thing was barely three feet wide. "I'm tired of putting myself out there," she mumbled.

"You can't keep letting this get to you." Ryan sighed, a deep and doleful sound that made Alice's face pucker. "It's not healthy."

She side-eyed him, matching his pity with irritation. "Because you have *so* much experience with breakups."

"We've broken up before."

"For like a week two years ago. And I won't name names, but I distinctly remember reading *someone's* terrible poetry blog in the name of friendship when that *someone* pissed Feenie off." She looked him dead in the eye. "*Someone.*"

"That was different. I was young and emotional." He laughed. "My poetry wasn't *terrible.*"

"It was. Still is. The Internet is forever and you never deleted that blog." She giggled as his eyes widened.

"Well." He cleared his throat. "This isn't about me. If you need to cry, then cry, but just promise me you won't do it in front of Feenie, please." He glanced at the doorway before lowering his voice. "I've already had to talk her out of driving to Margot's house this week. Twice."

"But she lives in Iowa."

"Twice," he repeated. "You know how she gets."

Feenie had always been (lovingly) overprotective of Alice. If she had told Feenie what Margot had actually said, Feenie would probably disappear into the night and her mug shot would be everywhere in the morning.

Technically, if it weren't for Feenie, Alice would have never met Margot.

The apartment complex ran specials for college students, waiving the need for a cosigner as long as they had proof of enrollment and paid three months up front instead of two. They had even allowed pets. (Their cat, Glorificus, was most likely snoring under the couch.)

Apparently Ryan's application for the apartment got accepted at the last minute and *apparently* it was too good of a deal to pass up. Instead of all three of them living on campus at Bowen State University, they had both ditched her in favor of shacking up together.

Angry wasn't the word, but Alice's hurt settled in with a nice bitter aftertaste. She loved them, so she got over it. Before she even had time to mentally prepare herself for living with a stranger, Margot had breezed into her life. . . .

"Again with the waterworks," Ryan said with affection. He pulled her into a hug, resting his chin on the top of her head. "There's a few more boxes. We'll take the truck back to the rental place so you don't have to worry about it."

He walked away, pausing at the door. "I know it sucks, but breaking up isn't the end of the world."

She loved Ryan, truly did with her whole heart, and wouldn't wish a breakup on anyone, but that boy needed some perspective. He was delusional if he expected her to believe that he wouldn't fall apart if

Feenie left. She was the only girlfriend he had ever had. Once, when they were ever so slightly high, he crowed on and on about how lucky he had been to find Feenie so early and how he wouldn't have to spend the rest of his life searching for The One.

"You believe in that?" Alice had asked.

"Yeah. Soulmates are real. God says so. Watch, one day you'll find yours and you're going to remember this moment and finally begin to respect and revere me for the prophet that I am. He has a plan for us all."

(Being high tended to turn Ryan's brain into sentimental and religious mush.)

Back then, Alice had shaken her head at him. She didn't even know if she had wanted to date yet, but she also didn't have any doubts about her asexuality. She had spent countless hours thinking and coming to terms with what that meant, the kind of future she wanted to have, and if that could possibly include another person.

The bottom line was her body had never shown so much as a flicker of sexual interest in anyone. But that didn't mean she liked being alone. That didn't mean she wasn't lonely. That didn't mean she didn't want romance and didn't want to fall in love. It didn't mean she couldn't love someone just as fiercely as they loved her.

THE AFTERNOON BECAME a blur of movement. Ryan followed her unpacking lead; his extra inches of height came in handy, and he was good with a hammer. Feenie mostly complained. They had stopped for lunch, sitting on the floor and using upturned boxes as tables, and decided to watch a show about an out-of-control police precinct with a hilarious cast of characters when Alice's phone rang.

(A large pizza—half extra cheese, half pineapple, and real bacon. Not that Canadian stuff.)

(It's ham. Canadian bacon is literally ham.)

"It's my parents," Alice explained, getting up and stepping out of the room. "Hi, Mom."

"How are you? What are you doing?" Her mom had a remarkably high speaking voice and her singing voice was the star of their church's choir. No one expected her to sound the way she did—like a Disney Princess in action.

"Good. I'm unpacking now." She braced herself during the extra beat of silence.

"I'm happy that you're happy, but I really don't understand why you couldn't move home for the summer. It's not too late, sweetie. Your room is still set up."

She leaned against the wall, suppressing a sigh. "I'm not moving back, Mom. How's Christy?"

"Tired, worried, but coping. Nothing unusual."

"And Adam?"

"He's strong for Christy. I know he wishes you were here right now."

"Mom, please stop. I feel bad enough."

Her brother, Adam, and his wife, Christy, were having a difficult first pregnancy. They had planned to move in with their parents for extra support and to save money on rent and child care for a little bit. The baby wasn't due until October. Alice had already written her speeches to plead, beg, and offer to donate her right foot to have the excused time off from school. It was imperative for her to be there when the baby first opened their eyes. And for their first smile. And first laugh. However long that took.

(Jesus, she couldn't wait to meet that kid.)

"You can be in charge of decorating the baby's nursery. I'm sure Christy would love for you to take over to help reduce her stress levels."

"I can't. Summer school, remember? Besides, I love California. California loves me."

"Online classes can be done from anywhere. Your school won't know you're ten hours away from campus. I checked your student account this morning—"

"Mom, you promised you wouldn't do that." She tried not to whine, but she was BUSTED. She had zero intention of attending the summer intersession.

"I wanted to pay for your class. Why haven't you signed up yet?" she said. "And it still says 'undeclared.' What did we talk about?"

They didn't talk about anything. Her mom had lectured her for an hour about how the foundations of a good law degree were rooted in political science. Alice came from a family of lawyers (her mom, her dad, and her brother) and local politicians (her newly elected sister, Mayor Aisha R. Johnson). The expectation was clear: Alice would attend law school.

(Or be disowned.)

(Probably.)

(Okay, maybe not, but the penalty would be steep.)

"I'm going to. I've been busy. I'm busy now." Alice sighed. "I have to go. Okay, I'm hanging up, I love you, kiss Daddy for me, bye."

Ryan had paused the episode while they waited for her to return.

(Her absence didn't stop them from devouring half the pizza, though. And she thought *she* ate fast.)

"I am having a terrible week," Alice announced as her phone chimed.

> I am going to pretend like you didn't just hang up on me, young lady.
> Call your sister.

"Damn it. Margot hates me or something, my mom is practically breathing fire at me, and now she wants me to call Aisha, who is really going to roast me. What's next? Am I going to fall and break both my ankles?"

"I wouldn't say that," Ryan warned. "Don't put that out there."

"All I'm saying is everything happens in threes. Something else is going to happen. I can feel it." She stretched out on the floor next to Feenie and rolled onto her back, groaning at the ceiling. "I love my mom. My parents take good care of me. I love my mom. My parents take good care of me."

"Is that some kind of mantra?" Feenie tapped Alice's nose. "Say it enough and you'll believe it?"

"No, I believe it. It can be *really* hard to remember that sometimes." She sat up. "She went into my student account to pay for my summer intersession class even though we agreed that I would do it myself."

Ryan gave her a funny look. "So what?"

"It's my responsibility. And now she's irritated because I didn't sign up yet or declare my major when neither of those things are any of her business."

"But you don't get financial aid?" He reached for another slice. "I'm failing to see the problem, Buttons."

Her parents paid almost all her tuition. The only reason why they made her pay anything at all was to encourage her to get a job instead of lazing about. She had found a quiet job at the county library, and for the first time in her life she had been able to tell them that she didn't need a spending allowance. She hated trying to explain why her sense of pride shot through the damn roof during that conversation. Most people didn't understand.

She wasn't rich—her parents were. They made that distinction quite clear to her anytime she stepped out of line. She had lived under their roof, in their house, and had to follow their rules. They expected courtesy and good grades and for her chores to be done. In return, they gave her the childhood they never got to have.

But she wasn't a kid anymore.

"She just told you," Feenie said. "It was Alice's responsibility. Momma J overstepped. I'd be mad, too. Intentions don't change impact."

"True, but it was a positive intention. You can still be grateful," said Ryan.

Alice puffed up her cheeks. "I *am* grateful. I just—I don't think wanting the tiniest bit of autonomy is a bad thing."

How else was she supposed to learn? Wait for the magical Adulting Fairy to show up and give her private lessons?

"If my mom did that, I wouldn't be complaining," Ryan said.

"Well, it's not your mom. So . . . ," Alice muttered. "And you're not the one she's forcing into law school. Free education or not, I'm not trying to be there, no way."

"Hear, hear!" Feenie raised her can. "Fuck parental expectations."

Ryan laughed. "What do you want to do instead?"

"Can I major in TV? I'll get my bachelor's in Netflix-ities and my master's in Hulu-ology." Alice grabbed the remote and pressed Play.

CHAPTER
4

Being on time pleased Alice past the point of reason. It put an extra bounce in her step, a song in her heart, as she entered the library.

Unlike the fancy college library that aimed for a sterilized, industrious, *all studying all the time* sort of feel, this one was run by the county and made its patrons feel at home. The automatic sliding glass doors opened to a large space with multiple high-arched windows that almost eliminated the need for artificial lighting. Books were housed on row after row of black metal bookcases and the carpet, originally installed long before she'd been born, had slowly transformed from its initial deep red to a dark purple, but managed to appear as if the color had been purposely selected.

To the left, the children's section was filled with bright colors and characters from books painted on the walls by local artists. All the furniture had recently been reorganized (by none other than Alice) to maximize the floor space for groups and create quiet nooks for solitary readers. The media center began on the right side. Row upon row of computers bordered the beginning of the massive fiction section and digital media available for checkout.

She waved at Cara Sanchez, the head librarian. At five feet even, she took home the award for World's Most Adorable Boss. Round and cheerful with a pixie haircut, she topped off her look with flawless makeup and a bold red lip. She made you want to pick her up, put her in your pocket, and then run because abduction was illegal.

Cara waved back before pointing toward the table closest to the elevator.

Alice looked—her Cutie Code™ immediately shot up to Red.

(That hadn't happened at first sight since the Victoria's Secret Fashion Show last year and never in the wild.)

She stopped in front of the elevator, facing forward, and pressed the button. A curious, nervous sensation wriggled and rooted itself down inside her chest. Alice looked over her shoulder again, blinking rapidly at the person reading on his phone, completely oblivious.

Only his profile was visible. Tanned skin. Dark eyebrows. Strong chin. And a tiny curl of hair brushing against his forehead. He held his thumbnail in between his teeth, his index finger curving over his top lip, the rest of his hand curled into a loose fist. Most likely to hide his smile—whatever he was reading was making him adorably happy.

Her Cutie Code™ ticked upward until it strained against the top.

The elevator pinged. Alice shrugged off the sensation and walked inside. Turning around, she pressed the button for the fifth floor.

Just as the doors began to close, the Cutie Code: Red person in question lifted his head, looking right at Alice. She staggered backward, clutching the banister as the elevator began to ascend.

Kill Bill sirens blared in Alice's head.

The elevator hummed and whirred, the floors illuminated and darkened as they were passed, and the air inside wrapped her in its warm, fake-pine smelling embrace. Same as always. Nothing had changed, magically making today the day she became moments away from suffering a massive heart attack.

Sure, she hadn't worked out for a while (see: ever) and her diet primarily consisted of ramen noodles during lean times (see: all the time), but this was a bit overkill. Her body had, at least, a minimum of fifteen years before she had to worry about that kind of thing.

Out of the elevator and in the hall, she took a moment to catch her breath. It was a hop, skip, and a jump to the break room and she wasn't sure if it was empty. The library didn't have many employees, but the last thing she needed was someone to spot her and ask if she was okay.

(In her mind, she was sure she had that whole *deer about to die in the headlights* look going on.)

Luckily, it was empty, giving her a few more moments to calm all the way down.

The designated break room also held all the employee badges and the time clock. It wasn't much to look at, nor could anything be done about it (Alice had already tried). A rectangular room with three tables in the center, lined on either side with chairs. The walls were covered with cliché inspirational wall art, government-required labor posters, and employee notices. It had built-in lights, but Alice turned them off, opting to use the natural bit of light that came in through the tinted window.

Essie had taped a Post-it to Alice's badge. Alice blew out a huff of breath. Right, then. Time for work. The continued cute analysis would have to wait.

(Maybe he would still be downstairs. . . .)

(FOCUS, WOMAN!)

(Right!)

She peeled the note off her badge, clocking in as she read it:

I had to step out—be right back! Please show Takumi how to clock in and make a copy of the handbook. THANK YOU!

"Who the hell is Takumi?" She folded the Post-it note in half before tossing it in the trash. Takumi Shibue had a temporary badge on the wall already, but it didn't have a picture yet.

Back downstairs, she stood behind the information desk waiting for the handbook to finish printing when she felt that *itch* between her shoulder blades when someone stared too long. She tried to take a sly peek to see who it was and . . . *Jesus.*

(Sweet God in heaven, have mercy on her soul.)

Her Cutie Code™ blasted straight past the Red zone. If it were a pressure gauge, the glass would have cracked right down the middle.

He was gorgeous—and that was not a word Alice threw around lightly. Not just *"Hi, I'm the new boy next door"* gorgeous, but the kind of gorgeous that would make you slap your mama. The kind of gorgeous you'd stab your best friend of twenty years in the back, set her house on fire, and drive off into the sunset with her husband for. *Have sex in the break room at work even though you know there are security cameras in there* gorgeous.

As if she'd actually do any of those things.

She always laughed at characters who lost every last drop of their common sense on TV and in movies when someone too attractive for words crossed their path. If this guy was on a show, he'd be considered the kind of gorgeous that would cause midseason plot twists and act-two spinouts, leaving the viewer on the edge of their seat because their beloved characters were goners after looking into those dark brown eyes.

And he stared at her.

(Too much cute.)

(A veritable cutie-induced overload.)

There was a place for cute and every cute in its place. Whoever he was hadn't just exceeded her scale. He had broken it.

Cutie Code: Black—the Next Generation.

It had to either be him or the heart attack had been replaced by a disorienting fever virus. This was how it happened in the movies: some poor soul (Alice) was doing great, having a perfectly normal (and punctual!) day. And then, in some innocuous way, they'd have contact with Patient Zero (*him*) and boom—uncontrollable sweating, fever, chills, hemorrhaging, and then . . . death.

This wouldn't kill her (possibly), but she had an idea what it was.

Attraction: The Final Frontier.

The Fatal-est Attraction.

Death Becomes Attraction.

"Do you really need all those copies?" Cara asked.

Alice snapped out of her internal loop. "What?" She looked down. "Crap!" Her finger must have slipped. Instead of one copy she had set it to eleven. She pushed the Cancel button over and over, as if that would make the machine get the message faster.

Cara chuckled. "You okay?"

"Yeah. Peachy." Alice rubbed a hand over her face. "Hey, is that guy over there waiting for someone to help him or something?"

"Yeah. You. That's the new employee, Takumi."

"*That's Takumi?*" she hush-whispered.

"Yes," Cara said slowly. "He's the one Essie wants you to intro."

"Him?" She cleared her throat. "You're sure?"

"He's the only new hire. You're the only assistant. I'm sure," she deadpanned. "Do you know him?"

"Nope. Never seen him before in my life."

"Right." She laughed. "Here he comes. If you need help, you know where to find me."

Oh no. Not yet. If she could just—

"You're Alice, right? Essie described what you looked like. I figured I should probably ask instead of staring at you," Takumi said.

He was tall enough to make her look up.

"Yes. I am. Alice. That is me," she said, shaking his hand. She prayed he didn't notice her clammy hands. That he didn't wipe his hands on his pants because she was pretty sure she'd die of embarrassment.

"I'm Takumi."

He smiled.

Her eye twitched.

Everything was going *fabulously*.

"This way." She held out her hand toward the elevator. Takumi had broad shoulders and strong hands and dark brown eyes, and THAT SMILE should have been criminal.

The elevator pinged as soon as she pressed the button.

"After you," he offered.

She felt like she was having an out-of-body experience. She didn't have the capacity to think about that other *thing*, so she focused on the cute. She had dreams about this level of cute. They were never supposed to manifest into reality.

He had such a nice jaw. And shiny, shiny hair that had been dyed darkest dark blue. And, and he smelled amazing.

When his gaze turned to her, her eyes zipped to her feet.

"Have you worked here long?"

"Yes."

"Do you like it?"

"Yeah."

He hesitated then said, "What's your favorite thing about it?"

The answer formed itself in Alice's mind. A beautiful sentence full of wit that would impress the hell out of him. But somehow, during the near-instantaneous route from her brain to her mouth, the words decided to have a sudden-death match. The sole victor? "Things."

He waited for her to continue and when she didn't, he chuckled. "You're not very talkative, are you?"

She shook her head.

"That's okay." He smiled, laughing a little.

The elevator pinged and opened. Takumi held out his hand (again!!!) for her to go first. Alice marched out of that elevator like she was in a band on a football field in the middle of the summer, complete with sweat trickling down her back. After she had opened the first door on her left, she stood in front of it to let him pass.

"This is the break room," she said, steeping in a nice cup of self-loathing.

He walked by her and she took a deep breath to calm herself—nope. That was a lie. Alice had had her first creepy moment, crowning herself the creepiest Creepy McCreeperton in existence.

"Badges." She pointed to the wall.

"Do I clock in?"

"Yes."

"And my badge should be on the wall?" he asked, already looking.

"Alphabetical. Last name."

"I noticed that."

"Right. Of course."

He grinned, making eye contact with Alice. She stood up straighter, holding her breath, counting to ten, and releasing it slowly.

Takumi twirled his badge between his fingers. "So what do I do?"

Alice pointed to the red box. "Just swipe it and you're set. Clock in and out for lunch. Breaks are paid time."

"Now what?"

"I'm not sure exactly. Essie only wanted me to show you how to clock in. I guess you can wait here for her to come back. I have to get to work."

"Is that for me?"

Alice handed him the forgotten handbook she'd been holding the entire time.

"Okay. Bye."

CHAPTER

5

hy are you crying? What happened?" Feenie's concerned face filled the screen on Alice's phone.

She had been curled under her blankets for the past hour trying to get it together. Gasping hiccups kept ripping out of her throat, her nose wasn't so much a nose anymore, rather a snot-filled mess, and her eyes were oh so swollen. She was so distraught she had even skipped dinner.

(Alice did not skip meals, ever.)

(That was tantamount to treason in Alice-Land.)

"H-he l-looked at m-me a-and I—" She hadn't cried this hard since she had watched the *Fringe* series finale.

"I can't understand you. Take a breath, woman."

She breathed in and it came out as a sob. "And h-he probably th-thinks I'm really stupid n-now."

"Oh, good God. I take an emergency break to talk to you and you're incoherent," Feenie mumbled. "Who is *he*?"

That made Alice cry even harder, because guilt was an abusive bastard.

"I can't help you if you don't tell me what happened." Feenie sighed. She pinched the bridge of her nose, shaking her head. "Would you rather talk to Ryan? He's better than me with the emotional crying thing."

"No." Feenie was the only person she wanted to talk to about *him*.

"Then suck it up and talk."

In elementary school, while all of Alice's friends had talked about boys they liked, she had kept quiet.

In middle school, she had pretended to have a crush on Patrick Furlong so she would have someone to talk about, too.

(This was where she had begun to perfect the art of playing along.)

In high school, Alice had gone all out, pretending to be hopelessly in love with Sam Oliphant. She had damn near snatched the *this love is our destiny* crown right off Theresa Lopez-Fitzgerald Crane Winthrop's head.

(*Passions* remained the only soap opera Alice had ever watched.)

But this had been where Alice messed up. Turned out, Sam had a thing for Alice, too. A different kind of thing, but a thing nonetheless.

He had asked her out. She *had* to say yes.

Alice had been trying to sort out the difference between romantic attraction (which she felt) and sexual attraction (which she didn't). By the end of their first week together, she knew for a fact that she didn't even want to be Sam's friend anymore. He was an awful human being. A human-shaped garbage fire. A waste of space and genetic material.

But finally, *finally*, she fit in perfectly with her friends.

(Peer pressure was a helluva drug.)

They all had someone and now she did, too. Normal felt like a constant state of despair, but they had stopped teasing her. Had stopped giving her pitying looks, calling her "innocent" and excluding her from sleepovers because she had nothing romantic to gossip about.

Fast-forward six months, she's dumped with a new nickname. The Corpse. Because kissing him had been an ordeal to overcome. Because she never seemed interested in touching him (see: jacking him off). Because she had just lay there while Sam had sex with her, and he had told everyone.

Whenever Alice thought about that time, two things stuck out:

One—Francine Loren's mock whisper in the locker room: "I heard she didn't moan. Not even when he went down on her."

Two—the curiously soft sound of Feenie's fist connecting with Francine's face layered with the instantaneous crunch of bone cracking.

Alice had stood there covering her mouth like all the other girls, except not in shock. She had tried to hide her smile. Cute girls were not supposed to be violent. Seeing Feenie, fists clenched at her sides silently daring Francine to get up, fierce and seething with unchecked rage, was kind of . . . liberating. Even if it was in a secondhand sort of way.

As harsh as it seemed, Feenie's confrontation had felt like a gift to Alice.

Feenie standing up for her gave Alice the courage to tell her friend the truth. She had confessed she thought something might be wrong, so one day, after health class, they had talked to their teacher, who then said the word: *asexual*.

Everything had finally made sense. And had given Alice a whole new set of challenges.

Through it all, whenever Alice entered crisis mode about anything ever, she turned to Feenie (or Ryan by proxy). So she told her about Takumi and their botched introduction. As she babbled, Alice's tears began to recede, her tone returned to normal.

(The sniffles didn't quite go anywhere.)

Feenie eyed her, keeping her face neutral. "And you think you're attracted to him?"

"What else could it be? It's not just me appreciating how cute something is like I usually do. He's *beautiful*, Feenie. I almost melted into primordial soup of Alice."

"And he's so beautiful, you think you want to have sex with him?"

Alice fidgeted in her seat. "I'm not sure."

Feenie gave her a withering look. "Okay, well, how did he make you feel?"

"Like I was stupid. I'm serious! Don't look at me like that. My mind went completely blank and filled up with white noise."

"That still sounds less like you were turned on and more like you thought he was exceptionally hot. He probably just exceeded the Cutie Code."

The Cutie Code™ was a fun game, but it was also a system used for critical analysis—Alice's way of processing the different kinds of attraction everyone else seemed to experience. She only shared her system/game with those whose opinions she trusted, to see how her coding compared to theirs.

It was about *feeling*—the level of emotions it could evoke from her, how likely it would be to make her *squee,* and most important, how did her body physically respond to it.

A naked, muscular male chest was Code: Red for Feenie. Meanwhile, it was Uncodable for Alice. Over time, it expanded to include *everything*, and Alice had become obsessed with it. She clamped her bottom lip between her teeth. A new wave of tears began to coat her eyes.

"Oh," Feenie said. "*Oh*. You checked?"

"After he left, I went to the bathroom. The *plumbing* was on."

Feenie softened, and said, "Oh, sweetie," which made Alice start crying again because Feenie was never *soft* for anyone.

"How could this happen?" Alice wailed. "He didn't even touch me."

"Sometimes it just happens," Feenie said, tone still *soft*. "For me, I just have to be in the mood. Ryan will look at me and it's go time."

A deep voice yelled Feenie's full name in the background. She turned in response, face wrinkled in undiluted aggravation and not so politely told him where he *and* his mother could go if he yelled her name like that again.

"I have to go," she said to Alice. "I swear to God this place would fall apart without me."

"Okay. I'll see you at home."

"That's right. You live with us now." Feenie beamed, a question forming in her eyes. "Fuck, I love you. I think sometimes my mind blocks out how much, so every time I remember feels like the first time I'm realizing it."

"Uh, thanks?"

"Take it and don't complain." Feenie rolled her eyes. "Wipe your face and push what happened to the back of your mind for now. Go do something, like start studying a second language so you can get a fabulous job once you're fluent. My future sister-wife can't be poor. Someone has to support my ass."

Feenie had always joked that she planned to marry both Alice and Ryan. And they would both spoil her rotten.

"Isn't that Ryan's job?" She wiped her eyes.

"Well, yeah." Feenie shrugged. "I figured he'd do all the house stuff and you could support my makeup habit."

"Sounds like a plan." She sighed. Only Feenie could have calmed her like this.

"But I'm really glad you called me about this. Everything is going to be okay. Try not to think about it for now."

"Okay. I won't."

"Love you."

Alice adored the way Feenie said *good-bye*. It was always some variation of "I love you." And if she forgot, Alice would get a text within thirty seconds letting her know.

Feenie was right. She needed to push it to the back of her mind, get some perspective. Tomorrow, when she got to work, everything would be the way it was before she ever laid eyes on Takumi. She'd call it a fluke, yes, a one-off event, due to her body short-circuiting from stress. It would *not* happen again.

CHAPTER

6

Oh dear God.

She had been wrong. So very, very wrong. The feelings, the sensations, came right back, flooding into her like they had never faded. Alice had always wondered what physical attraction would feel like, and while she didn't necessarily dislike it, she wished there were a button she could press to turn it back off.

Essie had somehow conned Takumi into leading Storytime in the children's section. The kids gathered around him in a rapt semicircle, gasping, shouting, and giggling at the appropriate times. He even used voices—it was the most dramatic (and entertaining) adaptation of *The True Story of the 3 Little Pigs!* she had ever heard.

And she was hardly any better. She watched the show from behind the picture-book shelf. Her back began to ache from the tiny chair (and she was sure she had felt the dangerous wobble of the tiny legs from her weight), but you couldn't pay her to move.

(Which, technically, the library was. She was supposed to be shelving, not watching.)

Takumi was still really, really, ridiculously good-looking (straight-legged light blue jeans with a soft-looking gray sweater pushed up his forearms. And okay, but seriously, those forearms? *Man.*) and she was still mystified. And attracted. Like a giant dumbstruck moth to a super-naturally beautiful bug zapper. Screaming was most definitely not in Alice's best interests, but that didn't stop the urge to want to do it.

"The end," Takumi said, closing the book. "Who's next?"

Almost all the tiny hands shot into the air. A few held their books above their heads.

"Let's do a riddle this time. Whoever guesses the correct answer first wins." Takumi tapped his chin. "Which letter of the alphabet holds the most water?"

"I know!" A little brown boy stood up. *"C!"*

"That's right," Takumi said. "Which book did you pick?"

The boy toddled toward him, book outstretched. "Can I hold it?"

"Sure. Come sit here." He tapped the spot next to him. "You have to hold it out so everyone can see," he said, helping his helper move into position.

"Will you do funny voices again?"

"Of course." Takumi laughed. "Everybody ready?"

Alice caught his eye and his grin grew into a smile that would launch a thousand ships.

She could watch him all day (like the stalker that she was). When was the last time she had ever been this fascinated by the look of a person? If ever? She wasn't an artist or musician (her creativity was reserved solely for aesthetics/decor) or even a writer (unless essays about her shows counted?), but if someone handed her a pen and paper, she'd probably start penning sonnets in Takumi's honor.

"Alice," Essie whispered, leaning against the shelf with her arms crossed.

Alice jumped and promptly resumed her shelving duties at triple the speed. "Hey, Essie," she whispered back. *What wormhole did she slide out of?*

"Enjoying the show?" She was almost Cara's polar opposite with the legs and neck of a giraffe. Elegant and feminine to an absurd degree, she never had a single strand of hair out of place. The way she wore her clothes was the stuff designers dreamed about, and she had perfect dark brown skin that made Alice weep with envy.

(Her own skin was a similar color, but hyperpigmentation was real.)

"What? No. I'm shelving." She lifted a book and made the pages flap.

"Uh-huh," Essie replied, eyebrow cocked. Her gaze drifted over to Storytime. "I think he's going to be really good for the library."

"Yeah. He'll be great."

"The kids love him." She zeroed in on Alice's full cart. "And I see they're not the only ones. Still not done?"

"Oh, um, the shelf needed straightening before I could start, so I've been doing that," Alice lied.

"It's okay." Essie laughed. "He has that effect on almost everyone at first. He is pretty cute. What code is he?"

Essie knew all about Alice's Cutie Code™ and thought it was both hilarious and fascinating. On days when Essie didn't go home for lunch (she lived super close to the library), they would spend the hour together scrolling through Tumblr, coding all of the pictures.

Essie was determined to crack the code. Once, it baffled her how a painted image of the aurora borealis could surpass her own Code: Yellow. Essie had spent a solid twenty minutes arguing how she was more attractive than some "weird, squiggly green lights in the sky."

There's no way Alice would admit that Takumi was Code: Black. Once she explained it, vainer-than-vain Essie might lovingly murder her.

"Cute? Really?" Alice reached for her maximum level of cool. "I did not notice."

"Liar." Essie laughed.

God, could she smell the lie on Alice? Was that an actual thing? It probably was, her signature scent being Eau de Struggle.

"You notice everyone," Essie continued. "I've been watching you watch him for almost thirty minutes. He's single now. Want me to set you up?"

Alice answered slowly, measuring each word. "Employees can't date each other."

"Wrong. Librarians can't date assistants," she said. "And it's not like I'll tell Cara anyway. As long as you two don't go overboard with the googly eyes, I really don't care."

Essie was one to talk—every other sentence out of her mouth was usually "Andrew this" or "Andrew that." She had met her boyfriend (the aforementioned Andrew, whom Alice had yet to meet) two months ago. He had swept her off her feet, and shortly after, they rode off into the sunset of magical Happily Ever After Land.

"Thanks, but I'm not interested in romance right now."

(Or dating.)

(Or love.)

(Or being happy, apparently.)

Essie side-eyed her. "Says the person who wrote an essay about the blatant romantic dissonance in *Sleepy Hollow* called *Ichabod and Abbie: The Greatest (Love) Story Never Told* and had it published."

Her ears went hot. For as much TV as she watched, Alice never got into fan fiction. Writing critical analysis essays about her favorite shows and ships were her drug of choice. She wrote them for herself and for her like-minded friends. Sometimes she got lucky and online magazines bought her work.

"I showed you that in confidence," she hissed.

A riot of giggles erupted from the group, drawing their attention.

Essie knocked on the top of the shelf with her knuckles. "Get to work or I'll move you to dusting duty in the Takumi-free reference section."

CHAPTER

7

The night air had a warmth to it that made it feel like the sun hadn't set yet. The haze from the city lights created an artificial dome that made the black night sky seem less distant. Alice sat down on the plastic bench under the bus stop's solar-powered awning.

She had ended up falling asleep before Feenie came home last night. And had also, maybe, possibly snuck out of the apartment before Feenie woke up to avoid her. She didn't want to talk about Takumi yet. Strangely, Feenie hadn't pushed either—after the first few messages:

I hear you. I see you. I'm everywhere

Feenie switched to inspirational ones:

I'm here when you're readyyyyyy
Insert relevant R&B lyric here

If anyone tells you to smile, punch them.
You be sad/mad if you want to!

> Never forget me and Ryan <3 you.
> I love you more, though (don't tell
> him I said that please)

Alice started and stopped several messages to Feenie but wasn't sure what to say. She rummaged through her bag—Ryan had found some "nutritional" protein bars that were on super sale (buy one, get two free). Two bites and she knew why they were so cheap. Chocolate dirt was too good of a descriptor for that travesty of a snack. A glob of it stuck to the roof of her mouth and the chalky aftertaste coated her teeth.

Her phone chimed again. Her sister, Aisha.

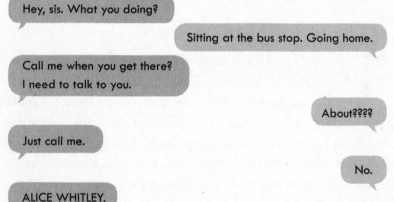

> Hey, sis. What you doing?

> Sitting at the bus stop. Going home.

> Call me when you get there?
> I need to talk to you.

> About????

> Just call me.

> No.

> ALICE WHITLEY.

Alice cackled. She could practically hear her sister's sharp screech, see her eyes widen and lips purse into a thin line. Was there a greater joy than antagonizing one's siblings? Probably not.

She took another bite of her chalky granola bar before tossing the rest back into her purse. Her taste buds didn't deserve the continued torment—not even to settle her demanding overlord of a stomach.

> Tell me why first.

> ...keep on. See what happens.
> You better call me. I mean it.

>> No. Nein. Nope.

She bounced in her seat, giddy as all hell. *God*, did she love pissing Aisha off. Considering their age difference, they got along great, but it was a lot easier to get away with this through text. In person, her sister probably would have put her in a headlock until Alice apologized and did as she was told. Sometimes Aisha sat on her lower back, pinning her to the ground, and pinched the skin between her shoulder blades.

(Her older brother never helped.)

(Being the youngest had a lot of drawbacks.)

> I am calling you at precisely 9:15.
> Answer. Your. Phone.

>> Nooooooo means noooooooooo

She'd only play with fire for a bit longer. Aisha could go from Tolerant Mentor to Evil Stepmother faster than a sparkly vampire jumping to save a girl from being crushed by a van.

"Hello, Alice."

"Takumi!" She jumped in her seat and stared at him, cheeks chipmunk full. "Hi!"

"I didn't mean to startle you." He laughed, a deep beautiful chuckle that turned Alice's dirt granola bar to ashes in her stomach. "Are you taking the bus?"

She nodded and swallowed. It slid down her throat in one solid lump.

"Do you want a ride?"

A ride. In his car. Alone.

Good God.

She shook her head.

"Are you sure? I don't mind."

"I'm fine. All the time. I mean, I take the bus. All the time." She gave herself a mental high five for forming actual words.

(Granted, with a wonky sentence pattern and cadence, but words!)

He sat down.

He sat down right next to her.

A whole bench and yet he figured shoulder-to-shoulder proximity was the way to go. The control it took to not lean away from him was the stuff made of legends. The effort of not moving made her rib cage shake like she was too cold.

"Are," Takumi began slowly, "you okay?"

"I'm fine. Why?"

"You seem kind of"—he moved farther down the seat away from her, eyes concerned—"tense."

"I'm fine. Really." She balled her hands into fists, pressing them into her thighs.

Talking to him shouldn't have been difficult. It shouldn't have taken so much effort to keep it together and stop herself from flailing like a long-limbed Muppet hopped up on sugar. The curious Takumi-induced nervous energy made her hands shake, her throat tight, and her heart-beat echo inside her ears. All she wanted to do was let it out. Maybe then she'd feel better and stop embarrassing herself every other second. And be able to say more than three words at a time to him.

He stared at the parking lot and around the area before turning to her with a determined look on his face. "If you tell me to leave, I absolutely will. I don't want to force my chivalry on you, but if you could possibly take pity on me and let me stay, I'd appreciate it."

"Pity?" Was her voice always that squeaky?

"Yeah. It's late. It's dark. You're sitting here. Alone."

"Well, if you say it like *that*—"

"Oh shit. No. I'm not trying to scare you—"

"Done now."

"—and I'm not implying you need to be protected or anything—"

"*Uh-huh.*"

"All I'm saying is two people together is better than one, sort of like how you're not supposed to split up in horror movies—oh my God. I am really messing this up," he said, laughing. He ran his hand through his hair. "I swear I'm not usually like this."

"Like what?" Alice was certainly *never* like *this.*

Carnivorous butterflies gnawed away at the inside of her stomach. She tried to focus on the flower pattern on her skirt, but her gaze kept involuntarily going back to him because her eyeballs had apparently developed minds of their own—how splendid. Why was her body so intent on mutiny?

"*This,*" he said as if she were supposed to understand. "Awkward, I guess? My brain is melting. I figured I could last at least a week before exhaustion set in from working two jobs."

When he caught her staring, she mumbled, "So, um, two? Jobs?"

"Yeah." He grinned. "This is my evening and weekend gig. Monday through Friday days, I'm a paper pusher in an office until the fall."

"Then what?"

"I'm going to be a teacher. Kindergarten."

"Really?" And suddenly, Storytime with Takumi made sense. Essie didn't force him—he probably volunteered.

"I'm pretty excited about it." He nodded. "It's the same school where I did my student teaching. I applied, the stars aligned, and they hired me."

"Congrats."

"Thanks. What about you? Is this your only job?"

"Yeah."

"Are you a student?"

"Yep."

"Still not feeling talkative, huh?" he teased.

"It's your fault," she blurted, making him laugh.

"Is that right?" He tilted his head to the side, smiling while biting his bottom lip.

A severe hot flash ripped through her, level: wildfire. It started in her head and scorched its way downward until it singed the coral pink nail polish off her toes. It may have been due to embarrassment or possibly desire (???), because, at that moment, they felt eerily similar to her.

She knew that look.

The Look. The one a person used when they tried to figure out if they liked what they saw enough to date. Not even a month ago, she wished people would stop giving her that look so she wouldn't ever have to explain about being asexual. Did she want Takumi to find her attractive? She wasn't sure, because what if he did? What if he asked her out?

What if, what if, what if?

Why, why, why?

Margot's smiling face popped into her head. A warning. This was the beginning, and regardless of what happened with Takumi in the middle, everything would end with that one word. He'd want to know. She'd have to explain.

"What's wrong?" he asked.

"Nothing." Her gaze stayed glued to the sidewalk.

"I'm sorry. I thought, um"—he paused—"I don't know what I thought. Sorry." He tilted his head back to watch the sky and muttered, "I have to stop listening to Essie."

Essie, her brain hissed. Payback would be swift and satisfying.

"You know Essie?" She kicked a pebble into the street. Of course he did. Would it kill her to stop asking stupid questions? "Outside of work?" she clarified.

He gave her his attention. "Yeah. That's how I got hired here: tangential nepotism."

The bus came rumbling down the road. Alice stood, getting out her bus pass.

"I'll see you tomorrow?" he asked.

"Probably," she said, eyes flicking to his face, then ran for the bus's doors. Once she sat, she checked out the window for him. Takumi continued to stand there, waving at her.

"I hate everything," she whispered to herself, slouching in her seat.

CHAPTER
8

'm home!" Alice said. She threw her bag onto the slightly used but well-loved quilted purple couch. Glory trotted to the front door. She yowled for food, head-butting Alice's shins. "I know, I know."

Talking to the cat amused Alice to no end. Glory had personality. She made her desires and feelings known through actions with a scary amount of accuracy. Like how she flipped over her green food bowl with a contemptuous look in her eye.

"Oh, don't be like that," she chided, replacing the bowl and filling it. "Sometimes I think you only love me because I feed you."

Dinner was an outstanding bag of popcorn washed down with Diet Pepsi. Alice wanted to lose herself in season five of *Supernatural* and pass out once her serotonin levels overloaded on the cutie patootie badass with the biggest heart named Dean Winchester. Snuggled down on the couch, wrapped in a blanket, she started the first episode. The house bills were split—she had convinced Feenie and Ryan to upgrade to the fastest Internet money could buy. Lagging sent her into a cataclysmic rage and buffering was her absolute kryptonite.

Two episodes later, Feenie came home, arms lined with shopping bags. "Finally! Good God, I thought I was going to have to stalk you from behind bookshelves just to see you."

"I appreciate your enthusiasm for my well-being," Alice said as Feenie passed her on the way to the kitchen.

"*Someone* has to look after you."

"By the by, you know you and your meddlesome ways are banned from my library, right?"

"What? Why?" Feenie snorted with laughter.

"You know why." Alice paused the episode and set her phone down, ignoring the question. "Want some help?"

"Too late." She dumped the bags onto the kitchen counter before trying to squeeze herself in between the back of the couch and Alice.

"You could just sit next to me." Alice frowned, moving over, barely hanging on to the edge of the couch.

Feenie bared her teeth and twitched her nose. "How are you feeling? Better?"

"Yeah. I've calmed down. Some."

"Ooh, that sounds ominous. Think you can make it through a conversation tear-free or do you need more time?"

"I'm tired, so probably not. What's new with you?"

Feenie had dropped out after one tenuous semester at Bowen, had a gigantic fight with Ryan about it (which resulted in them nearly breaking up), and currently felt smothered within an inch of her life by her parents (even though they lived ten hours away). She worked at a piercing-and-tattoo shop as a receptionist with no long-term life plans apart from marrying Ryan after his graduation.

"Nothing to talk about really." Feenie shrugged.

Alice's phone chimed—Aisha's name flashed on the screen. "Hey! Give it back."

"Nope. It's Feenie time." She pressed Ignore. "What does she want?"

"Well, *now* she'll want to kill me. Thanks."

Feenie laughed. "I'll be sure to sing the *Upper Room* at your funeral. Just call her back later."

"I don't want to call her at all, but I was going to answer."

"I got you, boo." She said each word as she typed: "Dear—Aisha—I'm—Alice's—favorite—so—fuck—off—for—the—next—hour—"

"Don't you dare send that!" Alice lunged for the phone. Feenie pulled back, but the couch provided a bit too much spring, launching them onto the floor.

"Ow. *My boobs*," Alice whined. "Get off."

Feenie laughed, rolling onto her stomach. She slid the phone across the floor where Glory promptly chased it.

"Why did you do that?" Alice tried to crawl away.

"NOPE." Feenie pounced on her like a bear cub learning how to wrestle. She locked her arms around Alice's waist, flipping her over and wrapping her legs around her thighs. She kissed her forehead too many times to count.

Alice squealed some wordlike sounds before dissolving into a fit of giggles.

"Because you're mine and I refuse to share," Feenie said. "Say it!"

"NO, DAMN IT!"

"Say it or I start tickling you," she threatened.

"Okay. I will." Feenie stopped, but then Alice said, "I don't negotiate with terrorists."

"Wrong answer."

Five minutes later, Alice's abs began to hurt from screaming/

laughing/crying so hard from Feenie's tickle attack. "Okay!" she gasped. "Okay. I love you the most!"

"Was that so hard?" Feenie asked. "I made you laugh."

"You're an asshole." She wiped her happy tears away, trying to catch her breath.

"The very best." Feenie lay down next to Alice but kept one of her legs slung over her.

"Can we get back on the couch?"

"There's more room down here. Hey. Cat. Bring us a blanket and some pillows."

Glory blinked at her from where she was stretched out on top of Alice's phone.

"We should have gotten a dog," Feenie muttered. "Now where were we? Tell me more about this Takumi fellow. Asian?"

(A *Who Framed Roger Rabbit* reference never failed to lift Alice's mood.)

"Japanese," Alice said. "And I already feel bad about calling you for that. I feel ridiculous as all hell."

"No, no, no," she said. "I've been waiting for this. I have a plan and it needs sharing."

When was the last time she'd seen Feenie this excited about something? Her eyes practically sparkled full anime style. It blew so hard that it had been triggered by Alice's crisis, but a beggar couldn't be a chooser and she was on her knees—she'd take her Feenie time anyway she could get it.

"Okay. Let's hear it."

"I think this is going to provide a perfect opportunity."

"For?"

"To sleep with him, of course. You need to have sex with him."

"Feenie." Alice sighed so deep, her chest hurt. Of all the things she had expected Feenie to say, that wasn't it. "I'm really going to need you to stop doing drugs. It's affecting your cognitive thinking at this point."

"Hear me out," Feenie said. "Please?"

Alice exhaled, pressing her lips into a tight line. "I'm listening."

"If you're attracted to Takumi, that means sex might be different. Remember how disappointed you were before?"

Every time Feenie brought that up, regret walloped Alice upside the head. After Sam but before Margot, Alice had begun to think that *maybe* she'd had sex too early and *maybe* she should try it again. The result was a one-night stand with a boy named Louis to see if *maybe* she had been wrong.

She wasn't. She had picked him randomly (he had seemed nice enough), they fumbled around for about thirty minutes, he managed to give her an orgasm, and . . . that was it.

Sex, Alice had decided, was like jogging. All the people in the world could say it's so amazing and great for you, but if you don't care about jogging, you'd rather spend your time with a Netflix queue and a box of doughnuts.

Orgasms, Alice had decided, were like stretching after exercising. It felt amazing in the moment, but who really thought about that perfect stretch two hours later? She certainly didn't.

"I was *not* disappointed. Some things were just confirmed and I was more affected by it than I thought I would be." Truth be told, Alice was relieved, but hadn't figured out how to explain why she felt that way just yet. She didn't need sex to be sure. She had always known.

"Yeah. There's a word for that. *Disappointment.*"

"Anyway," Alice said, eager to move on. They would never see eye to eye there. "I don't know if that's something I'm ready for. After Margot, it feels like there's no point in me having sex with anyone, not even to make them happy. I just don't want to do it."

Feenie's lip curled. She wasn't angry—just thinking. "Let me ask you this," she said finally, "would you want to date him?"

"I don't know him. I can't answer that."

"Yet. You don't know him *yet*," she said. "This happened for a reason. As the love of my life likes to say, *The universe is speaking to you.*"

"You hate it when Ryan says that."

"Yes, but we're not talking about me. There's something about him that you like without knowing why. I think we should investigate."

"We?"

"You'll need my help, of course. First, we have to figure out how to get his attention. We don't know much about him, so you'll have to play it by ear for the first week or so. Start off being your usual charming Alice self, report back to me, and we'll dissect and make a game plan for the next day."

"And I'm supposed to do that every day?"

"If that's what it takes." Feenie shrugged. "Think of me as your personal love coach."

"What about the other side? What if it never happens again? What if he is it for me? I only get one shot, it all goes to shit, and I go back to feeling nothing and thinking I'm broken. I finally feel balanced. I don't want to lose that."

Feenie flicked her right between the eyes.

"*Ow*, you ass." Alice rubbed her forehead.

"First of all"—Feenie pointed at her—"you are not broken and I don't ever want to hear that again. Second, being attracted to one person doesn't necessarily change who you are. Maybe you're gray-sexual instead of straight up ace. There's just something about the way Takumi's genetic code arranged his face and body that appeals to your brain chemistry. It's insta-lust. Enjoy it for what it is."

Alice didn't think it was possible to love Feenie more than she already did, but that moment tipped her over. Yes, Feenie's suggestion to have sex with Takumi was questionable. However, she wasn't suggesting he would *cure* her.

Graysexual.

In spite of everything, Feenie had acknowledged she was still on the spectrum where she felt most at home.

"It's not lust," she said. The words felt true. "It's something, but I don't think it's that."

"Let's find out for sure then."

"I have such terrible luck with dating, though."

"People have shit luck all the time. What the fuck makes you think you're a special snowflake?" Feenie laughed but Alice didn't.

"Because I want it more," Alice said quietly.

"You don't know that." Feenie sighed. "Inspirational, 'Kumbaya'-type shit is not my jam, so I'm only going to say this once: You can't let one or two bad experiences stop you from being happy. Maybe it's with Takumi, maybe it's not. But you're not going to know until you try."

With Feenie in her corner, things didn't seem nearly as hopeless.

CHAPTER

9

If Alice was truly attracted to Takumi, what did that mean for her? What should she do next? Feenie's plan had merit, but she hadn't witnessed Alice's epic failure.

Holding a conversation was an issue. She looked at Takumi and her brain short-circuited. All the words were there, but they began to jumble before even making it down the pipeline. She needed structure. Rules. Method.

Objectively, she was in a classic case of besotted befuddlement. The only thing she hadn't done (yet) was run into a door or fall down the stairs or something equally embarrassing and life threatening in front of him.

(God Almighty. Please no.)

The plan would form with time, but she wanted to talk to someone about everything else. Someone not Feenie, someone who didn't know her and could give an unbiased opinion. She had medical insurance under her parents' plan. Unfortunately, seeing a counselor meant getting a referral from her primary physician, and since her mom had access to her medical record . . . that was a solid non-option. She'd call Alice so fast—no, she'd probably skip the phone call and jump on the next available flight to find out what was wrong with her *baby girl* in person.

Her sister would rat her out.

As would her brother.

(Her family was thick as thieves. Everyone knew everyone's business.)

Her laptop sat all the way across the room on a stack of boxes, so mobile Twitter would have to do. She opened her DMs with Moschoula.

love me please

how much does your counselor charge? I have insurance but I'm trying not to use it

(Please remember I'm poor. If you can kick me a referral and swing a discounted rate we can barter something. I can write an essay or two for you?)

I can get you a free consultation on referral for sure. Just ask all your questions then and if he wants to see you again, you can totes say no.

Can I ask what's going on? You don't have to tell me if you don't want to.

Alice's inability to say "being asexual" plagued her. The words formed but lodged themselves in her throat. One night she had stood in front of the mirror repeating, "I'm asexual," over and over again. She had thought that if she could get used to hearing it, she'd accept it as truth faster. Alice knew it had made *sense*. She could check off all the little boxes. But she wasn't sure it was a title that she had necessarily wanted everyone else to know.

She didn't want to be known as Alice the Asexual. She wanted to be Alice who had an (admittedly) unhealthy obsession with all things cute and ate ice cream in the winter and taught all her friends how to make a *Soul Train* line and, and, and . . .

Being asexual would trump everything else about her, good and bad and weird.

If Alice had told someone, would they begin to use that as the primary defining characteristic for her from then on?

Oh, hey everyone, some person would say as they introduced her, *this is Alice. She's asexual. Sorry if you had any plans for her. She won't ever desire you, regardless of how much she likes you.*

Was it really anyone's business that Alice didn't feel sexual attraction when the rest of the world did? It was Alice's secret. She could guard it like Smaug hoarding gold if she wanted to.

> I just need to talk to someone about . . . stuff. Sex-related stuff.

Okay ☺

> I mean, it's nothing bad. I read some stuff online, some answered asks on Tumblr, but I kinda want something a bit more personal, you know?

Totally.

He's really great to talk to.

And I'm always here too.

> Thank you!! did you want the essays?

Her phone rang—Aisha.

She resisted the terrified urge to throw it against the wall. A deep breath and prayer to Jesus later, she answered in her sweetest voice. "Hello, sister dear."

"If you *ever*, in this life, ignore my calls again," Aisha hissed. The threat didn't need to be finished. (They never did.) "Do you hear me?"

"Technically, Feenie did that. Not me."

"Alice."

"Yes, I hear you, I'm sorry." She frowned. *"Dictator,"* she mumbled.

"What was that?"

"Nothing. So what's up? What's so important?" Alice crawled under her blankets, covering her head.

"I talked to Mom today. I signed you up for a seminar."

"A *what*? *Why*?" She kicked her legs out in a tiny tantrum.

"Watch your tone," Aisha warned. "Because Mom is worrying herself sick over you. You're going to law school. Hurry up and make your peace with it so she'll leave me alone."

"Ah, so this is about you. I feel so loved."

"That's not all you're going to feel. Keep on testing me."

God, she even talked like their mom now. Alice would always remember the moment her mom and her sister had their huge blowout. It was awful—Aisha stayed away from home for nearly three years, didn't come home for Thanksgiving or Christmas. But once she came back, she began to take the *like mother, like daughter* sentiment to new heights and then surpassed them.

"Fine. I will. What makes you think you can tell me what to do? If Mom can't make me do it, what makes you think you can?"

The silence on the other end of the line set Alice's bones on edge. She shivered and pulled her blanket tighter around her.

"Because I'm ten times scarier than she is," Aisha said with deadly calm. "You do what I say or else."

Alice knew firsthand that *or else* was a frightful terror to behold. "This is exactly why Adam is my favorite. He wouldn't treat me like this."

"I don't care. Don't waste my money. Go to the damn seminar."

CHAPTER

10

Alice's heart pumped faster than the 4/4 beat of the song she was listening to, and it had nothing to do with breaking out into a full run from the bus stop to the elevator. Feenie's plan burned in the back of her mind. Be normal. Act normal. Everything was fine. She wasn't attracted to Takumi at all. He was a normal level of cute. Alice was used to cute. Cute she could handle.

(Hell, cute was what she worshipped.)

Then two things happened at once: the elevator door opened and her phone rang.

Adam, her brother. He almost never called her, preferring to e-mail for some reason, but he was one of the few people she would willingly answer the phone for.

He cut her off as soon as she answered.

"Why do you mouth off to Aisha? Jesus Christ, Alice."

"In my defense, she deserved it." She ducked into a dead-end hall and leaned against the wall.

"She *always* deserves it, but you're not supposed to do it. How many times do I have to tell you that?"

"You do it," Alice replied.

"I'm not almost twenty years younger than she is. You are. She called me, screeching about you and how you're disrespecting her, and this shit with Mom and law school. What in the hell are you doing down there?"

She laughed. "I like to think I'm living my best life."

Adam sighed.

"Why aren't you taking my side?"

"I did. She told me to stop enabling you and hung up in my face." He paused. "I will never not be on your side. You know that."

"Thanks." She picked at a loose string on her bag. "What did Mom say?"

"Oh, she didn't *say* anything. She's passive-aggressively leaving me notes to call you."

"Why?"

"She thinks that you think you'll have to be a DA, and she wants me to reassure you that there are multiple careers someone with a law degree can select from. She also wants me to convince you to quit the library. There's an internship opening at De Tablan & Prince out there. She met them at a fund-raiser and talked you up."

"Unpaid? Sorry. I can't. I need money."

"Yeah. I tried to explain that to her, and just so you know, the notes intensified. She left one on the bathroom mirror about how it's very rude and ungrateful of me to assume *she* wouldn't financially support you."

"Which is the entire point." Alice stared at the ceiling and tried not to sigh. "I need to do this myself."

"I know. Aisha knows but doesn't want to fight with Mom again.

I think on some level even Dad knows. But Mom—" Adam paused. "If you really don't want to go to law school, figure out what you want to do instead. Quickly. In the meantime, just go to the seminar and whatever else they want you to do."

"I'd really rather not."

"I hear you, okay? I'll do what I can on my end, but you have to meet me halfway. Go to the seminar. I mean it."

"Fine." She grinned. "And I'll text Aisha and Mom to give you all the credit so you can rub it in their faces."

"That's all I ask."

"I'm not quitting my job."

"Of course you aren't. That'd be dumb."

She hung up and tilted her head back against the wall. Her brain felt stuffed—it was already chock-full of anxiety over how the next four hours would go and now . . . this. Summer was supposed to be chill— it had been in high school anyway. Why did things have to change so drastically from one year to the next?

(And why hadn't time travel been invented yet?)

(Forward or backward—anywhere but now would do.)

A deep breath later, she walked toward the break room. Her hand clutched the strap to her satchel tight enough to make her palms tingle.

And there went her calm.

Alice's gaze darted to the ground. More deep breaths—in through her nose and out through her mouth. She wasn't ready to look at him. Not yet. If she wished hard enough, maybe she could spontaneously develop the power of invisibility before they spotted her and—

"Hey, you," Essie called, smiling.

"Hi," she replied. Alice's simple black dress with the pretty crocheted hem and plain black flats provided a stark contrast to Essie's look: a dazzling orange-and-white dress that flowed in all the right ways and places with a small white knit shrug. One said life while the other said funeral.

"What's wrong?" Essie asked.

"My online class. I forgot a quiz was due and my already dismal grade plummeted." A truth, but not the current truth. That had actually happened months ago because that syllabus had been a complicated beast to be reckoned with.

"Once, I had a 99.7 percent in one class and then I bombed a test. My grade dropped to 89 percent. I cried for a week." Essie shuddered. "I do not miss school or that level of anxiety."

"When did your class start?" Takumi asked.

After taking a moment to center herself (*woosah*), Alice glanced at him.

Takumi had parted his hair on the left side, creating a slight pompadour to the right with sides closely cropped to his head. The asymmetry complemented his already balanced features and clean-shaven jaw.

Looking at him stressed Alice all the way out. That stupidly beautiful man was slowly giving her high blood pressure. Steam was mere moments from spewing out of her ears.

But.

But.

That was it. Nothing else happened.

Alice's lips ticked up into a smile, her breath came out as an excited laugh. She was fine. She was herself again. "A while ago."

"Do you still have time to fix your grade?" Takumi asked, eyes on her.

The head rush of eye contact hit her hard—Alice felt warm all over, her face blazing from the intensity. That was what had been driving her over the deep end. If she didn't look him in the eye, maybe she'd have a shot at normal interaction.

"Probably not," she said, busying herself with grabbing her time card. "I have a good feeling that I'm going to skim by with a C minus."

"*Whoa*, don't get too ambitious," Takumi said, tone light.

"Initially, I had hoped for a B, but after I read the first chapter in the textbook, I had to check myself." She clocked in, returning her card to its spot.

"It can't be that bad," he continued, moving to stand next to her.

"It can and it is. I am not a science person."

"What kind of person are you?"

She stared at the ceiling in mock contemplation. "The kind that likes to stay indoors and watch TV. I think I get it from my grandma. She never missed her stories, you know, soap operas. I'm like that. Except with Hulu's entire catalog and I'm not waiting for retirement to start."

He laughed. "I meant academically. What's your major?"

"Oh. Oops." She shrugged. "I haven't decided yet."

"Aren't you a sophomore?"

Alice bristled. "It's not uncommon to wait until junior year to declare. Besides, I'm still knocking out my general ed."

"I didn't declare until the end of my junior year, actually."

"Really?"

"Yeah. Let's just say I know exactly how much online classes suck, especially taking two at a time when they're only three weeks long. Four separate times so I could catch up."

"That's madness."

"I had to graduate on time."

"You two do know I'm still standing here, right?" Essie asked, eyes darting between them. "And you're both already clocked in?"

They turned to her.

"I see you're hitting it off." She placed her hands on her hips.

"Only because she took pity on me," Takumi deadpanned, making Alice snort.

"And you already have inside jokes. *Hmm*." Essie cocked an eyebrow. "It's a good thing, too. Dave called in sick. Alice, I want you with Takumi today. As long as you keep the volume low, you can play music down there."

"Not the basement," Alice complained.

(Goddamn it, Dave. You had ONE job!)

"That won't be a problem, will it?" Essie asked like she was implying that it better not be.

"Apart from the spiders, dust, and probable ghost haunting?" Alice pouted while they laughed at her. "Why do you do this to me? Why don't you want me to be happy?"

"This is a job. You're paid for your work, not your happiness," Essie said.

"True, but a happy worker is a productive worker. Or whatever that saying is."

Essie smiled, shrugged in the most feminine way possible, and sashayed to the door.

"We should go," Alice muttered, speed walking after Essie.

"You seem better today," Takumi said, keeping up with her pace. "Almost like a different person, really."

The three of them entered the elevator. Essie pressed the buttons for the first floor and the basement.

"I can see how you would think that. I was having an off day. I'm fine."

"You were *fine* last night, too."

"Last night?" Essie exclaimed. "Yeah, hi, still here."

"He meant at the bus stop. He waited with me."

"Alice, I told you I will give you a ride. Carpooling counts toward that carbon footprint thing."

"That's really why you want to take the bus?" Takumi asked. "You're worried about the environment?"

"Yeah," Alice began. "It's cheaper and better for the planet to get a monthly bus pass. I get a student discount and the stop is right in front of my apartment complex sooooo," she trailed off, baffled over why she shared quite so much. Did he really need to know all of that? "Besides, one of the security cameras points right at the bus stop, so it's safe."

Essie exited the elevator on the first floor, while Takumi and Alice continued on to the basement. It was deceptively small with no windows, packed with bookcases, two small tables with a computer on top of each—one in the center of the room, the other against the far wall. To the left was a stairway that almost no one used and to the right, a file room housing all kinds of archived paperwork, including the outdated card catalog.

Alice rubbed her nose, already feeling sneezy. "There's a ghost down here. I can feel it."

"Are you psychic?"

"No, but the warning signs are all here." She began to tick them off on her fingers. "Supernaturally cold, I always feel like someone is watching me, books move from where I know I left them, and sometimes I see things skittering out of the corners of my eyes."

Takumi thought for a moment, surveying the room. "Maybe the heater is broken, the security cameras are on, someone is playing a prank on you, and there are rats."

"Your skepticism is not appreciated."

"Hey, I'm not saying I'm not a believer, but if there's a logical explanation . . ." he said.

"Fine." Alice threw her hands up like she was done with him. "Go ahead and let your guard down. Don't come running to me when you get possessed." She picked up the clipboard with the week's schedule. "You can work on damaged books," she said, handing him the list.

"Just decide if it can be mended or if the library needs to order a new one, then follow the instructions for each process. They're on the cart over there by the drop chute. You know your computer log-in, right? I'll be over there finishing up the new intakes that are going into circulation since *Dave* felt compelled to get ill all of a sudden." She pointed to the table stacked with books and a computer.

"Maybe he's possessed. It usually looks like an illness at first," Takumi said, reading the list. He headed toward the farthest table stacked with the damaged books.

Alice tried her damnedest not to smile as she went to her table.

Ten minutes later, Takumi called her name. She ducked down lower behind her monitor—a knee-jerk reaction. His voice saying her name made her stomach flip.

"Alice?" he asked louder.

"Yes?" she answered, eyes on her screen.

"Are you going to play music?"

"Oh, sure," she said.

She plugged her phone into the small blue speaker Essie had purchased for the room. Without thinking, she pressed Play to pick up where she had left off this morning. The player kicked in at the chorus of "I'll Make Love to You" by Boyz II Men.

Her heart stuttered and stopped. "Shit!" she exclaimed. She'd never moved to stop a song from playing so fast in her life.

He smiled. "Have a problem with Boyz II Men?"

"No." There went her beloved boy band playlist. Alice adored cheesy love songs. Listening with Takumi in the room, however, might be her undoing. She selected another playlist, and the opening song from her favorite anime began to play, which was in Japanese. Stopping that one with the quickness, she covered her face and prayed to be put out of her embarrassed misery.

"What was wrong with that one?"

Alice answered, still using the monitor as a shield, "I turned it off before I could get accused of being culturally insensitive and then fired."

Takumi laughed. "You can play the song if you want."

"No, it's fine." She scrolled through her playlist, settling on *Instrumentals,* a playlist composed of blissfully wordless OSTs from movies.

Midway through the surprisingly quiet shift, Takumi left for his break. He hadn't spoken to her again after the musical snafus until she told him to go. Alone in the basement, Alice spun in her chair, waiting for Feenie to text her back.

"How are things?" Essie called from the elevator.

"Fine." She stopped midspin, pulling back up to the desk. "Takumi's on break."

"When? I didn't see him come up."

"He took the stairs for some reason."

Essie used a paper towel to wipe the tabletop before sitting on it. She always sat with her head held high and her legs crossed not at the knees, but at her ankles. Alice's grandma told her that's how proper young ladies were supposed to sit.

(And then she would tease her grandma by saying she'd settled for being a heathen and would probably slouch until the day she died.)

"I didn't really need to check on him," she confessed. "It's boring as hell up there."

"Umm, it usually is," Alice said.

"True. But today feels extra soul-sucking."

Alice laughed. "Do you even like your job?"

"They pay me a decent salary, I have health benefits, and I'm one promotion away from running the place. What's not to like?" Essie rolled her eyes, which made Alice think she was being sarcastic even though it didn't sound like it.

"What made you want to be a librarian if you think it's boring?"

"It wasn't any one thing." She gingerly flipped through one of the new arrivals. "After I graduated from college, I couldn't find a job anywhere else and ended up getting hired here. My expensive new diploma earned me minimum wage. After a year of abject brokedom, I decided to go back to school so I could defer my loans for a bit. Cara suggested library sciences since I didn't plan to quit, and six years later, I'm still here." Essie closed the book. "Boring isn't necessarily terrible. There are far worse jobs to have and a multitude of negative ways to feel about them. You'll see when you're older after a few more years of work experience."

Alice schooled her face. She didn't want to be disrespectful to Essie (somehow she managed to be both an almost-friend and a great supervisor), but she *hated* when people pulled out that *you'll see when you're older* line. How in the world was that supposed to be helpful? It was infuriating and condescending more often than not.

"In other actually interesting news," Essie continued, "Takumi was asking me about you before you got here."

"Really?" Alice perked up.

"*And,*" Essie said, "he notices how much you stare at him."

"No, he doesn't," she said, not that she would know. She had spent the majority of the shift looking at anything and everything besides Takumi's face. When she had to give him instructions, she looked at his shoulders or above his head at the ceiling. "I mean, he can't because I don't."

"I'm definitely getting a vibe."

"There is no vibe." She rolled her eyes before realizing this would be great information for Feenie. Was Takumi being friendly or flirting and why, oh why, couldn't she tell the difference? "But if there were, how would said vibe feel? Just, you know, wondering."

"Stop being silly. You know what I mean."

No, she really didn't, and she hated when people made that assumption. If she had known, why would she bother asking?

"How do you know him anyway?"

"We have my cousin in common. I owed her a favor so I gave him a job," Essie said. "So what color would Takumi be?"

"I have a color?" Takumi asked, walking back in.

"Yes!" Essie held up her hands like she was preparing to tell an epic story. "Okay, so Alice has this color system she calls the Cutie Code and she uses it to determine how cute something is. I'm Yellow-Orange, which is close to the top by the way." She actually began to preen.

If Alice weren't mortified beyond recognition, she would have gotten up and run for her life. The Cutie Code™ was sacrosanct. Essie didn't know Alice told only certain people about it—people she thought would understand and not ridicule her to death.

"Oh yeah?" Takumi asked, turning to Alice. "What color am I?"

Kneecaps were generally uncute, so Alice stared at his. She had only one option in this increasingly perilous situation: damage control.

"I don't know." She shrugged. "I decided to retire the Cutie Code. So."

"What? Since when?" Essie exclaimed as the intercom chimed— Cara telling Essie to come back upstairs. She huffed, standing up. "I'm pausing this conversation. I have thoughts," she called as she darted from the room.

"Could you unretire it for two minutes? If you randomly saw me, what would I be?" Takumi asked once Essie was gone.

"Why?" Alice said, ducking behind her monitor.

He walked to the other side of her desk. "I want to know. I figure I have to be Yellow-Orange. I'm at least as cute as Essie is."

His tone wasn't superior or arrogant or mocking, surprising Alice.

She lifted her gaze to his face. The amused way he smiled at her, interested and waiting . . . she felt like her answer would mean something to him. He cared about what she would say.

A spot in the center of her chest began to warm up.

"I don't know," she said, pushing her theory along. "Essie is very, very cute. Besides, girls typically rank higher."

"Personal preference, or am I sensing some sexist undertones?" he joked.

"Well, cats rank higher than everyone. Am I being species-ist?"

"No. Cats are everything. I swear, there are more cat videos on the Internet than porn."

Her eyes lit up as she made a shocked gasp. "I know, right? I have this theory that the only reason why the Internet was invented was so people could share pictures and videos of their cats with the rest of the world."

He laughed and she kept going because she desperately wanted to hear that sound again.

"There's this cartoon called *Futurama* and they have this episode where cats are actually aliens who come to Earth to disarm the human race with their cuteness and take over the planet. It's on Netflix. Or I could loan you my box sets."

He raised his eyebrows at that.

"I mean, if you want."

"I'll, uh, get back to you." He turned and walked toward the door.

Alice closed her eyes, rubbing her forehead. She had cleared one hurdle only to collide into the next one. *Yes*, she thought, *scare him off with your TV obsession, why don't you?*

"For the record," Takumi said, making her look up. "I think you're very, very cute, too." He smiled, took one step before turning back. "I realize that could have been construed as sexual harassment. I'm sorry. You said it about Essie and, uh, yeah. I'm sorry."

Alice, who had entered a slight state of shock, managed to say, "It's okay," without smiling hard enough to make her cheeks hurt, but, oh Good Lord, was it coming.

"If you could not tell anyone I said that, it'd be stellar."

Stellar. Oh, what a cute word that was. "It'll be our secret," she promised.

"Thanks."

"You're very, very welcome."

He grinned and left the room.

Alice sat back in her chair, letting her smile erupt over her face like a happy volcano. She texted Feenie:

> No initial response. Everything feels how it usually does.

> REALLY? Bummer

And Alice couldn't resist giving her a teaser for the conversation they'd have later that night:

> But . . . he thinks I'm very, very cute.

CHAPTER 11

"Hey, you're home." Feenie leaned against the door frame of Alice's room. "No work tonight?"

"I called in sick." Her first counseling appointment was in two hours.

(She wasn't nervous. Nope.)

"What's wrong?" Feenie was across the room in seconds, stretching out on the bed next to her.

"Nothing worth talking about." Alice had spent the morning thinking of exactly what she wanted to talk about with the counselor. Her list wouldn't stop growing—from one-word bullet points to paragraphs of frenzied exasperation. She wrote and wrote and wrote until her hand cramped, until she could barely read her own writing, until she was near tears and emotionally exhausted.

(This appointment was going to suck.)

"Everything is worth talking about with you." Feenie snorted. "Anyway, I've come up with some new rules for the Takumi Trials. It's good that you figured out you can't tell if he's flirting or not, but I think Essie is super unreliable, so anytime you and Takumi have an important interaction, you have to text me so I can interpret on the spot and we can plan the next steps accordingly."

"I can't do that. I'm supposed to be working."

"Like anything happens at a *library*. They're not going to care if you text me. Just don't be super obvious about it. I do it all the time."

"And," Alice continued, "Essie keeps pairing us together. He's always right there. He'll see me texting and will ask about it."

"So? Lie to him. Also, 'keeps'? Two nonconsecutive shifts is hardly a pattern."

"And I don't even know if I want him to flirt with me, though. I like that he goes along with my jokes."

"So you definitely want to be his friend?"

"I didn't say that." Alice rolled over onto her side. "I don't think it's going to go the way you want it to."

"And what way is that?" Feenie grinned. "Don't you get it? This is good! I need to know things like this. You're making progress, but I can't help you if you withhold information from me. He thinks you're cute and admitted it. That's like steps one through three already done."

"So? I think he's cute, too. It doesn't mean anything."

"I think it does."

"Well, I've decided it doesn't. Mind over matter."

"Okay, so you don't want to get to know him?" Feenie poked Alice in the cheek and left her finger there. "I'm getting confused."

"Because it is confusing. I don't really want to deal with it," Alice admitted, feeling wearier by the second. "Why are you so into this?"

Feenie shrugged, but Alice knew why and promptly felt terrible for asking.

A big part of Feenie felt like she was missing out on the dating world and was scared to admit that to Ryan. She didn't want to hurt his feelings or make him think she didn't want to marry him. If living vicariously through Alice's predicament helped Feenie feel fulfilled, Alice was willing to share this experience with her.

It was the least she could do for the one friend who had always stood up for her.

"Fine, but for the record, I think you're getting your hopes up for nothing."

Feenie scoffed. "Are you talking about my hopes or yours?"

Alice rolled over and faced the wall and shoved her head under her pillows. "Go away."

"I'm not going to let you bottle everything up about Takumi until you explode," she said, tugging at the pillows.

"Hello, my loves!" Ryan announced.

Alice felt his weight on the bed as he wiggled in between them. "This bed isn't big enough for three people," she complained.

"It's fine," he said. Alice looked at him—he had a severe case of gray under-eye circles but was alert and smiling. He beeped her nose. "Who's Takumi? What are we talking about?"

Alice and Feenie exchanged a look.

"Don't do that," Ryan whined. "Tell me."

"Girl stuff," Feenie explained.

"O-kay," he said, drawing out the word. "What kind of girl stuff? I want to know. Maybe I can help."

Alice sighed. "You tell him." She covered her head again.

THE COUNSELOR'S OFFICE walls were lined with floating bookshelves; a small desk sat right in front of the window. The room also upheld Alice's stereotypical fantasies of a therapist's office—a full-size couch was against the left wall and two small armchairs with a round table in between were on the right.

She took one giant step toward the armchair and perched on the edge of the seat. He sat cross-legged in the other chair, placing a manila folder and notepad on the table.

"May I call you Alice?" Alice nodded and he continued. "Okay, Alice. My name is Dr. Burris and I like to start my session with a bit of a disclaimer. This is a safe space and anything you say here will be kept confidential unless you divulge plans to harm yourself, harm others, or engage in any sort of illegal activity. Do you have any questions about that?"

Alice shook her head. Her hands had moved on from twisting the paper with her waiting-room number on it to holding her bag in a death grip. She needed to be there. *Wanted* to be there. Recognizing that as fact didn't make her any less nervous. She had to trust him to give her sound advice, and in order for him to do that, it meant talking about herself. Sharing parts of her she hadn't even told her parents about. And sure, he sounded like he'd be nice—his tone was rather pleasant to listen to. But what if he was a closet racist? Or homophobic? Or a religious fanatic who would try to subtly instill his beliefs in her?

"Excellent. We'll have thirty minutes today to talk about whatever you need to." He opened the folder. The form Alice filled out in the waiting room lay on top. "You checked off 'sexual concerns,' and it says here you have questions about 'stuff'?"

"Yes."

"And would you mind explaining what 'stuff' entails?"

"Sure. Okay. Um," Alice began and cleared her throat. "I, uh, recently, I experienced something and I was, am, a little worried about it."

"Are you comfortable sharing your experience with me?"

"Yeah. Um." Alice looked at him. That familiar feeling of fear mixed with shame burned in her stomach. "You know, maybe I could start by telling you a little about me first?"

"Please do."

"Okay. Well, my name is Alice. I'm nineteen. I'm a sophomore. I'm what you could consider a TV and minor film buff. I'm the youngest in my family—have an older sister and brother. I have a job that I'm pretty good at. Got my first apartment this year with my best friends. And I have a cat named Glorificus, but I call her Glory." Alice tapped her finger on her bag. "Those are the basics, I guess."

After a beat he asked, "Is there anything else you'd like to share about yourself?"

He didn't say "Perhaps why you're here," but she knew that's what he was waiting for.

"Yeah. Well, I have a problem," she said. "It's not really a problem, I guess? I've been dealing with it, dealt with it really. Did the whole *coming to terms with it* thing in high school, you know. Got my experimenting phase out of the way, and I've sort of lived my life since then, learning to work around everyone else's perceptions of how I should be. Everything was great. Fine. I was happy most of the time."

"And now you're not," he prompted. He tilted his head to the side.

"I wouldn't say I'm unhappy, but I am confused." She swallowed hard. Her jaw ached. "I don't . . . experience . . . you know, I'm not sexually attracted to . . . boys."

His face remained blank except for a small, encouraging smile. Alice practically saw the word *LESBIAN* flashing in his eyes.

"Or girls," she continued. "Or anyone."

And there it was. A subtle lifting of his eyebrows, one blink too many, the corners of his mouth evening out.

"While it's rare, it's not uncommon."

Great. Rare. That was the exact opposite of comforting.

"There is a name for it," he said. "Do you know what that's called?"

"I do." Alice fidgeted in her seat. "That's how I identify. That word."

"And is *that word* the *stuff* you have questions about?"

"Not exactly. Indirectly," she said. "At my job, there's this gu—umm, this person, and when I saw them, I felt something. Attraction. Sexual attraction, I guess."

He raised his chin, eyes thoughtful. "How did seeing the person make you feel?"

Feenie would make a great psychologist. She made a mental note to tell her so.

"Well, you see, there's something else you should know about me. I have an intense aesthetic attraction. I like cute things. Animals, clothes, makeup, decor, nature, pretty designs, you know, just things that are eye-catching, and that includes people. But it's not sexual at all. I get really excited about the way the thing looks and I like talking about it, so it can be confusing sometimes. For them, I mean. Not me. I don't feel anything. I don't get, you know, aroused looking at cute things.

"So when I saw Tak—I mean, the person, I thought that's what it was at first. They were just exceptionally cute, but then I got really hot and was having trouble thinking and there was action happening *down there* and I'm confused about stuff now."

"Did you want to have sex with this person?"

"I don't know. Maybe." She sighed. No point in holding back now. "I'm still figuring out how that's supposed to feel."

"Allow me to rephrase: Did you explicitly think of sexual activity in response to seeing this person?"

"No. I mean, it wasn't like I wanted to take him to the supply closet for a quickie or something."

"What about now? Would you like to have sex with them?"

"I haven't thought about it," she said.

Dr. Burris clasped his hands together, resting them in his lap. "A common misconception is the difference between arousal and attraction.

Arousal is a physiological response, whereas attraction is an experience, and they are not mutually exclusive. Does that make sense?"

"Yeah."

"Regarding your situation, it seems that your arousal may not have been a direct result of a desire to have a sexual experience with the person. Of course, it's possible that it was, but that's something only you can explore and decide for yourself."

"So what does that mean for me and who I am?"

"You seem to be uncomfortable saying *that word*, and if it's okay with you, I'm going to say it. I think you know what I'm talking about."

"It's fine."

"Asexuality isn't something that's black or white. There is a multitude of shades of gray in between. Being potentially sexually attracted to one particular person isn't as outlandish as you've convinced yourself it is."

"I know that stuff. There's this thing called the Internet, and it's quite handy," Alice joked.

Dr. Burris raised an eyebrow.

"I mean, thank you for saying that. It's very reassuring to hear. But I don't think I'm being clear. Everyone talks about sex like it's the greatest thing ever in the history of all the things, and I don't get it. I kept waiting to want to do it, to not have to be convinced all the time, to even think about it and it just never happens. But like, even knowing that I knew I could get aroused—I've experienced it before. That was just the first time it happened because of another person and I didn't even *think* about sex. My friend brought it up later. None of this makes sense and I need it to."

"Why?"

"Because how else will I ever—"

Alice snapped her mouth shut, promptly staring at her feet.

"Ever what?" he asked gently.

Alice closed her eyes. "Look, I know all of this. I've read books and articles and websites. I know what asexuality is and isn't." She opened her eyes, staring at the couch, defeated. "What I don't get is why this is happening to me now? I figured all of this out years ago and now all of a sudden, I'm changing? How am I ever going to explain this to anyone?"

"You explained it to me."

Alice slumped forward, head down. Wearing her asexualness, sharing that fact about herself with the world, wasn't something she was ready to do. One day, she knew the time would come and she had her speech ready (a typed paragraph, the paper folded five times, and hiding in her sock drawer). It was her safety net, the thing she held at night saying "one day, one day" while during the day she refused to think about it. And now that one day was here and she was speechless and lost.

"But you know!" she said. "You get it. I'm not trying to trivialize anyone else and what they have to do, but if I go to my parents and say I'm a lesbian, they would know what I meant. If I went to my siblings and said I'm bisexual, they would know what I meant. If I tell anyone I'm asexual, they're going to look at me like there's something wrong. They're going to tell me to go to a doctor. They're going to tell me I'm too young to know what I want or I'm still developing. Or they'll tell me how important sex is to finding a good man. Or they'll think they can fix me, that I'm lying because I don't want to sleep with them. It's hard enough trying to explain that word, so how in the hell am I going to explain I'm biromantic asexual? They're really going to think I'm making this shit up."

"You're worried whomever you choose to tell won't believe you. That's important to you?"

"Of course it is. How would you feel if you exposed your identity and the world pointed, laughed, and called you a liar to your face?

Would you ever want to do that again? How am I supposed to have any kind of romantic relationship with someone if I feel like I can't tell them the truth?

"My girlfriend broke up with me because she thought that since I didn't desire her, I wouldn't be able to love her, which is not true at all. I am very loving. I cry at the end of romcoms. My favorite movie is *Splash*. I want someone to give me flowers and take me on dates. I want to fall in love and wear a giant princess dress at my wedding. I want to have a happy ending, too, and all that other magical stuff. I want what books and TV and the world has promised me. It's not fair that I should have to want sex to have it."

Dr. Burris passed her a tissue box. "It would seem we've gotten to the root of the stuff."

"Well, I like to take the scenic route." Alice sniffled, wiping her eyes. "It's cuter."

"Not to mention far more informative. Have you come out to anyone, either before or after your discovery?"

"My best friends know. That's it."

"I'm afraid I don't have the kind of answer you're looking for." He folded his hands, placing them in his lap. Calm. Serene. "This isn't something where I can tell you to go read a book and it will methodically list the steps of how to come out. It is a personal and individualized experience. My advice to you is to be prepared to educate. It may feel unfair that the onus of that responsibility will fall on you, but when most people think the *A* stands for Ally, you will have to speak louder, with bravery and dignity, to be heard. You will have to be willing to inform and to educate. And you will have to know when it is time to remove yourself from situations and disconnect from those who either do not understand or are unwilling to. You have to do what is right for you."

Alice knew he had spoken the truth. Everything would boil down to her having to speak up.

Those were not the words she wanted to hear. It made her tremble inside. Her jaw locked into place, teeth grinding and vibrating in her skull.

Sam hadn't bothered to ask.

Margot couldn't be bothered to try to understand.

Alice didn't want to go through that again. How would she ever explain to the one person she might possibly be sexually attracted to that she was asexual? How would she explain to the next person that it was maybe possible her body could experience attraction, but she wasn't attracted to them?

Why did this have to happen at all?

Maybe it would be better to just ignore Takumi. So what if he'd been nothing but nice to her so far? Who said she *had* to be, too?

CHAPTER 12

Alice had splurged on pad Thai in a box for lunch, thinking it would be a nice variation on the two-for-one-dollar packages of ramen she'd been living on.

(Pad Thai was worth six packages of ramen.)

The trouble was, one box equaled two serving sizes. The Food and Drug Administration didn't know what they were talking about—one box equaled one Alice portion. Unfortunately, this sent her straight to Carb Coma City. And with the week she'd had, she needed it. Being around Takumi began to border on insufferable territory.

The counseling appointment had ripped a wound inside her that refused to heal. And Takumi wouldn't stop irritating the hell out of her like a man-size saltshaker. Feenie's guidance, Essie's raised eyebrow suggestions, Takumi *existing*, her own body's refusal to get its shit together—all of it was the tiniest bit thrilling . . . at first. Now? She wanted to duct-tape him to a chair, cover his mouth with a shipping label, and trap him in the elevator so she wouldn't have to deal with any of it anymore.

Pulling out a chair, she dropped the carton on the table and retrieved her book from her bag.

"You changed your hair," Takumi said, standing near her table.

"Yes. I do that often." The more stressed out she got, the more likely it'd be she would forget to take proper care of her hair, so until she sorted through all this emotional crap, a protective style would be her best friend. Fueled by pure spite, the thick, waist-length braids took two and a half hours to finish, instead of her usual four hours. "Anyway, it hasn't changed since the last time you saw me and you just got back from break. Why are you here?"

"To see you." He sat down. "I wanted to compliment you earlier but you seemed mad. It looks nice."

Her right eye twitched.

They'd been placed on basement duty again. Takumi for half the Saturday until his Storytime shifts started, in which Alice would then be left alone. To be consumed by spiders. Or possessed.

Whichever came first.

She pasted a smile on her face, and said in her sweetest voice, "Go back to work."

Takumi hesitated. "What are you reading?"

Alice held up the book for him to see the front cover.

"What's it about?"

She rotated the book for him to read the back.

"Is it any good?"

"No," she answered, placing it in front of her.

"Then why read it?"

"I finish what I start." Her Netflix history could attest to that.

"That's admirable," he said.

"More like compulsive." She turned her head toward him. Was it possible to marry regret? She sure spent enough time with it. No one should be allowed to look as amazing as he did. Did his parents sell their souls so he'd win the genetic lottery?

He nodded at her processed lunch for one. "You don't know how to cook?"

"Why?" She made a mental note (for the thousandth time) to stop looking at his face.

"You're always eating crap. Have you ever tried it?"

"What? Cooking?"

She had given up trying to learn when she created a gaping hole in her thumb knuckle on a cheese grater.

The week before that, she had sliced a quarter-of-an-inch-deep cut into her index finger pad trying to open a bag of rice with a serrated blade.

Two accidents, both drawing copious amounts of blood, were more than enough to deem the kitchen far too dangerous for her. Microwavable processed meals were much safer, and, on occasion, even tastier. Sure, she had to chug liters of water a day to combat all the sodium she'd ingested, but she'd rather be bloated than accidentally dismember herself next time she tried to chop a tomato.

"Yeah. If you need help, maybe I could give you lessons."

(*The Joy of Cooking*, indeed.)

On cue, Alice's heart rate went wild. She'd write that down in her journal later. Dr. Burris had given her homework: research different kinds of attraction and figure out which ones apply to her for them to discuss at their next session, which she wasn't going to.

(The homework seemed like a good idea, though.)

Aesthetic was a no-brainer.

What Dr. Burris had said was true: the Circle of Having Sex had yet to merge with the Circle of Takumi to create a Venn diagram, much to Feenie's dismay. Alice had placed a question mark next to "sexual" and moved on.

Takumi leaned in closer when she didn't answer. "I'll show you all of my secret recipes."

"Sounds like fun," she said, and then muttered, "I hope you have medical insurance."

"Fun?" He stared at her carton of food, thoughtful. "Cooking isn't my idea of fun, but I'm really good at it and I like teaching."

"What do you do for fun then?" She sat up straight and spoke to him over her shoulder. "Not that I care."

"It depends." He came closer, inches from Alice's face. She zoomed in on his long, straight camel lashes and watched him blink in slow motion. Takumi had such lovely eyes . . . since when was the color *brown* so captivating? They weren't even multihued brown—they were one solid color, pupil barely visible.

(*Brown, though? How?*)

He tilted his head to the side, glancing at her lips, then her eyes.

She sat there, paralyzed, unconsciousness waiting in the wings for her to pass out from lack of oxygen. Behind the wings, shame laughed at her. She told herself, staying awake too long night after night, convincing herself Takumi did not matter. So why did his presence do this to her?

It was confusing and awful and made her want to break things. More often than not, violence was the first thing that sprung to mind. This intruder was wrecking her life. But she couldn't bring herself to tell him to stop. Whatever this was, she wanted to get to the bottom of it. And the only way to do that was to stay near him, to keep interacting with him.

"Depends on what?"

"Now that I know you actually do *care*," he said, standing up. "See you in twelve minutes."

She closed her eyes. Remembering how to move, she placed her overheated forehead on the cold table. "Hey, body? It's Alice. I hate you," she whispered.

Lunch over, she headed back down to find Essie and Takumi engaged in a playful argument. She was so irritated their cuteness hardly registered.

Hardly.

"Be quiet, Takumi." Essie laughed. "You can't say things like that." She placed her hand on her chest, pretending to be offended as if she were a Southern belle in need of a fainting couch.

"Why not?" he argued. "Alice doesn't mind. Right, Alice?"

Alice sat in her seat and leaned around her monitor. "I mind. I mind so much, I'm going to report you and I don't even know what you said." Her inability to control her attitude bothered her, but she couldn't seem to stop. In all honesty, Alice was angry at herself, not him. It was difficult to tell the difference, to find who deserved to be snapped at when he was the catalyst.

Essie chuckled. "Whatever is going on between you two, leave me out of it." She stood up, hefting a stack of manila folders into her arms. "But be sure to invite me to the wedding," she whispered as she flounced away.

"I can't win with either of you," Alice muttered. She didn't want to look at him—she knew he was wearing that stupid grin that made her want to pick up a folding chair, pretend she was a WWE wrestler, and go to town on something.

(Feenie would be proud.)

But she didn't have to look. He walked across the room and stood beside her table.

"I'm busy," she said. Any time they were alone, he pounced like a sly, scavenging hyena (which were terribly cute and terribly misunderstood animals. And also massive in size. She saw one at the zoo once and nearly lost her mind). He *always* wanted to talk.

"Do you believe in magic?"

"What?"

"Do you," he said slowly, sitting in the empty seat adjacent to her, "believe"—he pulled out a pack of cards—"in magic?"

She exhaled through her nose like an angry bull. It took everything she had not to roll her eyes. "That's not real magic." She gestured at the cards. "That's sleight of hand."

"So do you believe, then? In *real magic*?"

"I didn't say that."

"You implied that there's a difference between this and the *real* thing." He slid the cards out of the box and into his hand. "Here. Shuffle them and pick a card."

"I'm not doing this. Go back to work."

He set the deck down on the table and pushed it until it stopped right next to her wrist. Then Alice made a very dumb mistake—she'd always been a sucker for a pretty face. Willy Wonka could wrap her in plastic, market her, and sell her as a limited edition fool-flavored candy.

"Fine. I'm only doing this once."

He grinned as she shuffled, and said, "That's all I'll need."

She side-eyed him but continued to shuffle—pulling stacks of cards out of the middle and placing them on the top, turning them faceup to make sure they weren't all the same card, and making sure she touched only the edges. For fun, because she hadn't done it in some time, she performed a riffle shuffle and a bridge. She smiled, pleased with herself for not messing up, and realigned the cards into a neat deck.

"Now pick one card and place it back in the deck."

"I know this trick," she said, deflating a little. "The back of the cards are marked."

Takumi turned around in his seat to face the wall. "Pick a card. Place it back in the deck when you're done."

Intrigued, she complied. Six of diamonds. "Now what?"

He spun around, took the deck, and shuffled for a moment before spreading the cards into a neat semicircle between them. He didn't hesitate—he picked up the last card on the left-hand side. "Is this your card?"

"No."

"Are you sure?" He squinted at it. "Are you really sure?"

"Positive."

He set it aside, selecting the next card just as quickly as he had with the first on the right-hand side. "Is this your card?"

"No."

He squinted again, clicking his tongue this time. "Are you really, really sure?"

"I'm positive."

Takumi selected a card from the middle. "How about this one?"

"Why do I get the feeling you know damn well that's not my card?"

He snorted with laughter, seemingly surprising himself—his eyes widened and he covered his mouth. "Sorry," he said, clearing his throat. "You're right. I do. I was trying to build dramatic effect." He rested his forearms on the table. "Let me ask you something: the concept of magic has been around as long as humans have. It persists even in the face of rapidly advancing technology and science. Why do you think that is?"

"Because people want to believe, Mulder."

"Yes, actually." His right hand hovered above the deck, slowly moving from one end to the other.

Alice waited patiently for whatever he planned to do. There's no way he could pick the card she had. Unless there was some sort of smudge on the back. She'd seen that before—the cards had been heat sensitive. She had been careful to touch only the tiniest corner with her fingernails when she selected hers.

"I wanted to do this to cheer you up," Takumi said, without breaking his concentration. Eyebrows tensed. Eyes relaxed. Lips parted slightly. Pausing for only fractions of moments over random cards before continuing his sweep. "You've been really upset lately. I know we only met two weeks ago, but I care. I've been thinking about you, wondering what I could do to help. You were right—people want to believe in magic, because when things seem terrible, magic and miracles give them hope. They want to believe something is working in their favor behind the scenes. Something good." His hand stopped, selecting a card again. He laid it on the table in front of her. "Something that will surprise them."

Alice sucked in a breath. "How in the hell?" She picked up her card, examining the front and the back. "How did you do that?"

"Magic." He shrugged like he didn't just impress the hell out of her.

"Do it again," she said, trying to put the card back with the deck.

"No," he said, cleaning up the cards. "That's yours. I want you to keep that card."

"But it will ruin the deck."

"It won't. I want you to keep it. I want you to have something miraculous to hold on to when everything seems awful."

His smile was kind—and her heart softly fluttered for a moment. She pressed her hand to her chest, cleared her throat, and tried to memorize that sensation. Tried to evoke that gentle feeling of surprise again on her own.

She couldn't.

"When you feel like you don't need that card anymore," he said, "give it back to me. I'll teach you how to do it, and then you can show someone else."

She stopped herself from setting the card back down. Giving in to anger, being combative, wasn't who she was or wanted to be. Graciously accepting his kindness felt true to her soul. It wasn't magic—she knew that. But the gesture made her feel warm. Made her remember that moment when she saw that it *was* her card, the feeling of seeing him completely confident and knowing. She'd rather have the card than know the secret.

(Or pass it on.)

"Okay," she agreed. "My turn. I don't have anything impressive to go along with it, but I am sorry. You were right about what you said earlier. I've been in a shit mood lately, and I've been taking it out on people who don't deserve it. Like you."

"That's okay. Everyone has moments when they're less than their best."

She bumped his shoulder and smiled. "Did you steal that off a Hallmark card?"

"Don't insult me, Alice." He raised an eyebrow. "I can come up with my own cheesy lines without resorting to petty thievery."

"My apologies, good sir."

"But," he said, "I was beginning to think you seriously didn't like me, which with the year I'm having would make sense."

"What do you mean?" She placed her elbow on the table and cradled her chin in her hand.

"I mean, I thought I must have done something and now you hated me because of it."

"I got that part. And for the record, I don't hate you."

"Good to know. I was one glare away from deducting cute points."

"No, not the points!" She gasped in mock outrage before laughing.

(*God*, did that feel good to do.) "I don't hate you. Not even close. I'm just . . . exasperated."

"With me?" He looked confused.

Alice decided to sidestep the truth. She didn't plan to lie, just sort of hopscotch around it. She settled on "I have a lot going on right now."

"Would you like to talk about it?"

"Not really," she answered immediately. "And, uh, I didn't mean to be rude earlier when you complimented my hair. Well, maybe I did, but I'm sorry. I get questions about it, and I hate feeling like I'm forced to explain every little detail about braiding and my hair, because if I don't, then they'll say I'm being mean or something because they 'just want to understand' and touch it, so I get defensive anyway and it's a terrible trap. But yeah. Thanks."

Takumi nodded. "My friend Melissa told me about that. She had an afro for a while and she would get really upset because her coworkers kept touching her hair without asking, but she couldn't show it because, um, what did she say?" He thought for a moment. "They'd say she was an angry black woman or something like that? Is that it?"

"Yeah. That's, um. Yeah, that's it," she managed, staring at him. "It's super weird to me for some reason that you actually know that. Hearing you say it kinda messed with me for a second."

"Why?"

"I don't know. I said 'for some reason' for a reason," she joked.

He crossed his arms, sitting back in the chair with a thoughtful expression on his face. "It would be more surprising if you knew any stereotypes for Japanese Americans. Not Asian Americans in general, but my people."

"Well, you're not wrong," she agreed. "I mean, but that's a good thing, right? That I can't think of any?"

"Not really." He had the same look on his face that her dad did when he was mildly disappointed in her about something but wouldn't say why. Like she was supposed to *know* better.

"Ah," she said to fill the awkward silence. "It's the deck, isn't it?" She pointed to the cards, wanting to change the subject. "The deck is rigged?"

He shrugged. "Or maybe I'm a magician."

The elevator dinged. They both turned their heads toward the door. Busted—too late to run, too late to pretend like they had been working.

"I leave for ten minutes and you two start *playing cards*?"

CHAPTER

13

Ryan didn't speak when Alice entered the kitchen. He pulled her arm, tugging her toward him, and placed his head on her shoulder. She rubbed the back of his neck. He had used the same cucumber-melon shampoo since middle school. Nothing smelled more like *Ryan* than that.

"Tired?" she asked.

"Exhausted. Tell me why I agreed to do this again?"

"This" meaning his overwhelming summer schedule. He had explained his plans to Alice right after the previous semester had ended. She had kept her incredulous face in check in order to appear supportive, but she knew this was coming.

Ryan had attended Bowen only because he was wait-listed for Dennard University. He received his formal acceptance with some bad news: some of his state-college credits wouldn't fully transfer to the university. Two summer school classes to catch up plus regular morning shifts twenty hours a week at a small, nearby pastry shop, and to top it off, he had regular volunteer shifts at a hospital.

"Because you love helping people *and* it's going to look amazing when you apply for medical school. Best of both worlds. Want me to sing the song?"

Ryan laughed. "Maybe some other time."

"Why don't you go lie down? I'll bring you your food when it's done." A pot of potatoes boiled on the stove. Mashed potatoes with sweetened yellow corn on top was his favorite comfort food, thanks to Feenie's influence.

"Sure you can handle this?" He eyed her skeptically. "I don't want you to hurt yourself."

"Yeah." She smiled. "This is perfect Alice-level cooking. There's nothing sharp around, I can handle a can opener, and I'll be careful when I drain the potatoes." She gave him a thumbs-up.

"Okay. Yeah. Thank you," he said on his way out.

"Oh, um, hold on." Alice glanced at the calendar they kept on the fridge with all their work schedules. That Friday had a giant red heart around it for Family Night. It had been a tradition for years—they almost never missed a single date. At first, they called it Horror Movie Saturday, then it changed to Dorm Room Dinners—now it had a simpler title. Something it should have been from the very beginning. "You're free tomorrow morning, right?"

"Free to sleep in."

"Sleep is for the weak," she joked. "You know you want to go to a law seminar with me."

"That sounds like the exact opposite of what I want to do."

She began to open the can of corn. "Oh, come on, please? I'll make my mom pay for you."

"It sounds awful, though."

"No argument there." The lid popped open. She drained the excess water and dumped the kernels into a glass bowl. "It's going to be dry and boring and I don't want to go by myself. Please? It's only three hours."

"Did you miss the bit about me being tired?" He leaned against the refrigerator.

"She's being unreasonable and has recruited my sister to browbeat me. I need support. And love. And affection. Please? Also, do I put extra sugar on this?"

"*No*. It's naturally sweet. Just microwave it." He sighed. "Maybe you should tell your parents the truth."

"I already did. I'm going to again when I figure out what I want to do instead. Adam is helping me stall."

"Any leads?"

"Not a one." She set the bowl inside their microwave and started it. Two minutes to be safe. Or was that too long? If she managed to burn the corn—

"What about computer programming?" he asked. "That could be fun."

"Fun for who?" She laughed around each word. "Surely you don't mean me."

"What about a language? Translators are always needed."

"You think I'd be good at that?" She bent at the waist to be eye level with the viewing window. So far, so good.

"I think you'd be good at whatever you put your mind to. You can be kind of indecisive."

"Kind of?" She glanced at him.

"Okay. Very. But you have a great memory and you do really well in structured environments. If there are set rules or instructions to follow, you can do it no problem and excel. Language is like that. It could work for you."

"My school does offer a few, I think." Alice opened the microwave door and nearly touched the bowl before remembering to use a pot holder. "Which one should I pick?"

"The obvious answer is Spanish or Mandarin. If you want, I can start teaching you Tagalog. Buy a couple of workbooks and I'll grade them during my lunch breaks."

"But you're so busy." She smiled at him. (And the corn. It smelled amazing and very unburnt.) "You'd do that for me?"

"Of course."

"Mm-hmm, but you won't go to the seminar with me."

"I have limits," he said, walking away. "My understanding only goes so far."

CHAPTER
14

If Alice had any doubts she felt some kind of way about Takumi, her REM cycle decided to do the honor of setting the record straight.

The dream began normal enough. One of her usual that occurred when she'd eaten her body weight in ramen while in between paychecks. She sat at an enormous dining room table, the kind found in a mansion in a historical movie. Dish after delicious dish of sweet and/or savory food appeared by magic, steaming hot and ready to be devoured. She was more than up for the challenge. Best of all, the table came equipped with a button that made it rotate. She could sit in one spot while she stuffed her belly to her heart's content.

Midway through a plate of prime rib (cooked medium rare) and mashed potatoes (buttered, salted, peppered), the doorbell rang. She looked around the empty room to see if someone *else* would open the door (BECAUSE FOOOOOD) and reluctantly got up when it rang for the third time.

(But not before cutting a huge chunk of steak and shoving it in her mouth.)

A giant ballroom, straight out of a Disney classic, packed full of costumed attendees, greeted her on the other side.

"Well, if this ain't some bullshit," she muttered to no one, still chewing. She stepped inside, glancing at at the partygoers twirling around the dance floor in a choreographed waltz.

The door slammed shut behind her. She leapt into the air before whirling around. The knob wouldn't turn and she banged on the door until her hands began to hurt.

"Stop abusing the door," a voice teased.

Moving proved to be a problem. Her pajama pants with the worn-out elastic waistband morphed into a giant hoop skirt and several layers of fabric. The deep emerald-green-and-black fabric adorned with frills and lace seemed to sparkle under the chandelier lights.

"*Oh no,*" Alice whined, looking down.

Bodice tight.

Lungs constricted.

Cleavage plentiful.

"You're so cute," he said.

Takumi smirked at her from behind the black-and-gold-feathered mask covering the top half of his face. Alice's almost fainting spell could have been caused by the lack of oxygen reaching her brain due to the corset. Or by Takumi, dressed as Mr. Darcy in a dark gothic fantasy version of *Pride and Prejudice.*

(*P&P2: The Fall of the House of Alice.*)

"This isn't happening," she whispered.

"Dance with me?" he asked, bowing slightly.

"Do I have a choice?"

Takumi paused. "Doesn't seem like it." He held out his hand.

After rubbing her fingers against her palm, Alice placed her hand in his. He escorted her out to the middle of the room as the dance floor cleared. The guests formed a ring of spectators around them. Spinning her in a small circle first, he stopped the movement of her body with his own. Her resulting squeak echoed around the vaulted ceilings, and Takumi chuckled low in her ear. Goose bumps erupted all over her skin. He kept one of his hands in hers, placing the other on her waist, right where the corset had squeezed her into artificial narrowness.

They swayed together as the first few notes from a violin filled the room before Takumi picked up the pace, gliding with her around the room in large sweeping loops. Now, Alice had taken dance classes since she was four and didn't stop until she was sixteen. She knew how to dance. But knowing and remembering were not synonymous in this dream. She stared at his gold rose boutonniere, managing to not step on his feet or trip over her dress while she counted to stay on track.

"Alice," he whispered in her ear.

"Shh! I'm concentrating," she whispered back, on edge. She didn't want the partygoers to know she didn't know what she was doing.

"They're all gone."

Everyone had indeed disappeared. The room was also now strangely smaller, complete with a lush bed large enough to fit a small army. The comforter, pillows, and canopy were a sumptuous black velvet.

"Are you ready?" he asked.

She stared at him with a surprising amount of terror rolling around in her stomach.

"For?" she squeaked.

"The last night of your life." He leaned forward, her body froze, and he placed a light kiss right in front of her ear.

ALICE SHOT UP in bed, panting, gripping her chest. Her nightshirt was drenched in sweat. Groaning, she plopped back down on her bed, staring at the ceiling in desperation and relief.

"Nothing happened." She laughed, covering her eyes. And then she groaned again, flopping on her bed like an angry fish on land. That awful dream had sealed it. If she couldn't even have a proper sex dream, she must not have wanted Takumi in a sexual way.

Then . . . how *did* she want him?

When he looked at her and she looked at him and all they could see was each other . . . her heart might or might not have begun having tiny reactions.

Nothing too radical. It was a light feeling—airy, twisty, and warm. It made her want to be near him, hear him laugh, and maybe try to poke him in the dimples when he smiled.

It was *possible* Alice had a tiny romantic crush on him.

It was *possible* Alice had a not-so-tiny romantic crush on him.

It was *possible* Alice liked Takumi far more than she was willing to admit.

Possible did not make it a conclusive fact.

"Are you up?" Ryan said, knocking on her door. "You better be up."

"Yeah. Why?" she called, checking the time before flying out of bed. How did she sleep through her main alarm *and* the fail-safe?

"Because that stupid seminar starts in thirty minutes. Are you dressed? And you're buying me coffee."

Alice opened the door, grinning as Ryan's frown intensified. "Gladly, Grumpy Bear. I just need ten minutes!"

Four hours later, she was ready for a nap. And some chocolate.

(And maybe to slip back into that dream to figure it out.)

She'd fallen asleep during each presentation—she even snored herself awake at one point. And of course, Aisha had called the second the seminar ended. Alice ignored the first call, wanting to eat before talking to her, but Aisha called back as they pulled into the library parking lot.

"Aren't you supposed to be working?" Alice answered. She covered the speaker with her hand. "Walk me inside?" she asked Ryan. "I want to show you the new literacy center. They let me codesign the layout."

He nodded, turning off the car and removing his seat belt.

"I'm not in the mood. Don't test me," Aisha warned. "How was it? Did you learn anything?"

(Dry as toast. Boring as a snail race.)

(She learned she should just buy a house with her tuition money, because she would end up sleeping through class. Might as well get some equity or whatever her dad was always ranting about out of that money.)

"Yeah. It was great. Ryan said he learned a lot, too."

"Keep your sins to yourself," Ryan hissed as they walked toward the entrance. "Don't put that lie on me." He didn't fare any better, but slept as silent as death. A pair of sunglasses and he was out cold in the first twenty minutes.

"Which field do you think you'd like the best?" Aisha pressed.

"Well, I don't know. I got some pamphlets and handouts. I think I need to review them a few more times."

"Okay. I'll tell Mom to expect a call from you soon."

"Yes. Soon. But not now or today or this week. I wouldn't even bet on this month, to be honest."

"Alice."

"Fine. I'll call her. Soon. Ish. I'm at work now. Good-bye."

Ryan laughed as Alice kicked the air in frustration. "Why are they doing this to me?"

"Pretty sure it's because they love you," he replied, ever determined to be the voice of reason she loved.

"Why does everyone keep saying that? I don't wonder whether or not they love me. I know they do. They don't trust me, which is just as important, I think. I'm the baby. I get it. I wasn't supposed to exist, but I do, so it's like they think they know what's best for me since Adam and Aisha turned out great. They have all the shortcuts figured out and I'm just supposed to take them because they say so."

"Sounds like you don't trust them either." He held up his hands when she gave him a death glare. "I'm just saying."

Alice led him to the right, past the media-center shelves. There wasn't much available space—it was a small old building—and any substantial renovations would require the library to close. They did the best they could with what they had.

"Ta-da," she said, holding out her arms. Light poured in from the large paned windows onto two rows of rectangular desks. The third row housed computers with their screens turned away from the sun in cubicles big enough for two seats. "It's not much, but I read a thing where it said it's better to study in natural light, so I tried to utilize the windows and skylight as much as possible.

"I wanted to put posters up, but they said no. They didn't want it to feel condescending since this section is technically for adults. I did get to do this, though." She pointed to three half-size bookcases that lined one wall just under the windows. "Staff, volunteers, and tutors get to select which books go here. It's supposed to be the books that made us passionate about reading. Anyone who visits the center at least three times is allowed to add to it. Essie set up a special donation fund to buy books specifically for this shelf."

"Nice," Ryan said. "But what did you pick? You don't exactly read a lot."

She pointed to the spine of her first book selection.

"I should have known." He laughed. "Remember how mad we were about the leaked TV pilot?"

"Oh God, it was *awful*."

She looped their arms together and tugged Ryan back toward the entrance. Sometimes it was easy to forget that they had a connection that didn't involve Feenie. They had their own inside jokes and memories and traditions. He wasn't always around, but she could go to him when it mattered. Ryan seamlessly filled the spaces that Feenie couldn't.

For her, they were two halves of the same whole. Alice needed them both.

"They don't listen to me," she said after a moment, wanting his advice. "My parents. I always did everything I was supposed to without complaining. It's my life, but I'm still waiting for my turn to be in charge."

"When you said that, I pictured you and your parents in a car and you're climbing from the backseat into the front, trying to take the wheel."

"Like Jesus." She giggled.

"Yeah, but you know how it ends, right? You're going to crash, Buttons. You're all dead."

"Wow. Okay. Um?"

"It's a very morbid metaphor, I know. If you can't work together or come to an agreement . . ."

"What do you think I should do then?"

He smiled at her—one that meant *I love you, but nope you're wrong.* "You don't want my opinion on this."

"I figured as much," she said, trying not to be disappointed. So much for being on her side. That traitor. That adorable, formerly chubby-cheeked turncoat . . .

Ryan agreed with her parents.

But didn't he realize that meant she wouldn't see him and Feenie probably for years? She would ship off to school while they stayed here married and happy with Glory, while she suffered.

Didn't he want her around?

"Let's say I did go to law school. I'd probably have to move away," Alice said.

"Understandable."

She frowned. "You won't miss me?"

"Buttons, you're changing schools, not dying." He laughed, shaking his head. "It's not forever. We'll still see you on breaks and holidays."

We'll.

They.

Together without her.

Delaying the inevitable never stopped it from happening.

They exited the library's front doors and idled around on the sidewalk. Ryan threw his keys in the air and caught them with the opposite hand.

"What time does your shift start?" he asked.

"Five. I'm going to head up to eat before it starts. I have some frozen dinners in the break room," she said. "I'm off at nine tonight."

"Do you want me to pick you up? Or would I be interrupting a Takumi Trial?" He raised one suggestive eyebrow and gestured to the left with his chin. "Is that the infamous bus stop where he waits with you?"

"You're as bad as she is." Alice rolled her eyes.

"She's serious. I'm just joking. Do you even like him?"

"He won't leave me alone to dislike him in peace, so yeah, I guess." She grimaced. "He's too nice to hate. And he has that whole *charming* thing going on."

"Oh, poor you. It must be terrible having to deal with that."

"Shut up." She tried to kick him but he dodged the move, laughing. "Feenie teases me enough, thanks."

"Speaking of my wonderful almost-wife, she says there's a costume party she wants to go to. Friday night."

"But that's Family Night." They had already voted to have a fancy spaghetti dinner and watch a campy horror-movie trilogy about the undead.

"We can outvote her if you want."

"No, because then she'll be mad at both of us."

"All right. Bring it in." Ryan opened his arms for a good-bye hug. She stepped into it, frowning.

"I don't really want to hug you because you're a jerk, but I love you anyway." She looked up at him. "Thank you for today."

"The feeling is mutual." He kissed her cheek. "All of them."

She turned to go inside, but stopped short, a hand flying to her chest in surprise.

"Hey, Alice," Takumi said, wearing jeans and a T-shirt, not a three-piece suit trimmed in gold. His hair was messy, not slicked back, and he didn't look nearly as manipulative as he had in her dream.

She didn't have to think about which Takumi she preferred.

"Takumi. Hey."

"Are you on break?" His eyes darted to Ryan and back to her. He carried a bright blue bag with him.

"No, I just got here. I had to go to this school thing, so I'm only working a half day today. This is Ryan, one of my best friends."

They shook hands. "I'll see you tonight," Ryan said, touching her shoulder.

"Uh, we live together," she said to Takumi. "We're roommates. Us and Feenie, my other best friend. He's giving me a ride."

"Okay." Takumi gave her a look and she realized that he hadn't asked any of that. He hadn't asked anything. She overshared because she assumed he would care. Again.

(Why, oh why, did she care if he cared?)

She rubbed her forehead. "I'm going in now," she said, leaving them standing there. In the break room, she plopped the precooked and flash-frozen generic breakfast bowl with semiplastic eggs, overcooked sausage, squishy potatoes, and delicious cheese down on the table before sitting.

"Wait!" Takumi called. He sat in the chair next to hers. "Don't start eating yet."

"Why?" she asked, definitely not thinking about the dream or ball gowns or velvet pillows . . . Oh, who was she kidding? Somehow, he'd know about the dream. He'd sense it and she would die of embarrassment. "What are you doing here anyway? You don't start for another half hour."

(No, she didn't have his schedule memorized.)

(Okay, yeah, she did.)

(Tuesday and Thursday: 5 p.m.–9 p.m. Saturday: 9:30 a.m.–6 p.m. Sunday: 1 p.m.–5 p.m.)

"I have a present for you. Do you want it?"

"Is it a cute present?" Alice joked, facing forward. Looking at him dead-on in close proximity continued to prove to be difficult. Her mouth tended to dry out, thoughts still went blank.

"Not exactly." Takumi pouted like he had gotten something wrong. "You'll like this present, though." Reaching into the blue bag, he pulled out two square glass dishes with lids. He pushed her breakfast bowl away.

"Japanese mabo tofu."

"Did you make this?" she asked as he pried off the lid. One dish had plain rice. The other contained slightly orange-and-white-colored cubes of something (probably the tofu?) with green onions sprinkled on top and a thick reddish-brown sauce underneath it. She sniffed the air—pork, garlic, and . . . ginger? Her stomach began to rumble. "For me? Why?"

"Well," he began, smiling, "I was talking to Essie and she mentioned you liked trying new foods. I thought cooking for you would be a good way to give your bad days a little pick-me-up and make your good days that much better. Don't worry—I cleared our dinners with Essie for the foreseeable future."

He held a spoon out for her.

"Thank you," she said, taking it.

"You're welcome." He scooped out half the rice onto a plate for her.

She took a bite. "Holy crap, this is good." It had the perfect amount of savory spice. "You seriously made this?"

"It's actually pretty basic."

"Doesn't taste basic to me. *Wow.*"

"Are you always so easily impressed?"

"Lean Cuisine is a basic food group for me. My taste buds have degraded. It's probably really disgusting and I just can't tell the difference." She shoveled more into her mouth, eyeing his plate. "Are you going to eat that? Because, you know, I will. Waste not, want not, and all that jazz."

Takumi laughed. And then he tipped his plate over hers and gave her half his food.

"I was kidding," she whispered as she covertly tried to slide her plate farther away from his. Just in case.

"It's fine. I'm not that hungry anyway." He smiled.

"I guess I owe you dinner tomorrow?" Alice asked when her plate was nearly empty.

"You don't owe me anything. I did this because I wanted to."

"Yeah, but," she said, "I should do something nice for you."

"Um, well, rumor has it you can't cook, and I'm pretty picky about what I eat."

"That's not a rumor. I'm awful in the kitchen." She giggled. "Do you have a ton of food allergies or something? My brother's wife is like that. Christy is super paranoid about eating out."

He shook his head. "I like to take care of my body. I stay away from calorie-dense, overprocessed, chemical-laden foods. Except for pizza. That seems to always sneak in there."

"Because it's pizza. I love Chicago-style deep dish."

He leaned back in his seat, sucking in a breath, pretending to wince in pain. "Why would you even say that? That is my absolute favorite."

"Really? You strike me as a thin-and-crispy, no-cheese kind of guy."

"Your instincts are wrong. Give me all the cheese. All of it. Just throw a pound of it on top."

"I suppose you can have points for that. Anyway, I literally cannot afford to be that selective about what I eat."

"Can you really afford not to, though? You only have one body."

"My teenager metabolism hasn't quit on me just yet. Besides, when scientists find a way to upload human consciousness into androids, all of this will be irrelevant." Alice scrunched her face. "Do you always eat all healthy and stuff?"

"Ninety-eight percent of the time."

"And the two percent?"

"Just pizza. And good beer."

She had an idea so crazy she thought Feenie's spirit must have left her body with the sole purpose of invading Alice's to make her think of it. "There's a costume party coming up and there will probably be cardboard pizza and average beer. You should come along as my guest. Costume is optional."

Takumi made a face. "A college party?"

"There will be college-age individuals there," she said, smiling at him. "It's not like it's at a frat or something. Besides, you're not that old."

"I'm not old at all."

"Oh yeah? Prove it. Stay out past your bedtime," she teased. Her phone chimed—a text from Feenie:

> Um. Excuse me. But why is Ryan saying he got to meet Takumi?? What the entire fuck? I'm banned from the library and he isn't???

Oops. She'd deal with that later.

CHAPTER
15

There's something powerful about making a grand entrance in a fantastic pair of red heels.

Alice had chosen her costume well. She managed to find an orange turtleneck sweater that fit like a dream. Her short brown bob wig swished across the tops of her shoulders. Her pleated skirt was the exact same shade of red as her fabulous shoes.

From the orange knee-highs to the black-rimmed glasses, she was the perfect Velma Dinkley from *Scooby-Doo*. She rang the doorbell and twirled a strand of her hair in her fingers while she waited.

The door swung open. A white guy wearing a toga and gold laurel wreath on his head greeted her with an enthusiastic, "Jinkies!"

She smiled, deciding to take that as a compliment.

Behind him, the party looked almost exactly how Alice had thought it would—most of the attendees stood around in small clusters, a few people sat on the couch. Everyone had a red Solo cup in their hands. The music was at the perfect volume to hold a conversation *and* dance.

"My mom loves *Scooby-Doo*," he said, noticeably not moving.

"Me too. It's pretty great," she said. "So it's a little cold out here."

"That's too bad," he said. Toga Boy's gaze dropped to her exposed thighs. He sucked his bottom lip into his mouth as he continued blocking the bulk of the doorway with his body. If Alice wanted in, she'd have to slide past him.

"Okay." A nervous, tittering laugh broke free. "Are you going to move, or . . . ?"

"You have to pay the toll first." He cocked his head to the side. "What's your name?"

"Alice."

"Feenie's Alice?" A sharp breath slid through his teeth. "Damn."

Toga Boy backed up, holding the door open for her. Outside, she had caught only a whiff, but now the smell of pot and beer slammed into her.

"How do you know Feenie?" Feenie and Ryan had arrived before she did since she didn't get off work until eight.

"I'm a piercer at Tim's. You should come by sometime. You'd look good with a lip ring."

"I'll think about it," she said, intending to never do so. She craned her neck around the room, looking for any sign of her friends.

"Great."

Alice turned around to reply. Toga Boy leaned to the side, trying to see up her skirt.

"Ugh!" she grunted with disgust. Marching away, she wound through the small crowd. There were quite a few costume standards—ghosts, zombies, vampires, maids, superheroes, and villains. She spotted (and complimented) Jane Lane, Quinn, and Daria Morgendorffer from *Daria*, a lovely Katniss from *The Hunger Games*, and someone dressed in an outstanding costume as Ace Ventura when he wore the pink tutu, complete with the football tucked under their arm.

(*Laces out!*)

"Buttons!" Ryan shouted from a couch in the next room, raising his hand. Feenie sat on his lap.

Finally, she thought, weaving through the crowd toward them.

They were dressed as a pair—a couple from the 1920s. She in a wonderfully sparkly silver flapper dress, he in a pinstripe suit complete with a hat.

"Where is he?" Feenie demanded.

"Hello to you, too. He'll be here soon."

"You better not be hiding him from me."

"He had to babysit his nieces for a few hours." She sat down next to them in a sliver of empty space. "His brother should have gotten home around now-ish."

"Likely story. As soon as he gets here, I want to meet him. I mean it. I have questions."

"You're drunk, friend." Alice tapped the top of Feenie's head.

"Newsflash. Everybody is. Even this one." She kissed Ryan's temple. His cheeks were redder than normal and his eyes were glassy.

"We pregamed," he admitted.

"You didn't drive, right?"

"Carpool," he said, downing his drink. "I should do this more often. Why don't I do this more often?"

"I'm sure you'll remember why tomorrow."

Ghostbusters played on the TV in front of them on mute. Alice knew why they had chosen to sit there instead of mingling. It was Ryan's favorite movie—he knew all the words, and as a kid, he used to act out the scenes in front of the TV. He had even made his own proton pack out of his school backpack and his sister's curling iron.

(There was a video of one of his *performances* floating around in Feenie's hard drive. After Ryan had showed it to them some years ago, Alice had secretly stolen the tape and transferred it to digital.)

No sound didn't bother them. Ryan recited each line like a one-man show while Feenie cackled and Alice giggled. When the credits rolled, Feenie yelled, "Play the sequel! 'Everything you are doing is bad. I want you to know this,'" she quoted, laughing. "I love that line. I'm going to start saying it to people."

Ryan grimaced, eyes half-lidded. *Lightweight* wasn't the word, and he'd probably drunk enough to intoxicate an elephant. "Sweetie, please don't," he slurred. "I just really need you to not get into any more fights."

"No one is going to fight me if I say that." She chewed on the rim of her cup.

"I think he's worried about them saying something back and you fighting them," Alice offered.

"Don't start none, won't be none." Feenie smiled.

"We can't keep bailing you out of jail. Our wedding-and-house fund is for our *wedding and house*. We can't keep using it for bail money," Ryan said.

"*Oh my God*, will you let that go?" Feenie rolled her eyes.

Earlier in the year, Feenie had gotten into a public fight and was arrested (again). Fortunately, the charges were dropped, but they still had to pay the bail money. Alice had never seen Ryan so mad and he clearly wasn't over it.

A pang of sorrow hit Alice in her heart. One day, Ryan and Feenie would get married.

(At the wedding, she'd be on double duty as the Best Lady of Honor.)

(She'd already picked out her tuxedo-inspired dress.)

They could joke all day when it came to marrying Alice, too, but it wasn't like she had access (or contributed) to that bank account. It wasn't like Ryan had given her an engagement ring, too. She never thought the day would come when their trio would genuinely become a duo, but lately all signs pointed to that future as inevitable.

Soon they'd have a life without her.

Soon she would be left behind.

(Growing up sucks balls.)

"Guys," Alice whined. "We're supposed to be having a good time. Family Night, remember? I'll get you both another drink and when I come back, I expect you two to be in family mode."

"Love you, Buttons," Ryan said.

She took their cups, and wandered back out the way she had come toward the kitchen.

"Where is he?" Feenie called behind her. "Tell him to hurry up."

But when Alice returned to the couch, they were gone. She tapped Fred Flintstone on the shoulder. "Excuse me, did you see where the couple that was sitting here went?"

He was stone-cold sober, too. "Upstairs."

"Oh, thanks." She turned to leave, but he gently took her elbow.

"You probably don't want to go up there. I think they wanted to be alone."

"Oh. Right. Thanks."

Alice set the beers down on a clear space of end table. Family Night was decidedly over.

Sometimes she really felt like she brought this on herself. Besides Moschoula (who was busy posting pictures of herself gallivanting around an island), they were her only nearby friends. She didn't regret following Feenie and Ryan to school, but maybe it was time to try to build a life for herself outside of Them.

(But she didn't want to, damn it!)

If she moved away for law school, Ryan would miss her, but he would be fine. Feenie would definitely protest, but would she actively stop Alice from leaving? Come up with some harebrained scheme to prove how much she wanted to keep Alice around?

(She hoped to God Feenie would.)

As Alice headed toward the front door to wait outside for Takumi, a boy wrapped his arm around her shoulders. An electric jolt of fear zipped straight through her.

"Can I get you a drink?" He shook his cup at her.

"No, but you can move your arm." She shrugged him off, twisting away . . . right into a corner. She was wedged into the space where the wall met the staircase with him standing in front of her. Yellow jumpsuit, giant flower buttons, oversize shoes, ruffled collar—clowns were the devil's minions. All that was missing was the red hair and white makeup.

By the grace of dignity, she managed not to start dry-heaving on the spot.

"What's your name?" he slurred.

"Thoroughly Unavailable. My parents were antihippies. Excuse me."

She stepped to the side and he matched her.

"The disrespect," he joked in mock horror. (She hoped he was joking anyway.) "I'm just trying to talk to you."

"Fine. Let's talk. Do you know where Feenie is?"

"Who's that?"

"The person I need to go find, so if you'll excuse me . . ."

"Wait, wait." He shuffled in front of her. "Why are you in such a rush? It's a party. Relax."

"I am relaxed. If I relax any further, I'll fall asleep."

"I don't live here, but we could borrow a room—"

"No." She shook her head, lips pressed into a grim line. "Nope. Don't even. I retract my joke."

Clown Boy laughed. "You seem chill. And pretty cute for a Black girl."

Alice wished she had accepted his drink offer. And wished she would have taken a sip right when he'd said that. So she could have spat it at him in shock. *Cute for a Black girl* was an insult disguised as a compliment.

"Was that supposed to be flattering?"

"Well, yeah. I mean, you're hot, and your legs look incredible," he said. "That's a whole lot of leg and thigh. They'd look even better wrapped around my waist."

Her shoulders hunched. She took a step back. The wall greeted her. (Nowhere to run.)

"Don't be like that. Come on," he said, standing in front of her. He extended his arm, placing his palm flat by the side of her head in that way boys seem to do when they want to corner their prey. "You know exactly how you look," he whispered. His tequila breath singed her nose hairs.

"And how is that? Like I'm ready to solve some mysteries?" Her nervous laughter sounded awful in her ears. Maybe her Velma costume wasn't the best choice for this night. She wasn't trying to be *sexy*. She loved this costume, the best kind of balance between smart, feminine, and cute. Maybe she should have gone with her first choice—Gadget from *Chip 'n' Dale: Rescue Rangers*. But the last time she did, people kept trying to steal her goggles.

(She knew her outfit wouldn't have made any difference to Clown Boy, but it was a slippery thought to hold on to.)

"Sexy as fuck. I've never been with a Black girl before."

Never been with a Black girl was code for being a fantasy on someone's checkoff list.

"Allow me to be the one to burst your bubble: don't think you're going to start here."

"You don't even know me. You should give me a chance." His free hand traced a line across her thigh, right below the hem of her skirt.

No, no, no.

Nonononononononono.

With tense movements, she reached down and moved his hand. She pushed him gently in the chest. "And you should back up."

"What—"

"You're in my space," Alice said loud enough to make the people next to them turn around. She refused to even blink.

"What the fuck are you getting loud for?" he whispered to Alice but moved away. His eyes darted to the Black guy dressed as a pirate who openly stared at them. Waiting. "Everything's cool, man. We're just talking."

"Is that right? You okay?" the pirate asked Alice.

Her heart quaked and her fists wanted to connect with something, both surefire signs she was ten seconds away from a panic attack. Her spidey-sense was full-on tingling and it all said one thing: Get. Away. From. Him.

She shook her head once and then pushed her way out of the corner.

"Hey!" Clown Boy shouted as she all but ran to the front door.

For a long time, Alice had believed she was Cutie Code: Green-Yellow to *everyone else*. That was the average amount of cute she felt on any given day. She worked hard to maintain her appearance (and her self-esteem).

Puberty forced her to come to terms with the fact that her self-coding assessment may have been low—others would code her much higher. Parts of her (possibly even the whole of her) were desirable to the opposite sex. To her own sex. To the guy who liked to yell about the size of her ass when she walked from the bus stop to her house. To the people who called her cute while only staring at her breasts.

It made her uncomfortable as all hell.

Alice clomped down the stairs outside, ripping around the corner to stand in the dark side of the house. She pressed her forehead against the cold wood, taking deep breath after deep breath. It wasn't enough. She kicked the side of the house, slapped it with her open palm. The stinging sensations pierced through her hand.

She clenched it into a fist to make it worse.

"Alice?"

She jumped back away from the voice. Why was he always sneaking up on her?

"What are you doing?" Takumi asked. He wore light blue jeans, a white T-shirt, and a red jacket. His hair had been slicked up to give him a bit of a pompadour. She couldn't tell if it was a costume or not. "Are you dressed as Velma?"

"Yeah."

"This might sound weird, but can I take your picture?"

"Why?" She frowned at him.

"For my nieces. One of the instructors at their day care got them hooked on *Scooby-Doo*. If I show them I met Velma, it'll make their whole year."

"You have nieces?"

"Yeah. Twins. My brother's girls."

"You have a brother?"

"That's what I just said. I also told you about them yesterday," he said. "Are you all right?"

"I'm sorry." She covered her face. "I know I'm being stupid and saying stupid stuff. It happens when I get overwhelmed, and I just assaulted a house because *that's smart*."

"Hey." He stood in front of her. "Calm down. What happened?"

"I just wanted to wear a cute costume, you know? And everything was great, but then Feenie and Ryan left me and boys are awful when they're drunk and I can't even get drunk to drown my disappointed sorrows because Jesus knows it's not safe in there. And I'm just so *mad* I could spit."

"Could you do it in that direction?" He nodded behind her.

"'Spitting is the epitome of unladylike behavior,'" she recited out of habit. "My grandma says that. You're only supposed to *say* you'll spit, not actually *do* it."

"Okay." Takumi's slight smile made her feel a little bit better. "You wanna get out of here?"

"I can't," Alice said, wishing she could say the opposite. "Feenie wants to meet you."

"But I thought you just said they left?"

"Technically. They're upstairs. They wanted to be alone."

"Ah. So Feenie and Ryan are together?"

She crossed her arms over her chest, deflating into a pool of misery. "They're getting married soon."

"Ah. Got it. My best friends got married a couple of years ago. What a weird thing to have in common." He put his hands into his pants pockets and rocked on his heels. "It must be tough. It was for me anyway, at first. Suddenly being the third wheel."

Alice nodded, feeling calmer. "I think they try hard to make sure I don't feel that way, and I truly appreciate it, but I'd be lying if I said it didn't happen. I'm pretty used to it, though. It's just tonight was supposed to be our thing and they made it a Them thing."

"Hmm. That sounds like you're off the hook for sticking around," he said. "They can have their thing and we can have ours." He held out his hand for hers. "Are you hungry? I know a place."

She stared at his hand for a moment, biting her lip. "I'm always hungry."

(Holding hands didn't mean anything.)

(People did it all the time.)

(He was being nice because she was upset.)

(He didn't want her to feel alone. Maybe.)

She took it—his callused palm and fingers warming her skin.

"Who are you supposed to be anyway?" she asked as they walked toward the driveway.

"You don't recognize me? I was sure this would impress you." He squeezed her hand.

She tried to figure it out, but her brain was too full of everything else to play Spot the Reference. He pushed a button on his car key. A dark blue car's light flashed as the doors unlocked.

"His first name is Philip."

"Fry!" Alice gasped. "Oh my God, so you do know *Futurama*?"

"It's actually one of my favorite shows." He rubbed his thumb along the back of her hand. "We should watch it together sometime."

CHAPTER

16

It had to be the grungiest diner in existence.

Their shoes squeaked on the checkered, black-and-white floor in desperate need of scrubbing. All the tables were purple and circular with green chairs, save for the bright yellow booths that lined the front and only window. The chaotic metal light fixtures hung from the ceiling, their lights kept low. Giant Xs made out of duct tape seemed to be covering cracks in the wall.

But not a single seat was empty. Several groups crowded the waiting area.

"Velma, oh my God! How cute! Where are you guys coming from? Heading to?" the hostess asked.

"From a costume party."

"I love dressing up. I can't wait for Halloween." She began to gather the menus. "Just the two of you? I might be able to squeeze you in now."

"Yes, but to go."

"Even better," she said. "Have a seat in the bar. The consoles are electronic menus. Order directly from there when you're ready."

"Thank you," Takumi said. He led Alice to the dimly lit left where they picked the first two available bar stools.

She leaned close to him to make sure he could hear her. "Where are we going after this?"

"Somewhere quiet. It's pretty loud in here." He kept his head close to hers.

"Do you come here often?" She commandeered control of the menu, flipping through the screens. "Do you know what you're going to get? What tastes the best?"

"Yes. Florentine egg-white omelet. And for you," he said, "grilled cheese?"

"I do love grilled cheese, especially with dill pickles. A friend got me obsessed with it. But I think I want pancakes."

They placed their order (complete with a large chocolate-and-marshmallow milk shake for Alice). "I need support," she said when Takumi eyed her as he paid. "I won't feel good until I at least attempt to eat my feelings."

"Isn't that why I'm here?"

"Do you really think you're capable of going head-to-head with a milk shake? Let me repeat that: a milk shake."

"Challenge accepted. Let's start the night over." He turned to face her. Eye contact. Sure, she could hold his gaze, no problem.

"Hello, Alice."

God, had someone turned the air off? Wasn't that illegal in restaurants?

"Takumi," she said.

"You look lovely tonight."

"As opposed to every other day when I look like trash?"

"I never said that," he said, amused and completely at ease.

"I like to read between the lines," she admitted. "Figure out what you're not saying when you say things."

"Is that so?" One of his eyebrows arched toward his hairline and that slight grin was almost too much for her. Almost. She was still in total control of all her faculties.

"You're doing a horrible job. Try one more time," he encouraged.

He leaned closer, shoulders hunched, their faces inches apart. Up close, Alice realized that Takumi's lip used to be pierced. Snakebites: two tiny holes rested just below his bottom lip in each corner.

He gazed at her like she was a painting—lingering over her features one small exquisite section at a time. Her face grew hotter by the second. She couldn't turn away from the soft, wondrous look in his eyes if she wanted to. He spoke again, slower, deeper, a captivated whisper escaping from between his lips. "You are so lovely."

And that's when she lost it. Bubbly giggles erupted out of her—total *fangirl after her long-suffering ship had their first kiss* giggles. If there were room, she would have fallen backward and kicked her legs in the air.

"I'm sorry," she said over and over again. In a swift move, she plucked a random flyer from a tray and hid her face behind it. "Oh my God, that was ridiculous."

She put the paper down, fighting against the smile. If he looked at her like that again? Words. There were none. But there were questions all floating around a word she'd heard and seen on TV but never in real life.

Did he desire her?

More important, did she want him to?

"You should be an actor," she said. "Go to a casting call for a romantic indie movie or web series. The Internet would lose its collective shit over you."

"I meant it. You're beautiful, Alice."

"Thanks," she said with a tiny laugh. "But that doesn't mean you still can't act. You have to mean what you say, really get into character or your performance will suck. I think you'd be good at it."

"I'm happy being a sort of librarian and a teacher," he said. "I decided to stay on past the summer. Every other weekend for Storytime shifts."

"I've been wanting to ask you something—" She paused. "It's kind of personal."

"Go for it."

"Why did you get a second job?"

"My, uh, roommate moved out," he said. "Our lease wasn't up and I couldn't find someone to cover their share of the rent, so I decided to try to find another job."

"That's super shitty."

"Yeah. Well. That seems to be the kind of person they are."

Semi-awkward silence descended upon them. In true Alice fashion, she decided to fight awkward with silly.

Face scrunched, she asked, "Can I bite your nose?"

"What? No. You can kiss it, though." He tapped his nose. "Come on."

"I am *not* kissing you." She shook her head, laughing.

"Why not? It's a perfectly valid offer. You should take me up on it." He picked up a straw, unwrapped it, and began to chew on one end.

"Don't crumple the paper. You have to do the thing." She took the paper from him and tied it into a knot. "You're supposed to pull it apart. If it breaks close to the knot, it means someone is thinking about you." She handed it to him.

He pulled. "I wonder who that could be?"

"It's probably me," she admitted. "It's only fun to do when you're alone so you can speculate."

After their food arrived, they headed back to Takumi's car where he drove them to the waterfront. He pulled a blanket out of the trunk of his car.

"'Tis a fine evening for a picnic," he said, offering the crook of his arm.

She giggled and looped her arm through his. They sat on the grassy lawn as close as they could to the metal barrier. The moon shone overhead, full and bright, and rippled upon the water. The clear sky was decorated with stars. No one was around—just the two of them in their own private moment.

The edge of his egg-white omelet called her name. "Eww," she groaned as it hit her taste buds. "There's like no flavor in this."

"It tastes fine." Takumi laughed.

"No, it doesn't. The food you made for me was amazing. Why would you subject yourself to that?" She speared a piece of pancake and swirled it in the buttery syrup. "Here."

Her hand shook the tiniest bit as she held up the fork. Was she really about to feed him?

(Yes. Yes, she was.)

He shook his head, pressing his lips together.

She kept one hand under the fork to keep syrup from dripping onto his blanket. "Open up."

"Wow." He smiled with his mouth closed as he chewed. "That is really sweet."

"The proper term is *a tiny taste of triangular heaven*."

"If you say so." He wiped his hands on a napkin and pulled out his phone. "How about some music?"

"Can I pick?"

"No," he said, and laughed. "It's my turn. Your basement musical selections, while interesting, have not really been for me."

"Are those your nieces?" she asked, after seeing his lock screen. In the picture, he stood in a doorway with one girl on each hip. Someone else stood behind him, but only the top part of her face was visible above his shoulder.

"That was on their second birthday. They're not even my kids, but they're two of the best things to ever happen to me."

Soft instrumental music began to play. She didn't recognize the song, but knew jazz when she heard it.

"I'm going to be an aunt soon. Any tips?"

"Not really. I didn't spend any time with my nieces when they were first born. Ask me again in a few years."

"Really? That's surprising."

"It's not that I didn't like them or anything. I loved them before they were born, but I was scared." Takumi closed the lid on his empty take-out box and moved closer to Alice. "They were born a month early so they were really small. Multiple-birth babies usually are, I think, but this was extreme. I had never seen a baby that tiny before. They had to stay in the NICU, but we were allowed to visit them, and I remember being terrified that if I held them, I'd do something wrong. So I didn't and I might have developed a slight phobia. Winter break ended two weeks later and I had to go back to school."

"But you got over it?"

"Eventually. My college was about four hours away. I only visited during holidays and maybe one weekend a month. I almost never saw them in person, but I Skyped with my brother a lot, so they got used to seeing me. On that day," he said, tapping the screen on his phone, "as soon as I walked through the door, Mayumi spotted me. She got up and *ran*—I didn't even know they were walking yet, and she ran straight for me. I reached down, picked her up, and she hugged me. Megumi wasn't far behind, so I picked her up, too. My brother took the picture." He held up his phone to show her his lock screen again. "Anyway, I have a question for you."

"I might have an answer."

"Do you like me, Alice?"

Her heartbeat began to echo in her ears. "I wouldn't be here if I didn't."

"No." He tore at the grass, pinching the blades between his fingers. "I mean, really like me. I know you're attracted to me."

"Is that a fact?" She leaned away.

"You're not exactly subtle about it."

Well. That wasn't embarrassing *at all*. She made a mental note to work on her poker face.

"Oh. Sorry."

"Don't be." He grinned, but was also wringing his hands. "But that's not all it is, right? You like me as a person, too?"

It took everything Alice had to not laugh at the universe's perverse sense of humor. Her Personal Living God of Confusing Attraction, Takumi, wanted to know if she, Asexual Alice, liked him as a person.

Takumi covered both his eyes with one hand, tucking his chin into his chest. He murmured his next words so low, she almost didn't hear him. Her pulse twitched in surprise, suddenly surging like a river flow. There was no way he had just said what she thought he'd said. It was a brief delusion created in Alice's mind and projected onto him.

"Is it okay to say that?"

"Say what?" she whispered.

"That I like you," he whispered back. "Everything you do and say is so endearing, and it's ridiculous because I can't stop thinking *I need this person in my life*. I need to be near you. If I could stand close enough to you, maybe I could absorb some of your shine."

"You are the most adorable parasite ever," she said, hoping this wasn't a delusion. Life could be cruel. But it could also be wonderful.

"I really want us to be friends."

Her resulting breathy laugh was about as awkward as you'd imagine it to be.

"What?" he asked. "Why are you looking at me like that?"

She fell backward, covering her face with her hands.

He had made the distinction between her liking him as a person and her being attracted to him. On his own. The former point seemed to be important to him, which did something strange to her head. Hope was for the heart, not the mind. At least, that's where hers lived. Takumi saying that meant he might possibly understand if she chose to tell him she was asexual.

Because he could separate attraction from emotional connection.

Alice inhaled, deep but shaky. He had one of those faces that would never stop surprising her. It had been stupid to try to hate him for something he couldn't control. It was even stupider to hate herself for being unable to control her reaction to him. She decided to let it go. All of it. From that moment forward, none of that would matter anymore.

What mattered was this: the unshakable feeling of being exactly where she wanted to be and with whom she wanted to be with.

"Hey, what's wrong?" His tentative touch at her elbow almost made her smile.

"I'm fine."

He stared at her for a moment. "You know you don't always have to be *fine*, right? It's okay to not be okay."

She shrugged. "I don't like bothering people with my stupid problems."

"You're not bothering me." He made eye contact with her and held it. "Talk to me anytime about anything. I'll listen."

Her palms began to tingle. She flipped over onto her stomach, reaching for his phone.

"My music's not that bad," he joked.

"I'm giving you my number," she said, entering herself as
♦ ♦ ♦ ALICE ♦ ♦ ♦. "Anytime you want to talk, I'll listen, too."

CHAPTER
17

"And then what happened?" Feenie asked, clearly distracted. Her palpable disinterest somehow managed not to kill Alice's buzz. She was probably hung over and unhappy at work. If Feenie were truly upset about something, she wouldn't have answered the video call.

"We talked for a few hours. Then he brought me home."

"And?" Feenie asked, impatient. "Did you kiss him?"

"No, we didn't kiss." Alice bit her lip, trying to fight her smile. "We did hold hands."

"Oh my God, are you guys totally going to go steady now? Did you let him see your ankle? Oh God, the scandal! What will the neighbors think?"

"Shut up, you ass." Alice giggled. "It wasn't like a date. We just talked and ate pancakes. Well, I had pancakes. He had an egg-white omelet."

"Did he pay? Because if he did, it was a date."

"It wasn't!" Alice said. "He is pretty amazing, though. He's really into family. He loves them so much. And he's a photographer! Not professionally or anything, but he's super passionate about pictures and documenting his life. And he has his own apartment and he—"

"And, and, and." Only Feenie could roll her eyes with a smile like that and have it come across as endearing (even if Alice wasn't sure if that's the way she meant it). "You are so gone on him."

"I am not. Not in that way. I mean, I could see it. But it's still kind of *jumbly wumbly*."

"Not sexy-wexy?"

"Not even a little, you jerk. There's definitely something, though. Which is good."

"I'm going to say a name; don't get mad," she said. "But is this how it was with Margot?"

"No. Dating was her idea and I went along with it." It was hard to think about Margot without thinking about the last thing Margot had ever said to her.

"Not that. I meant did you get all *jumbly wumbly* around her?"

Alice thought about it. "Not really. Margot was mostly into physical stuff. It wasn't like we had long candlelit conversations or went for semiromantic strolls in the moonlight."

"No strange foodie nonsex dreams either?" Her laughter cut right into Alice's chest.

"Don't make fun of me. Please?"

"I wasn't." Feenie sighed. She had no limits—everything was fair game to her. Anything could be used as ammo. "Part of your problem is you're way too sensitive about this. Relax. It's supposed to be fun."

Alice took a deep breath, pressed her lips together, and breathed out through her nose.

Something had been up with Feenie from the moment she'd answered. She knew the signs: flippant, hot and cold, and manipulation— someone or something had royally pissed Feenie off.

(Was it her?)

"Anyway, Margot didn't care about romance. I do."

Feenie rotated her lip ring with an index finger. "Do you want to see him again?" She lowered her voice and raised her eyebrows. "After hours?"

"To hang out, yes."

"And if he asks you on a date? What will you say?"

"I think I'd say yes. Just to see. I think I might have a serious squish on him."

"The fuck is a squish?" Feenie sucked her teeth, shaking her head. "You know what? I don't want to know. It seems like you're romantically attracted to him, so there you go. Grand Mystery solved. I hereby resign from my love-coaching duties."

"Maybe," Alice said, trying to decide if Feenie's answer had been sarcastic. "But also maybe not. I don't know if I'd want to kiss him."

Feenie grimaced. "You've always liked kissing. That's definitely not a good sign, then."

"I haven't even wanted to hug him yet."

"*Oh, Jesus.* It's always out of the frying pan, straight into the fire with you." She pinched the bridge of her nose. "Hey, I need you to do me a favor. Can you call Ryan? He thinks you hate him."

"What? Why?"

"He's mad at himself, which extends to him being mad at me because he thinks we ditched you last night."

"You *did* ditch me." She laughed a little.

"Yeah. Well. Anyway, just call him."

Alice couldn't even pretend to be mad. Ryan had to be the sweetest person on the planet and besides, it had all worked out. "So you're just not going to apologize?" she joked.

"Are *you* going to apologize?" Feenie shot back.

"For what?"

"For fucking leaving."

(Ah, there it was.)

(*Damn it.*)

"Um, well, not to be petty, but you left me first."

"We went upstairs. You actually left the party. That is not the same thing." She looked Alice right in the eyes. "I'm not going to apologize for having sex with my boyfriend when you fucking jumped ship the first chance you got because you couldn't stand being alone for thirty minutes. Miss me with that bullshit."

Alice's jaw dropped. Unsure of what to say, she stuttered for a moment before mumbling, "I'm hanging up now. I'll see you later."

"Whatever."

Alice set her phone on the table facedown. She stared at it like it would bite her before sliding it farther away with a single finger.

Did she really do something wrong? Because it seemed like that's what Feenie implied—she had expected Alice to be there. But that hadn't been the first time they'd disappeared on *her*. She didn't want to be left behind (and sure, they always came back), but they didn't really expect her to wait around for them forever, right?

CHAPTER
18

S o," Alice said, watching Takumi make her tacos in the break room at the library. "Are you going to make me dinner every day? I'm not trying to get my hopes up or anything, but *foreseeable future* makes a certain kind of promise."

"I could," he said. "Then again, at that rate, you'd probably eat me out of house and home."

"I'm a growing girl. I need my nutrients." She smiled, resting her chin in her hand. "I do really appreciate this, though. It's very sweet of you."

"You're welcome. I like cooking. You like to eat my food. It works."

"Indeed. Cheers." She held up her water cup before taking a sip. Would she ever do something like this for someone? She didn't think of herself as a bad person, but she certainly wasn't in line for sainthood. She remembered birthdays, anniversaries, and other important dates, but random acts of kindness for the fun of it weren't on her radar. Being thoughtful was a bit of a struggle.

"Did you do anything fun on your days off?" he asked. "Let me guess: it involved TV and not getting out of bed."

"If only."

She had spent them locked in her room, hiding from both Feenie and Ryan, whom she never ended up calling. Not even the gnawing emptiness of hunger would make her venture out. Around noon she'd overheard the beginning rumblings of a fight between them and slid out of the apartment before they noticed. Nine whole hours spent wandering the mall, eating everything under the sun like she had nothing better to do.

(She was convinced Cinnabon, aka *The Final Resting Place for Her Blood Sugar Levels*, and Hot Dog on a Stick, aka *The Mother of All Lemonade Stands*, existed solely for the purpose of providing solace to the emotionally weary.)

When Alice had finally meandered on home, all the lights were off, the house dead quiet. She had scooped up Glory and slipped back into her room.

The urge to pout was oh so strong. "Leaving the party turned out to be a bad idea."

"What? Why?" He set her plate in front of her.

Alice filled Takumi in on the tail end of her video call with Feenie. "Everything is super awkward right now because I don't want Ryan to keep feeling bad about ditching me since he actually acknowledged it, but if I talk to him, that means I'll have to talk to Feenie, too, but the thing is, I really don't feel like I did anything wrong. If I don't talk to her, then she's going to accuse Ryan of taking my side, so they're going to fight and then of course he'll take her side because he has to and I'll be stuck on the outside."

"Something tells me this has happened before."

"Once or twice. Or ten times," she said, cheeks full of tacos.

(Shredded pork, cheese, and extra sour cream—Good *God* it was amazing.)

"Tell me about them. What do you like most?"

"Ryan is the literal light of my life. I don't think I've ever met someone as considerate and driven as him. He's all-around amazing. And Feenie, well, she's my oldest friend and soulmate. Her word, not mine, but I believe it," Alice said before laughing at a random memory that popped into her head. "When we were little, people used to call us Ebony and Ivory, which is kind of offensive now that I'm thinking about it."

"But she's dating Ryan? And you're okay with that?" The back end of her taco fell onto her plate with a small bit of it landing on her shirt. Takumi passed her some napkins.

"Oh, it's not like a romantic kind of soulmate," she said, dabbing her shirt. "Feenie's pretty hardcore, but she has her sentimental moments. Once she said if reincarnation were real, we'd meet each other in every single life because nothing can keep us apart. We're meant to be."

He looked confused. "If you're soulmates, aren't you supposed to be in love with each other? That's how it works."

"I suppose it *could* be romantic or whatever, but she has Ryan. They're meant to be right now, but we're meant to be forever, if that makes sense."

He finished chewing before saying, "Not really."

(She made a mental note to stop talking with food stuffed in her cheeks.)

(It was unlikely, but she'd give it a go.)

(At least she didn't chew with her mouth open.)

"I tried." She shrugged. "Anyway, I love her a lot. She was really looking forward to meeting you. I think she's mad about that, too."

"When you talk to them, remember that the worst thing that can happen is the three of you could stop being friends. If you don't want to get to that point, everything else will seem easier to get through. But, in the meantime, if you want to stay at my place you can. I have an extra room with a futon if you really don't want to go home."

She blinked at him, pausing to figure out if he was serious. "You'd let me live with you?"

"I'll let you crash. Temporarily." He grinned. "I never lived with my best friends, but I know what it's like when they start dating and suddenly, everything feels like them versus you and they're all you have. You don't have to slink around feeling terrible. If you need space, I have space."

She wanted to kiss his cheek.

Kiss. His. Cheek.

She eyed the table, surprised by the sudden feeling. "That's awfully kind. For all you know I could snore like a chain saw."

Takumi laughed, but asked, "Um, you don't, though? Right?"

"How should I know? I don't have to hear it."

"Crap," he mumbled under his breath. They laughed together, and for the first time in days, Alice felt like Alice again.

"Are you busy tonight?" she asked. "I don't need to sleep over or anything, but it's better if I can go home around midnight. I know they'll be asleep by then. My plan was to keep ordering coffee at a twenty-four-hour diner."

"As long as you don't mind kids," he said. "I am apparently baby-sitting tonight and am on preschool carpool duty tomorrow before I go to work."

"I love kids. Kids love me."

HOW COULD HE abandon her like this?

"Mayumi! Put that down." Alice hefted the four-year-old under her arm, who began to giggle with maniacal glee. "Give me my phone. That's not yours."

"Finders keepers!" She had reached that point of kid joyous laughter that made your heart melt in viral videos, but Dear Lord was it far, far more sinister in real life. "Finders keepers!"

"Alice, Alice, Alice! Look at me!" Megumi stood on the arm of Takumi's couch. She lifted her arms in the air and somersaulted onto the cushions. "Did you watch me?"

Alice clutched her chest with her free hand. "Please don't do that again."

Mayumi wriggled out of her grasp—Alice had to set her down to keep from dropping her—and bolted across the room. She abandoned her prize with a casual toss and she hopped onto the couch. "Me too! Watch me!"

It took everything Alice had not to pick up her phone and call Takumi screaming, *When are you coming back?*

They wanted chicken nuggets for a bedtime snack, he said.

He had to go to the grocery store for chicken breasts because he *had* to make them from scratch. Going to the McDonald's around the corner was out of the question.

Twenty minutes, he said.

What kid needed chicken nuggets before bed? Wasn't warm milk and a bedtime story the standard?

She checked her phone:

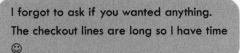

I forgot to ask if you wanted anything.
The checkout lines are long so I have time
☺

"Jesus Christ, MEGUMI, NO!" Megumi had begun to climb up the bookcase. Alice flew across the room so fast she barely registered jumping over the coffee table.

"Pick me up, too!" Mayumi hopped up and down, arms outstretched.

"No, Alice is mine!" Megumi wrapped her arms around Alice's neck. She blew a raspberry at her sister, getting spit in Alice's hair.

"Why don't we sit on the couch, okay?" she asked, trying not to sound as frantic as she felt. "We can sit together."

"No!" Mayumi latched on to Alice's leg. Alice began to drag Mayumi across the room like that, which only made Mayumi wrap her tiny legs around Alice's calf and laugh like she was on a pony ride at a birthday party. She even said, "*Wheeeee!*"

"Couch. Down. Now," Alice said, imitating Aisha's favorite tone— the one she reserved specifically for giving Alice orders.

Both girls jumped onto the sofa with a clear space between them.

"You can sit here!" Megumi.

"Sit with us!" Mayumi.

"*Oh God*," Alice muttered under her breath. "Who likes cartoons? Do you like cartoons?" Takumi (thankfully) had only one remote that controlled everything. His Netflix had an account labeled *Twins*. "How about Winnie the Pooh?"

"What's that?"

"We like *Bubble Guppies*."

Alice didn't know what unholy underwater hell a Bubble Guppy came from, and this was not the day she planned to find out, if ever.

"Pooh Bear it is."

Nice, calming, relaxing Winnie the Pooh.

Wrong.

The second Alice began to sing along with the opening credits to help them get interested, they wouldn't let her stop. Mayumi swiped the remote and hit rewind while they both shouted, "Again! Again!"

"There are other songs in the show. I can sing those, too," Alice said.

Five repeats later and she still had hope they'd see reason. At least they'd stopped climbing and flipping over everything. And had stopped fighting over who got to sit in her lap.

Small victories.

When the front door opened, Takumi took one look at Alice's face and burst out laughing. "Be glad I didn't ask you to give them baths. It would have been way worse." He took the groceries into the kitchen.

"Be right back, girls," Alice said, jumping up and helping Takumi with the bags.

To her surprise, they didn't protest.

(They probably never acted like tiny terrors from planet Toddler when they were with him.)

"Never let them see you sweat," he said, unloading one of the bags. "Once they figure out that you'll overreact, they won't stop. They think it's hilarious."

"You didn't tell me that," she said.

"You did fine. Cheated a little bit with the TV, but I'm still impressed. They're not hurt, you didn't lose one of them, and they like you."

"Like to torment me, maybe." She crossed her arms.

"That wasn't torment, trust me. It's why I watch them so often— no one else can handle them. All the other babysitters quit."

"And you left me alone with them?"

He turned on the oven. Weren't chicken nuggets supposed to be fried?

She decided not to ask.

"I had a good feeling. They're looking for extra help if you're interested. Pay is generous for nonfamily members."

"I do like money." She glanced at the twins. "I'll think about it."

Takumi placed the raw chicken in a colander and rinsed it. Should she volunteer to help? He did say he would teach her how to cook.

She decided not to ask.

"They've never seen Winnie the Pooh," he said. "I thought it might be too heavy for them, but they seem okay."

"Why?" She lined up the ingredients in a straight line, labels out, to make herself seem useful.

"Because they're smart. There's an anxious piglet, a depressed donkey, and a bear with clear boundary issues. They're going to have questions."

"Yeah, that's true, but the show itself sends a good message about Eeyore and Piglet. Both are surrounded by friends who love and support them, but it doesn't fix their mental problems. They're doing the best that they can and it's enough. If the maniacal munchkins ask questions, just explain why it's important to be a good friend."

"Oh yeah," Takumi said, squinting at her as he wiped his hands on a towel. "Essie told me about that. You like to write essays about TV shows."

"Only sometimes," she mumbled. "I have to be moved and in the right mood for it."

"Alice!" one of the girls called.

"It's a new song!"

"Come sing to us!"

"They also really like music," he said, gently nudging her out of the kitchen. "You probably shouldn't have started singing."

"Screw you, damn it."

She trudged back to the couch, leaving Takumi chuckling behind her.

CHAPTER
19

Takumi used the second bedroom in his apartment for storage and projects. A large desk, his computer, and camera equipment were set up against one wall. Another wall had a black futon with a lamp next to it.

Alice lounged on the futon while Takumi worked on editing a video he planned to give to his brother as a present. In an hour or so, she'd leave to sneak back into her apartment. She hadn't seen or heard from Ryan and Feenie all week. Part of her worried she was taking advantage of Takumi's offer, but it wasn't a big enough part to make her stop. Why on earth should she confront her problems when running had such delicious benefits? Takumi had made her crab cakes and roasted asparagus for *second* dinner that night.

"Are you moving into a two-bedroom when your lease is up?" she asked him when the silence began to bore her.

"One," he said, still focusing. "Or a studio if I can find one I like."

She thought of her own struggle to fit into her 0.5-size room. He had at least four times the stuff that she did. "What are you going to do with all your things if you get a studio? Are you keeping any of it?"

"The plan is liquidation—everything must go. Sell what I can. Donate what I can't. Trash everything else."

"You know what's strange? I totally knew that. The vibe is way too heavy in here. Your style"—she thought for a moment—"your style is simple. Soothing colors, like greens or blues but not black, with muted gray tones for accents. Not a lot of furniture—open floor space would be best—and the walls would still be filled with pictures like it is now; just add in some mirrors. You should totally let me decorate your new apartment."

Takumi rotated in the chair to face her. "Do you enjoy doing that?"

"Decorating?" She paused. "Promise not to laugh?"

"No." He shook his head. "Only because you always make me laugh. I can't control it, but it's not *laughing at you* laughing. It's more like delighted surprise laughing."

"I suppose I can accept that." She pursed her lips. "I like to go to furniture stores and put rooms together. I can spend hours in IKEA by myself browsing and taking pictures. They're like puzzle pieces to me. I see a couch and I immediately look for pillows, because every good couch needs that extra bit of comfort. There's nothing like a good pillow hug after a long day. After that, I do walls next, followed by floors. I *love* rugs, by the way. Coffee tables can be very off-putting if there's not a lot of space to work with, so I'm a fan of side tables.

"Kitchens are always fun because you can color coordinate the appliances. I'm really into chalkboard paint and classic kitchen aesthetic—gingham, apple pie, that whole bit—but I can also appreciate a futuristic look with chrome, especially if the room is exposed to a great deal of sunlight. I love how *clean* it feels."

"Interesting." He nodded, turning back around. "Okay. You're on. When I'm ready to move, you can be my creative consultant."

Alice kicked her legs and fist-punched the air in triumph. She lurched and rolled off the futon, landing with a tiny *oomph* onto the floor.

"Hi," she said after she finished rolling to the desk.

His eyes had a bleary, unfocused look. "Hi."

She stood on her knees to look at the computer screen. "Is that your brother?"

There was no mistaking the Johnsons were all related. Alice's features looked similar to her siblings—just much younger.

(Black didn't crack, but it did level up.)

(When the time came, she hoped her looks settled at twenty-four years old and then stayed that way for at least twenty years.)

Takumi and his brother didn't really look alike. They were the same height, but that was all they had in common features-wise.

"Yeah. Steven," he answered.

"Really?" she asked. "So, uh, Steven and Takumi, huh?"

"It's a long story."

"A story you're going to tell me?"

"Maybe someday."

Alice nodded, letting go of her next question. They were still new—she didn't want to upset him. He usually tended to be fairly open to whatever she said or asked, but occasionally he used a certain tone that meant she was close to crossing an arbitrary line. She noticed it the first time she asked about his parents.

"What are those?" She pointed to the open closet. The inside had shelves filled with what she thought were books at first, but she wasn't sure.

"Photo albums."

"Really? There's so many. Can I look at them?"

"Sure. Make sure to put them back in order, please."

Giddy, Alice went to the closet. Each album spine had a year written on it. They dated back to when his elementary-school days should have been—the one she picked up was from high school. She turned page after page, learning about the life he had lived long before her.

"Why did you start doing this?" she asked.

Takumi rubbed his eyes, sitting back in his chair. "I took photography in middle school. Our final project was to document our life for a month and then choose the best moments to display. I sort of never stopped."

Alice snorted. "Sort of?"

"It's more of a habit than a hobby. I'm not a freelancer or anything. If I'm in the middle of something with other people, I don't make everyone stop so I can take a picture. It has to feel right. I do it because I love it and I think it's good for me." He laughed under his breath, shaking his head. "I don't even show people now. Usually."

"I wish I could do this," Alice said, replacing the first album and grabbing another. "It's so cool."

"It's never too late to start." He turned his chair to face her.

"I'm not a fan of pictures of myself."

"Why not?"

"It feels weird. My mom is like you. She takes pictures of everything. She always says, 'When I'm old and lose my memories, pictures are all I'm gonna have,' which is the most horrid thing ever. It guilt-trips me right into posing for a picture."

"Good to know." He smiled.

"Don't even think about it."

He laughed. "Why don't you like pictures of yourself?"

"It's not that I don't. I just don't want them to spread. Like once it hits the Internet ether, you have zero control over it. It's gone. Someone else can use your face and your body however they want, and I don't like that."

"Use instant film." He shrugged. "No negatives. Every picture you take will be one of a kind, as long as you don't scan it or something."

"Oh," she said, thinking about it. "That could work."

"Now stop bothering me." He grinned. "I need to finish this tonight."

Alice stuck her tongue out at him and resumed flipping the pages. Takumi had gone to prom and looked amazing in his tuxedo. He'd played basketball and football in high school. He'd gone to summer camp. He'd shaved his head. He'd competed in and won bicycle races. He'd gone to the beach often. He'd eaten pizza a lot. He'd driven speedboats and water-skied. He'd gone to Las Vegas. He could snowboard.

Alice sucked in a breath. He also liked to take pictures while kissing. She steeled herself—the pictures weren't vulgar, but they were hard to stomach for some reason. From what she could gather, Takumi didn't have a "type." All the girls she saw so far were different races, shapes, and heights. Some had average looks, others were conventionally attractive, and quite a few were model-worthy. She figured out if there were a lot of pictures of one girl in particular, they must have dated a long time.

She stopped flipping the pages to stare at him.

Back when Alice had lived in the dorms, there was a girl, Sharon, who was obsessed with online dating.

Some of the girls from Alice's hall would sit in the common room, eating ice cream and scrolling through profiles for fun. It was fine at first, until another girl, Janice, suggested they play a game. They would all make profiles and see who got the most messages.

Alice could still remember that sense of dread that began to eat at her when Sharon turned and stared at her for a few seconds too long. "You're super cute, Alice," she had said, "but you're probably going to lose, so don't be too disappointed."

"Why would she lose?" another girl asked.

"Because she's Black. Black girls and Asian guys are always ranked the lowest on dating sites. I saw it in an interview with a guy who owns a dating app."

Through it all, being demeaned and feeling disheartened and dispirited, Alice was expected to be *nice*. To overlook the microaggressions when they continuously rained down on her and find solidarity wherever she could. She was expected to endure in silence.

And so she did. She was *tired*, but she wasn't out.

She had smiled, flipped her braids over her shoulder, and said with more confidence than she felt, "We'll see about that." As long as she didn't have to go on dates, she was willing to play.

(AND SHE GOT SECOND PLACE.)

(Not even an act of God could stop her from gloating in Sharon's face.)

(It was one of her pettier moments.)

Judging by his photos, Takumi didn't seem to have any problems getting dates either. With his height and face, he often looked like he was waiting for a flash and a shutter click before effortlessly gliding into another flawless pose. Vulnerability thinly masked by sharp angles and high-fashion arrogance.

She couldn't fathom anyone ever turning him down.

Soon, though, only one girl showed up in the photos. A lot. *A lot* a lot. She appeared in the second half of that particular album almost more than Takumi did. They weren't always together in the pictures, and if they were, it was a group photo.

Alice thought she was pretty. She had a body like a stereotypical ballerina: pale skin, very thin with a long neck and limbs. Her dyed-blue hair was cut into a blunt bob that slowly grew out (while her black roots grew in) in each new picture.

Closing that album, she picked up the next one, flipping rapid-fire through the pictures. Takumi on stage in front of a mic. Takumi in a suit. The girl. Takumi with his guitar and headphones on. Takumi with blond hair. The girl, again. Takumi in Times Square. She was there. Takumi sitting on a couch with his arm around her. Takumi with a blond Mohawk. Takumi in the backseat of a car looking out the window. Takumi camping. She was there, too.

Near the end of the album, it happened: Takumi and the girl kissing.

"Wow, you're real fond of that whole kissing thing."

"And you're not?"

"I don't dislike kissing." Alice closed that album and picked another. "I also don't take pictures of myself while doing it."

He raised an eyebrow. "Are you judging me?"

"Slightly. Yeah."

He surprised her by laughing and giving her a wide smile. "How about we just say to each their own and let it go?"

"How about no?" She chuckled. "Why do you do it? I mean, isn't it weird to look at these after you break up or whatever?"

Takumi pushed the chair back and stood, stretching his arms toward the ceiling and standing on his tiptoes. His shirt rose above the top of his waistband.

(Nothing but abs as far as the eye could see.)

(Who in the hell worked out that much?)

She poked at her soft belly. "No one should be that lean," she whispered to herself.

"I wouldn't say weird." He dropped into a squat before sitting on the floor next to her. "It might hurt a little or it'll make me laugh if it's a good memory. If I'm going to document my life, I should try to capture as many important moments as I can, right?"

"So," Alice began, drawing out the word, "kissing is important to you?"

"Honestly expressing my feelings is important to me." He flipped a page. There were several pictures of a bonfire at night. A Southeast-

Asian guy with dewy brown skin was wrapped in a red blanket, laughing in one photo. "Sometimes that means kissing. Or spending three days editing photos and videos together for my brother. Or letting a girl I just met stay in my house and look through my pictures because she's scared to go home."

"I'm not *scared*. I just don't want to fight with her." She fidgeted. And then poked him in the thigh. "Can I tell you something?"

"Why do you always ask first?" He laughed. "Let's just throw a blanket statement on that right now. Stop asking me and just say whatever you want."

"Fine." She made a face at him. "I spend a lot of time trying to figure stuff out. Like, my feelings and sorting through my thoughts. I don't think I overthink, but I like to know why things are the way they are for me and why they're different for someone else."

"I think everyone does that."

"No, they don't. At least, I don't think they do. Not the way I do it," she said. "So. Like. If I ask you something and it seems strange, I'm not being weird, I'm trying to understand."

"I haven't noticed anything strange."

"Yet." Alice paused, chewing on her lip for a moment before mumbling, "What kind of feelings do you have for me then?"

Takumi didn't hesitate. "I told you already. I care about you. I worry."

She kept her eyes on the photo album. "Why?" He had already done so much and it was beginning to weigh on her.

"I don't know. I don't think it's important to figure that out right now. I know how I feel—that's good enough for me. But I get why you're asking. I know how this seems." He gestured to the album on her lap. "Yeah, I've dated around some, but I'm actually really picky about who I decide to date and sometimes, even be friends with."

"How come?"

"Well, for dating, sometimes I can't tell if someone likes me or if they like me because I'm East Asian and moderately good-looking."

(MODERATELY. OKAY.)

He continued, "One girl stopped talking to me when I asked her to stop calling me Oppa because I'm not Korean."

"Yikes." Alice winced. "I've gotten the Black-girl version of that before, so I know how that feels."

"Yeah, but I didn't know that, which was why I was unsure about you at first. Part of me was like 'She's so cute' and the other part was like '. . . What if she's one of those girls? I should stay away from her for my own good.' But then *you'd* say something completely out of left field and smile, and it would reel my right back in."

"You like my smile?" she asked, trying not to do that very thing.

"It's a good one." He jumped to his feet and held out his hands. "Let's go for a walk."

"Ew." She let him pull her to her feet. "Exercise isn't compatible with my lifestyle and it's super dark outside."

"There's a park around the corner. I go there all the time when I can't sleep."

After a bit more whining (Alice) and negotiating (Takumi), they settled on a deal. He would make her a chocolate mug cake when they got back. He was a fast learner—bribe her with good food and she'd do just about anything.

NorCal summer nights were some of the best Alice had ever experienced. A dark sky, wisps of gray clouds, a bright moon, and a surprisingly warm breeze—she wished night could always be like this. They walked together, silent but comfortable, toward the park and pond only a few minutes away from his apartment.

"Do you know how to skip rocks?" he asked when they reached the edge of the pond.

She shook her head. "But I don't want to disrupt the wildlife."

(Her phone began to ring.)

A pair of sleeping swans huddled together in a grouping of reeds. She couldn't remember if geese or swans were the hostile ones. Maybe it was both. Either way, she didn't feel like being chased, tripping, falling, and getting pecked to death. When she told him that, he laughed.

"As long as you don't throw the rocks directly at them, it'll be fine," he said, but kept walking.

(Her phone rang again.)

Takumi tilted his head back, exposing his Adam's apple. "You can answer. I don't mind."

"It's just my brother," she said. "I might have a slight habit of hiding from my problems."

"Ever so slight," he said, eyeing her.

"I'd put my phone on silent, but I'm paranoid about missing something important."

"How do you know he's not calling about something important now?"

"Because he isn't," she said. "My mom is, uh, being kind of overbearing about school right now and she's recruited my siblings for reinforcements."

"How many do you have?"

"Just a brother and a sister. I'm the baby by about two decades." She laughed, and explained the problem.

"That sounds rough. I wish I could help."

"Can I ask—" His sharp glare made her laugh. "Sorry. Habit. How did you decide to be a teacher?"

"It's because of my nieces. I didn't realize how much I liked being around kids until I started spending time with them regularly. My brother couldn't believe I was able to teach Mayumi how to read when she was three. Megumi still isn't that into books, but she loves music. I'm thinking about signing her up for piano lessons."

Alice frowned. "Okay, but how did you get from that to teaching?"

"Because being a teacher seemed like the easier path than taking my would-be business administration degree and trying to find any job that would take me."

She snorted. "I almost declared business. My mom wouldn't have it, too vague, so we settled on temporarily undeclared as a compromise."

(ADAM. STOP CALLING.)

Alice slumped forward, throwing her head back and dragging her feet.

"There, there." Takumi rubbed her back.

"Do you ever feel like everything terrible always happens at once? It can't just be one hard thing—oh *no*, the universe or God or fate or whoever points at you, and says, '*YOU WILL HAVE ALL OF THE PROBLEMS. ALL OF THEM. RIGHT NOW.*' And then just drops an existential crisis on your head for funsies."

"It doesn't seem that bad?"

"It feels like it and I'm *lucky*. I have the uncanny ability to literally push all my responsibilities to the corner of my mind and pretend like they don't exist. Alice Bubble is a Thing." She stood up straight. "But this time, people won't freaking let me. Every time I check my e-mail there's like ten messages from my brother. My sister texts me every morning at 5:45—like she wakes up and her first thought is to torment me. Oh, and my mom is the worst of all. She doesn't even use words anymore. Emojis are her new best friends."

"That sounds funny."

"It's not! It's diabolical and how she tricks you into responding," she said. "I'm ignoring them with all my might. And I don't even have Feenie to commiserate with."

Takumi wrapped his arm around her shoulders, pulling her into a half hug.

"I'm tired of talking about my problems. Let's talk about yours. Do you have any?"

"No," he said. "I've managed to adult successfully this year. Minus one thing, I've been coasting."

"How nice for *you*." Alice sighed. "I miss her. Whenever I fought with my bio family, I had my found family to lean on. I miss them."

"I won't lie—I like having you around, but if you need to cut out to go be with them, I'll understand." His slight laugh made her look at him. "This was just supposed to be a nice, leisurely walk in the park. I figured you would make darling and hilarious commentary, I would smile and laugh a lot, and you would stare at my face because that is a thing you do that I've gotten strangely used to, you know? Our usual. Good times had by all."

She leaned on him, resting her head on his shoulder. "Do you really feel like I stare at you a lot?"

He nodded. "It took some getting used to, but then I realized if you're staring at me, that means I can stare back."

"You should take a picture of me. It'll last longer," she joked, feeling warm from mild embarrassment. "I mean, if you want to."

CHAPTER
20

The receptionist let Alice know her appointment with Dr. Burris would start on time. Turning around, she flopped down in the first available seat in the waiting area.

She hadn't planned on coming back to see Dr. Burris, her initial idea being to take her consultation and run, but then he had e-mailed her to check in. She told him about her insurance, her parents, and why she couldn't come back—and he offered her an extremely generous discount for two sessions per month.

"Alice?" Dr. Burris gave her a warm smile.

In his office, she settled into the same armchair with only half the nervousness she had experienced at their first appointment.

"Last we spoke," he began, "you were experiencing some anxiety and uncertainty regarding your sexuality."

"Yeah, that's still happening. Sort of. But not *really*."

"All right." He wrote something on his notepad. Alice craned her head to try to read it. "Would you like to continue discussing that?"

"Also not really." She shook her head. "It's like, my problem is everyone else. I'm not ashamed or uncertain or whatever. I'm ace. It's cool. I just don't want to be anybody's poster child. I'm not made for the front lines. I'll wither and cry under pressure, so it's better if I keep it to myself for now."

"Interesting." He shifted in his seat. "Have you thought about joining any clubs on your college campus as a means to build a support system for yourself? Engaging with others who identify as you do could help bring about a level of comfort that will enable you to speak freely."

Alice resisted the urge to snort. "Nah. I think those are great for some people, especially if you're the right color, not bi, and certainly not ace. So."

"Ah, I see. It's unfortunate that you've experienced that. What about groups online?"

"I use Tumblr, which is probably the best support system for me right now. I mean, it's a super garbage fire of discourse sometimes, but really, we all just hyper-love everyone and everything and want our ships to sail, regardless of canon or what anyone else thinks. And there'll be posts with literally thousands of notes that'll make the rounds saying things like, 'If you're Black and you're ace, you're valid and I love you,' which is really nice to read when you're not expecting it. You know that saying, 'love is love,' right? I've heard it thousands of times, but I learned it, internalized it, because of the blogs I follow on Tumblr." She laughed, feeling good and lighthearted, but wanting to change the subject. She was paying for this after all. "Anyway, I can use this time for whatever I want to talk about, right?"

"This is a safe space," he reminded her.

"Do you think it's okay to only have like two friends? I'm a firm believer in quality over quantity in the friendship sector, but I'm starting to think I might be wrong."

"First, to answer your question, my opinion on the number of friends any one person should have is irrelevant. What matters is how you feel about it."

"Well, I felt fine. My best friends, Ryan and Feenie, have been dating for what feels like forever, so I'm used to third-wheeling it. Lately, though, it's like"—she paused to think—"it's like, you know how motorcycles can have sidecars? Well, they're on the bike, I'm in the sidecar, and whatever holds us together is falling apart. They're turning and going one way while I have to keep going straight because I don't have anything to help me steer. Or an engine to keep me going. Or anything. I'm just stuck waiting for my little car to run out of momentum."

His eyebrows pinched together. "So, if I'm interpreting this correctly, you feel as if you and your friends are on two different paths— their path is an active choice, while yours is not?"

"Yeah. That's it exactly!" He summarized and clarified on the first try. The man was magic. "I read this article once that said most people aren't friends with the friends they had in high school anymore and that it was *normal*. There's all this weight put on college friends, but, like, that seems dumb? How is losing touch with someone you spent fifteen years with a good thing? Moschoula and Takumi are great, but that's not an equal trade.

"On the other hand, I can see how it can happen and why people think that way, because we change and grow apart, but aren't you supposed to fight for them? I feel like instead of fighting for them, all I do is fight *with* them. Like now." Alice explained what happened at the party while he nodded, taking notes.

"And Takumi is another friend?"

"Yeah. Definitely friend. But also, um." Alice's mouth went dry. "He's *the person*. You know. From before."

"Ah." He smiled. "This is fantastic. What did you—"

"Wait, let me stop you right there," she said, laughing and holding up her hand. "Nothing *fantastic* happened. I'm sorting, not sorted. I mean, I'm not sexually attracted to him, but there's another problem."

"All right," he said, pen ready.

"Sometimes I don't think I have enough room for everything. I have my issues—I guess that's a good enough word—then there are Ryan and Feenie, plus my family, and I want to squeeze Takumi in, too, but it kind of feels like too much right now? He's so good to me. Too good. I feel like I'm never going to be able to repay his kindness."

"Is Takumi asking you to?"

"He doesn't have to." Alice rested her chin in her hand. "When I compare myself to him, I'm not good enough anyway. And I don't really get why he's bothering with me in the first place."

"Can you tell me a little bit more about why you feel that way?"

"It's like, he's not nice to me because he expects something. I know what that feels like. He does all this stuff for me and he's just there because that's who he is. He's a better person than I am. Do I really want someone like that in my life? Someone who makes me feel less than? I don't know how to see the other side. He's not inspiring me to be a good person—I just end up feeling bad about myself when we're not together and I think about him. That's not his fault, I guess, but it feels like it is." She slid to the edge of her seat. "But this is the kicker: do I *really* want someone like that in my life?" she repeated. "If it's Takumi? Yeah. I do." She threw her hands up in the air. "I don't even know what to do with myself."

Alice took a deep breath. Last time, it felt like she had to break before spilling her heart in his office. She didn't even hesitate this time and it felt so *good*. Even if Dr. Burris didn't understand, she had said it, got the words out instead of holding them in until she pushed them down so far they began to grow roots and infect her.

Maybe she should start speaking up more often.

"Perhaps your unresolved issues with Feenie and your worries regarding your relationship with Takumi are related," he suggested. "Would you be comfortable talking about your family?"

"Immediate or extended?"

"Whichever you'd like."

"Sure." Alice checked the time. "I'm Black and grew up in the suburbs, whereas the rest of my family did not. You might want to strap in for this ride I like to call *Not Black Enough to Be the Black Sheep of Black Excellence.*"

CHAPTER

21

Ryan caved first.

After another week of late nights spent at Takumi's house, he had waited up for her. She opened the door and there he was, sitting on the couch. He didn't say a word. He simply stood up, hugged her, and all was right with the world.

Almost.

Feenie took longer to come around. No one mentioned anything, let alone apologized. Her *simply* consisted of asking Alice if Family Night for that week could be on Thursday. When she had learned Alice had been hiding at Takumi's, she curiously had nothing to say, no questions to ask, no teasing jokes to make Alice squirm.

Things were good, though.

"I'm hungry. You hungry?" Ryan asked. Feenie had crashed a few hours ago, but they were both wired and awake, at one thirty in the morning, marathoning season two of a postapocalyptic show centered on teenagers.

"I have no food. I'm on that rapid weight-loss diet called Starvation

Because I Spent My Last Six Dollars on Laundry." She glanced at him. "I don't get paid until Monday."

"Pizza or Chinese?"

"Chinese, please." There was a twenty-four-hour Chinese place downtown. "I mean, if you're absolutely positive you're willing to risk feeding me after midnight."

"You're happier on a full stomach, Gizmo."

"I do like it when you feed me."

"My phone is . . . somewhere." Ryan leaned over and tugged her earlobe. "Where's yours?"

"I'll get it." Alice walked toward her room, unconsciously rubbing her hairline. Three missed calls. One from both her mom and her dad. He also sent an e-mail, which was probably the length of a dissertation. The last call was unexpected—Takumi, not even five minutes ago. He'd blown her off earlier. Something about *having plans.*

(Okay, so maybe he didn't actually blow her off.)

(Maybe she just felt like being petty. And clingy.)

Takumi answered on the second ring, slurring her name. "I knew I could count on you."

"Takumi?" she asked. "Are you okay?"

"Um, are you busy right now?"

"Not particularly. Watching TV with Ryan."

"Do you think you could give me a ride?"

"I don't have a car."

"Oh. Right. Yeah. Sorry."

"But I might be able to borrow Ryan's," she said. "Are you drunk somewhere? Did you drive yourself?"

"Yes. No. Thank you."

"I haven't said yes yet. Don't assume. It's rude." She smiled as she grabbed the dress she'd worn earlier. "Text me the address? I promise I'll be there soon."

A few moments later, she shrugged on a hoodie and exited her room.

"Going somewhere?" Ryan asked. He had already started the next episode and paused it at the beginning. She sat next to him.

"Yeah. Can I borrow your car? A friend called. They're stranded at a bar and need a ride."

"Have them call Uber or a taxi."

"Too late. Already agreed to do it."

"It's Takumi, isn't it?" He sighed, throwing an arm over his eyes and leaning back against the couch. "This is me, being jealous, dramatic, and irrational."

"Of what?" Alice laughed.

"This is *our* first all-nighter of the summer in *our* apartment as a capital Me ampersand capital You."

"Sorry. The significance of whatever you're hinting at is lost on me."

"I'm saying we should be spending this time together and we can't do that if you're playing chauffeur."

"Still going. You know how I feel about DDing. If someone asks—"

"—You're going. Yeah, yeah, you're a wonderful human being." He pouted. "Can I have something to ease my heartache from being abandoned?"

"Like what?"

"Like you staying here. Didn't he have other plans? That's what you said, right? That's why you miraculously had time for me?"

Alice hesitated before asking, "Are you serious right now?"

"Of course not." He smiled, but it didn't reach his eyes. "Can you at least try to be back in an hour? The food will be here by then."

She kissed his cheek. "Deal."

ALICE ARRIVED AT the bar in under twenty minutes.

"Sorry. We're closing in ten," the massively built bouncer barked. He had more in common with the brick wall behind him than the entirety of the human genome.

He. Was. Magnificent.

"I'm here to pick someone up." She tried to stop smiling at him, but couldn't. "He called me for a ride."

The bouncer glanced behind him. "Okay. Hurry up," he said, returning her smile.

(He was probably one of those huge, intimidating guys who were nothing but pure marshmallow fluff on the inside.)

She scanned the bar for Takumi. The house lights had been turned on. A giant dance floor, or, at least, the one made by the mass of gyrating bodies, filled the majority of the space. White couches bordered the sparkly black walls on all sides. Gold staircases (steps, banister, and all) led to a second floor. If Alice had a nightclub, she wouldn't let the interior designer responsible for this tacky mess anywhere near it.

She spotted Takumi leaning across the bar, speaking to a female bartender with light blond hair streaked with pale orange highlights and the kind of light skin that probably tanned beautifully in the summer. His head turned a fraction of an inch, enough to spot Alice.

"There she is!" he called across the room, then turned back to the bartender to say something.

"Alice, this is Jennie, the bartender. Our dads are friends. We're friends, too," he said when she joined them. "Jennie, this is my Alice."

My. Alice.

"Hi, My Alice," Jennie said, smiling.

"Hello, Jennie the Bartender."

Takumi hugged Alice, squeezing her within an inch of unconsciousness.

"Too tight. Can't breathe," she gasped. He let go only to place his hands on her face and rub their noses lightly together. He pulled back and laughed, then wrapped his arm around her neck, holding her to his chest.

Alice's heart hammered against her rib cage. Part of her wanted to laugh and the other part (a very serious part that had been starving for affection and was apparently ready to devour Takumi) wanted him to do that again.

"Good-bye, Jennie," he said.

"Have a good night, you two." She turned around, wiping down the bar behind her.

"Come on, Drunky," Alice said, her breathing back to normal.

"Aye, aye, Captain. That's SpongeBob," he said, pausing to swallow. "Do you like My Little Pony? My nieces love it. It's very cute; you would like it."

"It is very cute, but it's a little simple for me. I like my cartoons with a bit more emotional *oomph*."

"That makes sense. You're so smart."

"Thanks." She unlocked the car door. "In you go."

After making sure Takumi was in, Alice walked around to the driver's side, hopping inside. "Are you going to puke in the car?"

He had the wherewithal to do a self-assessment before answering. "Probably not." She helped him click his seat belt into place after watching him struggle for a minute.

"Bad night?" she asked. She doubted this drunken episode was part of his allocated 2 percent of *unhealthy* indulgences where he decided to drink beer.

"You could say that."

Takumi stared out the window, head leaning back. When they reached his apartment, he opened the car door, managing to make it to his feet. One step forward, however, and he grasped the side of her car for purchase. She sighed and took off her seat belt.

"Come on," Alice said, placing her hands on his waist to steady him.

"I'm okay, I'm okay." He turned to her, eyes unfocused. "I think that last drink kicked in."

"You don't say?" She laughed. Before Takumi could protest further, she looped his arm over her shoulders and her arm around his waist. He leaned into her, mumbling *thank you* in her ear as they walked up the stairs to his apartment and went inside. She didn't not notice that she was touching him, he was touching her, closely again.

"Do you want me to get you anything before I go? Water or Tylenol?"

He sat on his couch, head resting against the back. He took a deep breath. "No. Aren't you going to stay?"

"I need to get home. Ryan's waiting for me." She turned to leave and turned right on back when he took her hand.

"Stay. Please. Just for a little bit."

Takumi begging was hazardous to Alice's soul. Her breath caught as she looked down at him, his eyes drunk and upset, but pleading with her to stay. She sat her hopeless self down, right next to him on the couch, but slid her hand out of his. He frowned at that.

She wouldn't have minded continuing to hold his hand, but he was drunk. It wasn't right.

He sat up. Moved closer. Their thighs touched.

"If you were dating someone, and you knew they loved you with their whole heart, had absolutely no doubts about it, could you cheat on them?"

Obviously, that question sent her mind into overdrive, connecting all the dots. A roommate who moved out suddenly. A part-time job to cover his rent. Essie telling her he's single "now."

Takumi had a *someone*.

A *someone* who had, apparently, cheated on him.

The girl in the photos. It had to be. Alice was nearly caught up with her photographic Takumi History—the girl was still in every single album Alice looked at.

He stared at Alice, waiting for an answer. Meanwhile, she wanted to keep her mouth shut to keep her jaw off the ground.

"Me personally?" she asked finally. "No. I mean, it's highly unlikely."

Cheating on someone was one of those things she was destined to never understand. Choosing to not have sex with someone else didn't seem like that hard of a concept to grasp, and yet she had comforted more than one person who had been cheated on.

"I don't get it." He shook his head. His fingers were intertwined, hands clenched together until spots of pink and white began to appear. "We were together almost four years. Four fucking years." At first, Alice thought he was talking to himself and she just happened to be there, but then he turned to her. "We were going to get married."

Married?

Marriage—for better or for worse, until death do they part.

Jesus.

Takumi had opened his house to her, listened to her family drama, trusted her to watch his nieces—why did he choose to keep a failed relationship a secret?

(And even though she had seen the pictures, she wasn't going to just *ask*.)

She had seen people talk about the weather and who they were dating in the same breath. Some would whip out their phones to show pictures. Minutes after a breakup, people changed their status on Facebook. Everyone seemed to love sharing their love.

(She was just as guilty—when she and Margot were together, she told anyone who would listen.)

"If she wanted to take a break, why couldn't she just say something?

Why cheat on me?" He asked Alice that question as if she had an actual answer to give him.

"I don't know," she said, keeping her voice as gentle as possible. "I'm also a little confused."

So he told her.

All of it.

Everything Alice did and didn't want to know.

Takumi and his ex-girlfriend and former almost-wife, Rena, had started dating in college when they were nineteen. And it just . . . worked. They had gone to the same college, lived together for two years, and then earlier this year, she cheated on him. She had always been a social butterfly (his words) and an innocent flirt (her words), but when it came to some guy named Thad (Alice's words: "Really? That's his name?"), that innocence fluttered. Except it wasn't only Thad. She cheated again with someone else. And once more for good measure before they broke up.

They began talking again a few weeks ago, very tentative (his words). Tomorrow night, they were supposed to have dinner to talk about being friends again and *possibly* seeing if that could lead somewhere back to being together, but he had seen her kissing some guy downtown earlier. Which was why he was so drunk. He realized that even though she might have missed him (her words), she didn't really want to be with him anymore (his words).

Takumi didn't cry, but his voice broke like he would start at any moment. He wanted Alice to say something. He wouldn't have spilled the proverbial beans if he didn't want some kind of guidance. They had made a deal to be there for each other.

She wouldn't let herself let him down . . .

. . . but her own dating experience was severely limited. Thinking about four years felt like thinking about forever or something equally impossible. Six months seemed to be Alice's cosmically chosen limit— on or around that mark, she got dumped. Both times. For the same reason. What hope did she have of keeping someone interested in her for *four years*? Maybe Rena got bored with Takumi?

(MADNESS.)

Maybe it was just about sex? Maybe Rena wanted to experiment? Alice's Tumblr dash was full of *those* stories—her mutuals deciding to try everything and then blog about it. Some of them were even in long-term relationships. She had talked to a few aces who had mentioned something similar—if their partner wanted to have sex, they were allowed to do so with someone else without consequences.

(Hard pass and a firm no thank you.)

Maybe that could work for Takumi and Rena . . . or not. He said Rena should have asked to take a break instead of cheating, but an open relationship wouldn't *be* cheating, right?

(*WHAT WAS SHE SUPPOSED TO SAY?*)

"But that's good, right?" she tried. "Maybe it's for the best?"

Takumi stared at her so long Alice began to think he was contemplating the most painful way to throw her out of his apartment.

"Okay," she said, tension getting to her. "Maybe that wasn't the most helpful thing to say right now."

"You think?" His face didn't move a single muscle.

(She could do this.)

(She could totally be helpful and return all his kindness.)

"From the outside looking in, all I can see is the bright side," she explained. "Like, I keep picking the wrong people, it never works out, and I get hurt. At first, I always feel like it's a hundred percent my fault, but then I start thinking that it's better we're over now, instead of later when it's too late. Stay with me on this. I swear there's a point in here somewhere."

His bloodshot eyes focused on her face, lids seeming so heavy that if he blinked, he'd probably fall asleep. The look was wretchedly adorable in a drunkard kind of way.

"I know you're thinking that she shouldn't have done it in the first place because you two were together, but I don't think she was thinking about you at all when it happened. People don't just cheat for the hell of it. Contrary to what people like to say, I don't think it just *happens*. It's a choice she made that had nothing to do with you."

"I don't think that's true." He took a deep breath and put his arm behind her on the back of the couch. He placed his head on his upper arm. "Why do you think your breakups are your fault?"

"I'm working on learning how to not think that, actually. Progress has been slow." She shrugged, trying not to slip into a whirlpool of abject failure.

(*I don't think that's true.*)

(Why couldn't he need help with something else? Why did it have to be relationship stuff?)

He poked her waist. "I told you mine, now you tell me yours."

"Maybe some other time," she said. No way in hell, no how in heaven, was she about to tell Takumi that she was asexual right there, on the spot. "When you're not drunk."

He rubbed his face with his free hand. "All right."

At the door, he wobbled a bit, not fully able to be upright yet. She thought about volunteering to let herself out so she could help get him into bed, but those words in her mouth? Nope. Not happening.

"Thanks for the ride." He sniffed, shoving his hands into his pockets. "And for the talk."

"You're welcome," she said, thinking. Redemption would be hers. "You know what you need? An Epic Wallow Session."

"What's that?"

"Me. You. Monday night. It's happening." She nodded. "Prepare thyself."

"I still don't know what it is." He rubbed his face again—a smile peeking through his fingers. "But okay. Whatever you want, if you think I need it, let's do it."

And then he was reaching for Alice. She was on the inside of a Takumi hug, his arms wrapped around her shoulders squeezing her tight, his warm cheek pressed against her blazing one, their bodies in extremely close proximity. Her hands moved on their own, finding his waist and matching the intensity of his hug. He felt firm, muscled and lean, and smelled like tangy alcohol with the tiniest hint of a nice-smelling laundry detergent.

"I'm really glad I met you," he whispered in her ear.

Chills rolled up her spine, making her head snap back. "Me too."

CHAPTER

22

Would her phone ever stop ringing?

Glory leapt onto the bed, pawing at her shoulder. She purred when Alice scratched under her chin. "That's not an alarm. It's too early to eat," she huffed, rolling over to check the screen, and then sucked in a breath through her teeth. Her thumb hovered over the Answer button, afraid of what would happen next.

Answering could mean death—a verbal evisceration the likes of which had never been seen. But not answering had the potential to be even worse. Ignore *her* long enough and she would magically show up, in person, like a thief in the night bringing the apocalypse with her.

"Hey, Mom," she said with a gravelly voice, faking *I was asleep and you woke me up* noises.

"Alice." Whenever she used that tone, her *I know you weren't asleep, I'm your mother, I can sense you* voice, a lecture was on the way.

She had honestly tried to remember to call, set alarms for it twice that week, but sometimes that Silence button could be really convincing, like it was using mind control to make her push it.

"Mom, I'm sorry. Things are really stressful for me right now." Glory jumped onto her chest and stretched out, kneading her in solidarity.

"It still says undeclared, Alice."

"Couldn't you have at least tried to pretend that wasn't what you were calling about?"

"Why? I want you to know that I know."

"I'm changing my password," she mumbled.

"I'll make your dad ask you for it."

Damn. Alice could never tell him no. "That's cheating!"

"That's love. I don't understand what the problem is. You clearly seem to think your future is a game, since you keep lying."

"*Lying* is a very harsh word. It's more like forgetting. On purpose."

"Alice."

"Mom." A vocal fry rumbled in the back of her throat before petering out into a whine. "Okay. Do you promise not to get mad?"

"I'm already mad."

"Fine. Madder? I've been wanting to tell you something, but I wasn't sure how to do it without disappointing you."

Her mom was silent for a moment. "You rank me being disappointed above me being angry?"

"Well, yeah. I mean, I don't want to make you cry."

"What on earth could you possibly say to do that?" Her amused laughter came to an abrupt halt. "Oh, Jesus, *no*. Alice, are you *pregnant*?"

"I'm not." She smiled at the ceiling—her plan had worked. Babies before twenty-five were her mom's worst nightmare. Anything she said now would be compared to that and seem less frightening by far. "I just don't think law school is for me. I *want* to stay in school, absolutely one hundred percent, but studying something else."

"Like?" Her mom's voice strained around the word.

"I have a couple of options in mind. I'm researching. My plan was to give you and Dad a presentation outlining my new, improved, and slightly magical six-year plan."

"And when would this happen?"

"Um, three weeks?"

"Fine."

Damn. She should have asked for more time. "A month?"

"Three weeks. I'll put it on the calendar."

"Thank you for giving me a chance and hearing me out," Alice said, chest loosening.

"I haven't agreed to anything beyond that." Her mother, ever the lawyer, just had to get technical and ruin the moment. "I have to go. Your dad is taking me to a fancy breakfast in the city. I think I hear him barreling down the stairs. I swear that man is half elephant."

In Mom-speak, "I have to go" translates to about thirty more minutes of conversation. She held Alice on the phone, talking about the baby and Christy, their dog Simon's failing health, current family drama over an upcoming family function, and anything else that flitted through her head. Her mom probably had already been seated at the restaurant when she finally hung up.

Alice didn't mind.

Still tired, she wanted to crawl back under the covers but dragged herself out of bed anyway. In the hall, Feenie's angry growl filtered through her closed door. Alice recognized that belligerent, mocking tone—Feenie only used it when she spoke to one person: her mom.

She still hadn't talked about PartyGate with Feenie. If she went in Feenie's room, odds were good Feenie would lash out at her.

She decided to risk it. For friendship and the greater good.

(Suddenly, she craved cookies. Being the bigger person should come with an automatic reward of sugary goodness.)

"Hello?" She knocked on the door twice. "Everybody decent?"

"Come in, loser," Feenie called.

Alice poked her head into the room. "Ryan's gone?"

"Josh called him to fill in a shift at some ungodly hour." Her eyes were red and the skin under her nose had been rubbed raw. "I think he slept maybe an hour."

Alice had no clue who Josh was.

Talking about the party didn't seem like such a good idea anymore. Alice settled in next to Feenie under the blankets and tried to uncurl Feenie's fists, but Feenie snatched them away.

Feenie had to swallow before commanding, "Don't."

"Okay," she whispered. "I love you."

The sun had come up and begun filtering through the closed blinds when Feenie finally said, "Sometimes I wonder where I'd be if I didn't have you and Ryan. I'm sure I'd still hate my family. I'd probably still be alive. I don't think I'd kill myself or anything, but that's Happy Me talking. I've been happy too long to remember what it was really like."

Feenie never opened up for the hell of it. She had something she wanted to say, and it would be a one-sided conversation until she was done. Then they would pretend it never happened.

Alice slid closer, taking Feenie's hand again. Feenie allowed Alice to hold it.

"Marie called me yesterday." Marie—Feenie's mom. "She worked whatever connections she has and had my case for fighting that dude in the bar last year thrown out. Apparently, that gave her the right to interrogate me. She wanted to know when I was going back to school, why I was wasting my life, why I was *embarrassing* her like this." Feenie exhaled. "I want to have a family with Ryan because that's what's right for me. I don't get how me wanting to get knocked up and be a housewife affects her. She doesn't want me to have kids, so she's never going to see them. Even if I die, she will never see them."

Alice knew that. She'd known it for years.

In elementary school, when they were told to be doctors and

astronauts and firefighters, Feenie stood up and said she wanted to be a mom. Back then, her favorite game had been House. Feenie was always the stay-at-home mom, while Alice was the working mom, and they had seven stuffed-animal children. Feenie did all the cooking, cleaning, and made sure Alice had her newspaper when she got home from work.

She wanted to be everything Marie hadn't been for her even then.

Their relationship ultimately died when Marie wished Feenie had never been born. She said Feenie ruined all the plans she'd had for herself.

"If I never met Ryan," she continued, "I think I would've started training to fight professionally. Probably MMA. I think I'm too scrappy for boxing, and kicking the shit out of people is fun."

Alice stared, mouth unabashedly open. *Fighting* and *Feenie* in the same sentence gave her heart palpitations. Feenie had been threatened with expulsion in high school until Marie stepped in to save the day and Feenie's diploma. After that, she somehow managed to control her urge to smash and break people's faces. In the past year, she'd gotten into only two, both ending with her getting arrested. Fighting wasn't a phase to grow out of—she knew Feenie liked, no *loved*, to fight, but she never knew she had considered going pro.

"Don't look at me like that—I already know," she said. "Besides, you're not in my alternative life either. If I hadn't met you, I wouldn't have figured out I like protecting people. I'd be a helluva lot meaner. Selfish. You make me be kind and have *feelings* no matter how hard I try not to."

And then she looked at Alice, the hard look sliding from her eyes.

"Maybe training isn't such a bad idea," Alice said quietly, unsure if it was okay to speak yet. "It would make sense."

"No." Feenie smiled, tilting her head so it touched Alice's. "I would've been damn good at it, though."

"If you really wanted to fight professionally, maybe you could talk to Ryan? Postpone your plans for a few years?"

"He already knows. The look on his face when I told him is probably going to haunt me for the rest of my life."

Alice wanted to ask but decided not to pry. "I think our moms coordinated their efforts. I just got off the phone with mine."

"*God*, could they just not be friends?" Her lips pulled back over her teeth in disgust. "Marie probably asked Momma J to take care of my case."

"My mom didn't mention it if she did, not that she would. She says hi."

"What did she want?"

"Same old *go to law school* spiel. I have to come up with an alternative to present to her and my dad in three weeks."

"Is foreign language out? Ryan told me he was going to teach you."

"Not out, but it would only be a minor. I think it's too late to try to pick a language and major in it, if I want to graduate on time," Alice said. "Takumi is helping me, though."

"Helping how?"

Alice smiled. "Mostly he helps me not think about it. He's really good at that whole emotional support thing and distracting me. My mental state is quite happy that we work together *and* then we hang out at his place after. It's all Takumi, all the time."

"Really? *Wow*. I had *no* idea. It's not like I stare at your empty room every night, waiting for you to come home or anything." Feenie rolled her eyes. "I have a headache."

"Do you want me to make you breakfast in bed?" Alice asked quietly.

(She didn't want to fight.)

(Not again.)

(But really, Feenie. *Really?*)

"*No*," Feenie said. "I'll cook for us. The last thing I need is for you to burn down the kitchen."

"Aw, I love you, too. Scrambled eggs and coffee, please."

Feenie kissed Alice's forehead just as Glory howled from somewhere else in the house, also ready for breakfast.

CHAPTER

23

Takumi barely glanced at the onesie before saying, "No."

"Oh, come on! It's a Rainbow Fish! Like the book!"

"I'm not wearing that." His voice still hadn't lost that morning-after edge—a half rumble an octave away from vocal fry—even though it was already nine thirty at night.

"Do you know how hard it is to find these in the summer? It's lightweight with a breathable fabric." She shook it in his direction, plastic scales shimmering in the comfortable lighting of his living room. They sat together on the couch, Alice's Bag o' Goodies at her feet.

"No one told you to buy that."

"You said I knew best. Onesie is best."

"When did I say that?"

"Last night right before I left when you agreed to the wallow sesh."

Takumi frowned, dark eyebrows pinched together, struggling to remember. Eventually, he sighed. "Can you believe I've never been hungover in my life? I ruined a perfectly good six-year streak."

"Six years? Someone started drinking early," she teased. "Totally not judging, by the way. So, onesie, yes?"

"It hurts to even look at that thing. Why is it so *vibrant*?"

"Because it's actually mine." She grinned and pulled a second onesie out of the bag. "You get to be the brown bear. Look, it even has little ears on the hood."

"You are way too excited about this." He took the onesie anyway.

"It's true. I am. I'll calm down in a little bit."

After changing, gathering blankets and pillows, making all the junk food she thought he would at least try, and selecting the first movie of the night, they returned to the couch and settled into their blanket nest.

"And so," Alice said, "it begins."

He wasn't a fan of horror movies, but had agreed to try one. A low-budget film about a haunted hotel where every room led to a different hell dimension.

(She pretended not to notice each jump scare that worked its magic.)

(She also pretended not to notice how he moved closer to her during every suspenseful scene.)

"Relax," she whispered, closing the gap between them to sit shoulder to shoulder. Takumi chose the next one—an adventure movie about a group of people who had a lethal imbalance of adrenaline to common sense and decided to scale an infamous snowy mountain for fun.

(Because *what* could possibly go wrong?)

"These people are dumb," Alice said, biting her slice of pizza clean in half. "I don't care. I'm judging them and their life choices because they're just dumb and they're making me physically uncomfortable. If I'm going to risk my life, it had better be to save someone else."

One of the hikers slid down the mountain feetfirst and collided with a jutting rock. His bones popped out of his legs upon impact.

"Jesus Christ!" Alice burrowed under the blankets so she wouldn't have to watch. "You promised it wasn't gory!"

"I forgot about this part." He tugged on the blankets. "It's okay. Come out."

"HIS LEGS. TAKUMI. HIS LEGS." She uncovered her head to glare at him. "This better make you feel better, because if I sit through this whole movie and you're still upset—"

"I'm not upset." He tapped her nose. "Thank you for tonight, but I don't want you thinking that I go around moping and getting drunk over my ex, okay?"

"That's not what I meant." She huffed, turning completely away from the TV screen. A wolf had appeared. That wouldn't possibly end well for the hiker in the red jacket. "I shouldn't have said that. It's okay to miss her or what you had because it was special to you, I think. When someone you love does something terrible to you, everyone tries to make you feel better by saying you'll get over it and that you should hate that person, but you don't. Maybe you can, maybe you should, but you don't want to. So, yeah be upset. Sorry."

"That was a lot," he said lightly.

"Seeing that guy's bones outside of his body put me on edge. I talk a lot when I get nervous."

Takumi turned the volume down (right when the wolf attacked! *Gosh*). "I don't have any more energy to waste on her. I don't want our past to feel like one giant mistake, you know? I don't like thinking she's a horrible person all the time, because she's not. Or she didn't used to be. I don't think"—he took a deep breath—"I don't think it's wrong to cut people who feel toxic to you out of your life even if you love them. She's pretty mad about that."

"You talked to her?"

"She called me today."

"So it's over?" she asked gently.

"Permanently."

"Are you okay?"

"I will be," he said. "I tried to speed up the being-okay process by drinking, which was really stupid."

"It wasn't, because if you hadn't, you wouldn't have called me and we wouldn't be having this life-affirming conversation right now in our fabulous onesies. Ryan thinks everything happens for a reason and happens exactly the way it's supposed to. Sometimes, like now, I agree."

He leaned over and placed his forehead on hers. She scrunched up her face to keep herself from laughing. When he pulled back, she straightened his hood, tucking the wispy strands of hair that had escaped into it. His sweet smile as she did it made her feel so happy.

(So wanted.)

"Is it your turn yet?"

"Nah," she said, knowing exactly what he meant. "Tonight is for you. I don't want to intrude with my tales of woe."

"It's not intruding. It's sharing. It's what we do."

"Fine." She took a deep breath. "I'm not ready to share. I don't want to tell you."

It was his turn to fix her hood. (He knew not to touch her hair.) "Okay," he said. "You don't ever have to tell me anything you don't want to."

But part of her *did* want to. Her secret shouldn't even have been one—it should have been a nonissue. Why couldn't being asexual just be accepted?

Why did she have to spend the rest of her life coming out over and over and over . . . ? And once she did, would people *always* expect her to talk about it? It would always be a huge deal, she would always be subjected to questions, and she would always have to defend herself.

Would it ever stop feeling like A Thing, a barrier, between her and everyone else?

"You know what? We look ridiculous," he said. "We should take a picture."

"We look adorable," she corrected. "And yes, we should."

Takumi jumped up and sprinted for his spare bedroom. When he returned, he sat next to Alice and put one arm across her shoulders. "In close. Faces together." He held the camera out in front of them.

"Are we smiling?" she asked, leaning into him. "Or should we act scared to commemorate watching this awful movie?"

"Smile first. We can always take more later."

(We.)

Alice gave the photo her best and brightest smile.

CHAPTER
24

Alice's hand trembled as she unlocked the door. Thirty minutes later and she still hadn't recovered.

"Ah! Get back here!" She chased Glory down the pathway, picking her up before she got too far. Glory liked to run for her life when she got a whiff of the outside world, often getting lost until she settled down in one spot, howling at the top of her kitty lungs for someone to come find her.

(The management and neighbors were getting real sick of Glory's shit.)

"Hey," Alice said to Feenie, who sat on the couch with Alice's purple comforter wrapped around her.

"Hey, yourself." She didn't look up from her laptop. "Where have you been?"

Alice flung her purse across the room, kicked her shoes off, and leapt onto the couch like a homicidal jungle cat hyped up on pixie dust. "Paragliding."

"What?" Feenie's head snapped up. "But you're afraid of heights."

"*I know*. And I am thoroughly wrecked." Alice held up her hand. "Look. I'm still shaking. I had an absolute *fit* in the air. I called him everything but a child of God." She had actually dropped to her knees and kissed the ground once they landed. "I must have used every curse word I've ever heard. You would have been proud."

"*'Him'?* And you went willingly?"

"We traded. Takumi's terrified of horror movies, so we made a deal about a week ago. Fear for fear. I got my old-school, gore-free horror marathon and the smarmy bastard just happened to be a licensed paragliding instructor who got us a deal for free-ninety-nine with his old company. He just dropped me off because he had to work at the library today."

"I can't even get you to go on a Ferris wheel." Feenie made a disgusted noise. "I'll be right back."

Alice watched her go for a moment and then peeked at her laptop screen. Wedding dresses.

(Wasn't it a bit early for that?)

"Here." Feenie held out a card. "I started talking to this guy who came into the shop to get his tat filled in and it turns out he runs his own interior-design business. He's looking for an intern to start in September. I told him you're into all that shit and he said he'd interview you, if you were interested."

Interior design.

Intern.

His own business.

The words tumbled around inside Alice's head. She could do that? As a job? That was something she could actually study, get a degree in and then get paid to do? She'd have to research, of course, but thinking about that, interior design, as a career, *made sense*. Her mom admired entrepreneurs and made it a point to support Black-owned businesses whenever possible. She might actually be thrilled Alice's education and career path might have the potential for her to become her own boss someday.

."Thanks." She took the card. "This is great."

"I am great." Feenie settled back into her spot. "Don't you fucking forget it."

"How could I possibly?" Alice tugged the blanket until Feenie let her in. "So dresses?"

"Yep."

"Find any you like?"

"A few." Feenie turned the screen away as if she didn't want Alice to see.

"Is this shop local?"

"Why? Are you going to go with me if it is?"

"Well, yeah. I mean, don't you want my help?"

Feenie clicked her tongue. "Sure you can pry yourself away from Takumi long enough to spend time with me?"

Alice sighed and stood up. Feenie didn't stop her.

CHAPTER

25

"Hey, Buttons," Ryan called when Alice stepped out of her room. He sat on the floor, building a tan-carpeted *something*.

"What are you doing?"

"Building a cat tree. It was on sale, so I said, why not?"

"She seems to like it." Glory had already stuffed herself into one of the lopsided circle baskets, watching Ryan work. The screw jutting out of the bottom made the basket rest on its side like a spinning top. "Do you want any help?"

"I got it," he said. "Why didn't you answer your phone yesterday?"

"I was doing my hair." She sat next to him. "I can only do it on my days off."

"Are you seriously saying it took you all day to wash your hair? I called six times," he said.

"When did I say 'wash'? Doing my hair is a four- to eight-hour experience."

"It doesn't take that long." He looked at her head. Her twist out didn't come out the way she'd wanted, but it would last a few days at least.

"You've known me forever and a day and you seriously don't know how long it takes me to do my hair?"

"I thought you woke up like that. All flawless and such."

She cocked an eyebrow, deciding whether or not to accept the compliment. "You're not nearly as smooth as you seem to think."

"You love me." He laughed. "Where are you off to?"

"Takumi is probably sick, so I'm going to check on him."

"Probably?"

"Yeah. I haven't heard from him in two days, but he called in sick on Saturday."

Ryan twirled the screwdriver between his fingers, focused. "Are you sure he's actually sick?"

"It's either that or he's packing and needed some time off." Alice shrugged. "He already signed the lease for his new place."

"Maybe he's doing something else that doesn't involve you."

"What's that supposed to mean?"

Ryan's face was so open, so honest. It always told the truth before he was ready to speak.

(Basically, he couldn't lie to save his life.)

"I just think it's funny that you talk to him and see him every day and all of a sudden he disappears and doesn't tell you why. I mean, you're guessing he's sick or packing. You don't actually know."

"He doesn't have to tell me every little thing he does with his life," Alice said. "And I've been busy, too."

Honestly, it hadn't even bothered her. It wasn't that she didn't notice or didn't care—more than once she had checked her phone, thinking she had heard the personalized chime she'd given him, but didn't have a message—but between the interview and interior-design research, Takumi sort of got pushed to the back burner.

(Wow, that sounded awful.)

She did text Takumi, though. He just didn't reply, which was super unlike him, so he *must* have been sick, right?

(Damn it, Ryan.)

"Okay. Forget I said anything." He smiled. "He can't come to the wedding, though. Feenie says no."

Alice laughed. "I have like two years to change her mind. I think I'll win that one."

Ryan's hand stilled in mid-screwdriver twist. Slowly, he lifted his gaze to her. "You mean six months."

"I'm sorry, what?" Cold shot through Alice as if she'd been stabbed through the heart with a giant icicle.

"We set an actual date. Next year, mid-February, because the venue she wanted had a tentative opening. We should get the confirmation with the actual date this week." He placed the part he was assembling to the side. "Feenie didn't tell you?"

Alice misaligned her jaw, exhaling in a miserable huff. "Apparently not."

"Hey, did you and Feenie ever actually talk about what happened at the party?"

"No. We've sort of just glossed over it." She also realized she'd done the same thing with him. Ryan and Feenie were a couple, but they were also individuals.

"I think you should," he said softly. "She's still mad."

"I know, but I don't get *why*. It's not fair—why does everything always have to be the way she wants it? It's like she doesn't care about my feelings."

He sighed—his expression was so pained it made Alice's stomach flip. "You really need to talk to her."

TAKUMI'S EYES WERE bloodshot—the reddened skin around them swollen and drooping.

"Are you okay?" Alice asked.

"Yeah," he said, completely stuffed up. "I think I might be sick."

"Might be?" She laughed.

"What time is it?" He rubbed his eyes and stepped back to let her inside. "I was asleep."

She slipped off her shoes in the entryway. Boxes, Bubble Wrap, and packing tape had commandeered the corner between the couch and the sliding glass door that led to the balcony, but he hadn't actually begun packing.

"Guess this means I have to take care of you." She smiled, more than willing to help nurse him back to health.

"No, it's fine. I'm fine." He sighed, coughed, and cleared his throat. And then closed the door behind her anyway.

(He totally wanted her to stay.)

(Obviously. Of course he did.)

Ryan the Meddler had her on edge. Everything was fine. Takumi was actually sick, not hiding something from her. He leaned against the door, breathing heavily, as if the movement used up the last dregs of energy he had. She had the feeling if he let go he'd fall over.

"Just don't breathe on me and infect me with your germs." She reached up, placing a hand on his forehead, and had to stop herself from saying *yeesh*—his skin flamed under her palm. "You wouldn't happen to have a thermometer, would you?"

He shook his head. She touched his cheeks with the backs of her hands. "Okay, you. In bed. Now." She helped guide him to his bedroom.

"You really don't have to take care of me. I'll survive. Somehow."

"Don't be so dramatic." She giggled. "But if you want me to leave, I will."

Takumi climbed back into bed. She pulled the covers up to his chin and tucked him in. Starve a cold, sweat a fever? That was it, right? She made a note to Google it later.

"You don't mind staying?" he asked quietly.

"Not even a little bit." She sat on the edge of the bed. "You rest. Relax and be wowed by my phenomenal cosmic nursing powers."

"Don't make me laugh. Everything hurts." He curled toward her. She rubbed up and down the center of his back.

"Wait here. Gonna go look for stuff."

She rummaged through his kitchen. She poured him a glass of water, diluted half a cup of orange juice, and grabbed a carton of yogurt, placing it all on a small tray she found.

(She hoped it was a tray anyway.)

(Too late. It was going to function like one.)

A bottle of Tylenol was stashed way in the back of a cupboard. She could sense the battle she'd have to fight to get him to take actual medicine. Why did health nuts always have a problem with lifesaving modern medicine? The treatment for the common cold could probably be 100 percent trusted at this point.

Back in his room, she slid the tray onto the nightstand before heading to the bathroom to soak a washcloth in cold water.

"You probably need to take a shower," she said, draping the cloth over his forehead. "But I don't want you to pass out in there."

"You could give me a sponge bath. You're a nurse, after all."

She narrowed her eyes at him as she opened the yogurt. "That was a joke."

"It was." He smiled.

"Eat."

He sighed, taking the container. "I'm not hungry."

"That's the fatigue talking. But my grandma said you have to coat your stomach before you take pills, so." She shook the Tylenol bottle.

"I have Tylenol?"

"I was surprised, too." She checked the bottle. "It's not expired or anything. I'm probably going to head to the store soon for medicinal reinforcements."

He groaned. "Don't leave." He rolled over and placed his head in her lap, arms wrapped around her. "I tried not to be needy, but I am," he mumbled. "Help me. I think I'm dying."

"That didn't take long." She laughed (trying to pretend like him asking her to stay didn't just make her happier than a panda bear in snow). She removed the washcloth and pushed back his hair from his damp skin. "I'll wait until you're asleep before I go." She laid a light kiss on his hairline. "You won't even know I'm gone. Deal?"

"I'll know you're gone. I'll feel it."

"Needy *and* overdramatic. I like it."

"I like you," he mumbled.

(Oh, Jesus.)

(What was she supposed to say to that?)

"Obviously," she said, smiling at him. "I'm amazing."

In the silence, she counted to 137. Takumi's hair covered his forehead and eyes, his lips were parted, and his deep breaths were in time to her numbers.

At 138, his gentle snores began to tickle across her skin.

Wriggling carefully, she managed to break free from his grip and place his head gently onto the pillow. She left a Post-it note on his bedside table (only after convincing herself not to stick it to his forehead for giggles):

So . . . this is kind of awkward, but I borrowed your house keys.
Kanye shrug Off to the store and to do a few Alice things. Be
back soon! (Drink the juice and water, please?)

When she returned he was still sleeping, curled around the pillow. She touched his forehead; still too hot with sticky skin.

Alice remembered exactly how he liked his oatmeal: steel-cut oats, quarter cup of soy milk, one tablespoon of butter, two teaspoons of brown sugar. She managed to get him fed and medicated with little to no fuss, but he seemed to be getting progressively worse. He struggled to keep his eyes open, he groaned a lot, every time he spoke he had to clear his throat, and he said he felt "foggy." Getting him into the shower nearly fried her nerves—she hovered just outside the bathroom door, alert for sounds of him collapsing.

Whenever she could slide away from Takumi, Alice ended up on the couch. She napped in two-hour bursts, but by the time her body got comfortable, four hours had passed, her alarm blared, and it was time to dose him again.

By late afternoon, she was all napped out and decided to try her hand at cooking.

(Soup. She could make soup.)

(No problem.)

All she had to do was measure ingredients, put them in a pot, and allow it to simmer until it turned into delectable soupy goodness. It would be fantastic and not at all too salty.

(Her panic attack lasted for about three minutes of chest constricting, hyperventilating terror before she pulled herself together.)

She had memorized the recipe, word for word, but still triple-checked each step before moving on and she only hurt herself once—a minor burn on her forearm while draining the noodles.

But the soup? The soup would be *amazing*. A masterpiece. Her pièce de résistance. Her grandma always said the way to a man's heart was through his stomach.

(That was also the way to Alice's heart, so bump those gender roles.)

But if that gross generalization was true, Takumi was about to fall madly in love with her.

"You're cooking," Takumi rasped before clearing his throat.

"Why are you out of bed?" she demanded, tapping the stirring spoon on the rim of the pan before replacing the lid. He looked distinctly ill: swaying as he stood, eyelids at half-mast, and patches of his flushed skin contrasted with paler portions.

"I heard you in here. It smells good."

"Almost done." She checked the food timer. "Fifteen more minutes."

"Did you buy the whole store?" He grinned, sifting through the contents of the plastic bag on the counter.

She walked over to him and placed a hand on his lower back. "I didn't know what your symptoms were. I bought everything to be on the safe side. What hurts? How do you feel?"

"Throat, headache, really tired." He looked at the stove. "Hungry."

"Under your tongue," she instructed, holding up the new thermometer.

He complied. It beeped after ten seconds. "One hundred point four." She scrunched her face. "Better than I thought, but not good." She measured out two tablespoons of cherry-flavored cold-and-fever reducer medicine.

(Let's get real: cherry was the only worthwhile flavor.)

Takumi raised an eyebrow before shaking his head. "Can't I take these instead?" He pointed to the box of pills.

"No. This will soothe your throat now. You won't have to wait for the medicine to disperse through your body. Those are for when you go back to work."

He swallowed the medicine. "Ugh, that's gross."

"Don't complain." She set the medication timer for four hours. "Okay. Back to bed. Now."

"But I want to watch you cook. For the safety of my security deposit."

"I'm only a danger to myself when I cook, not property." She glared, passing him to go to the bedroom. After setting the drinks down, she straightened the bed, adjusting the blankets and pillows.

Takumi touched Alice's back, and when she stood up straight, he hugged her. His hold was weak, he swayed a little, and she held on to him to keep him upright, before guiding him back to bed, pulling the covers up around him.

"How long are you staying?"

"As long as you need help, I guess?" She sat facing him. "I can spend the night, but I work tomorrow, so tell your body to hurry up."

"I don't feel as bad as yesterday."

"Good. I'm gonna go check the soup. Do not get out of that bed. Call if you need something."

The timer had two minutes left. She gave the soup one last swirl. It had the perfect consistency and smelled exactly how chicken noodle soup should smell. Elated, she grabbed a bowl, spoon, and another makeshift tray for Takumi to set on his lap. She scooped out two portions, making sure to get plenty of chicken in each.

He sat up in bed, his back against the headboard with his eyes closed.

"Ta-da! Chicken noodle soup," she said, setting the tray down.

"Getting up took all my energy," he said. "I'm too tired to lift my arms. Can you feed me, please?"

She waited for him to laugh or smile at the very least, but he asked her with a straight face. "Okay," she agreed. Holding the bowl, she stirred it. "If you don't like it, I can go buy something else." She blew on a spoonful to cool it down. "But I'm telling you, if gods got sick, they'd kick ambrosia straight into the underworld and eat this instead. I made it perfectly *and* from scratch."

She watched his face for any sign that he didn't like it. After he swallowed, he looked at her expectantly. She fed him spoonful after spoonful. He ate slowly, but finished the entire bowl.

"Can I have some more?"

"You want seconds?" She could barely contain her joy as she darted back into the kitchen, filled up his bowl, and headed back to the room. He ate just as slowly, but still finished all of it.

"That was really good. I knew you could cook."

"I still hurt myself." She showed him the burn on her forearm. It was important to stay humble . . . but . . . She did it! She cooked! And didn't maim herself! And it was good! "Doesn't mean I could do it again."

Placing the bowl on the nightstand, she helped him drink some water. "You should sleep. I'm gonna hang out in the front. Call me if you need me."

Before she could walk away, he reached for her again. "Please stay."

"All right. Only until you fall asleep," she warned. Lying with her back to him, they spooned, his arms around her waist and forehead on the back of her neck.

Alice awoke to the medicine alarm begging to be thrown across the room. She shut it off and rolled over. The sun had already gone down.

His body curled toward her, but his hands were shoved under the pillow and only a quarter of his face was visible.

(If Alice got sick, then she got sick, because she was in too deep to back out now.)

She pushed back that bit of his hair that never seemed to want to stay with the rest.

She kissed the small patch of cheek exposed to her.

He inhaled deeply in his sleep, mumbling her name.

She decided to let him sleep longer.

The spare room was also filled with boxes, but a few were already sealed. The futon was gone, all the pictures had already been removed from the walls, and the closet was nearly empty.

An emerald-green photo album still covered in plastic wrap sat on top of the desk. Loose photos were strewn across the top—Alice froze, heart hammering in her chest. The majority of the pictures were of her.

Was he really going to put her pictures in there?

She made it into his photo collection?

Really?

Alice trembled as she sat down on the desk chair, legs over the armrest. A few pictures of her at work made her frown, a couple of her sleeping made her cringe, but most of them were from when they were out and about (including one of Alice in her Velma costume from the first night they had spent together!). She picked up one: their first basketball game together. He sat behind her with his arms around her, holding the camera. She leaned on his chest, their cheeks touching. Wearing matching hats, they cheesed together, gums and teeth out in full force. Smiling, she set it to the side.

Another one: after he'd convinced her to go on a hot-air-balloon ride. She had refused to let go of him the entire time—her knuckles locked up from holding on to his jacket too tightly. In the picture, Takumi looked fantastic and smiled like he was paid to do it; Alice looked scared and stressed with her face turned slightly into his. The world stretched out as far as the lens could capture it before fading into the blue sky behind them. She set that one to the side, too.

The next one she picked up made her chuckle: it was of her trying not to laugh/cry as she bottle-fed one of the abandoned puppies at the animal shelter. She had gasped and let loose a high-pitched whine of "Oh my God, he's peeing on me!" while the puppy, unbothered, continued to eat. Takumi had laughed so hard he turned bright red.

Alice paused to count—how had they crammed so many moments Takumi considered important into such a short period of time?

"What are you doing?" Takumi stood in the doorway, disheveled and topless, rubbing his eyes.

"Looking at pictures," she answered. "You seem to have misplaced your shirt."

"It's hot," he said, leaning against the wall. "Are you going to come back to bed?"

"It's probably not a good idea for me to continually bask in the presence of your royal germiness. If I get sick, how will I take care of you?"

"We can be sick together." He closed his eyes, forehead on the wall. "The wall feels nice."

She laughed. "Takumi, go back to bed."

"But you're in here." He pushed off the wall, sighing and lumbering toward her. "Stand up."

Alice stood, giving in, and prepared to follow him, but he sat instead.

"Come on." He tugged her into his lap, resting his head on her shoulder.

His fever made him more like a heat rock than a person. And she was a lizard, curling around him like a lazy cat in the sun.

"Oh," she exclaimed, picking up two of the pictures. "Can I have these?"

Takumi cracked one eye open. "I accidentally broke the SD card for one of those. Let me make copies before you take them."

A picture of the twins caught Alice's eye. "Who's this?" A white woman kneeled in the grass with them.

"Their mom."

"Oh. She's white."

His abrupt laughter was cut short by a coughing fit. "Is that a problem?"

"Um, no? Why would it be?" Alice thought about it—his question felt like a setup. Takumi may have been sick, but that didn't seem to be enough to stop him from trying to get her to talk about things she'd rather . . . not. "You know what? No. Nope. Not doing this. That is so far out of my lane and I'm gonna stay right here." She tucked her legs to the side, curling all the way up onto his lap.

"I see you," he said, but tightened his arms around her anyway.

"Sorry." Because it felt like she had to say something.

"I'm too tired to care, but just do better."

Alice side-eyed him. "You are way too perfect for my liking. I'm gonna need you to develop some flaws so our friendship can have some balance, okay? It's stressful." She managed to speak without laughing, but the smile on her face was beginning to make her cheeks hurt.

"I have flaws."

"You do not! I haven't seen any."

"Maybe because I'm constantly being my absolute best so you'll like me."

"Why do you keep thinking I don't like you?" she asked, worried. "I really do. But I don't like Perfect Takumi all that much. I complain about you to my counselor." She laughed. "I want you to feel like you can be yourself with me."

"I'm always myself. But okay." He nuzzled her neck. "Can we please go back to bed?"

His face right in that exact spot, his breath against her skin, did funny things to her heart rate. She prayed he couldn't hear it.

"If you're going to use me as a human body pillow, I should receive some sort of payment. There are girls on the Internet who are paid handsomely to snuggle."

"What do you want?" He looked up. She brushed his hair back from his forehead. As she did it, his eyelids drooped, his head leaning into her touch.

"A promise," she said, thinking before speaking. She would've liked to have asked him to never leave her, but she couldn't bring herself to do it. So she settled for the next best thing. "Will you—"

"I adore you," he said, looking into her eyes. "You know that, right?"

(*Oh*. Okay. Well. Okay.)

Alice experienced every cliché ever written: her heart skipped a beat and then thundered in her ears, she held her breath, the world slipped away, and she felt like she was falling.

"I do now," she whispered.

His hand cradled Alice's jaw. He pressed his lips closer to the corner of her mouth than her cheek.

"You're going to get me sick." Her voice trembled more than she wanted it to.

"I'll always take care of you."

"You're under the influence of cough syrup. You don't know what you're saying," she joked. "Always is an awfully long time and I might hold you to that."

"Promise?"

"Wow." She laughed. "How strong was that stuff?"

"It's not the medicine." He smiled and bit down on his thumbnail—the way he always did to keep from laughing. She had stared at his face long enough to read him with little to no struggle. Takumi was thoughtful but not animated. His expressions were subtle but not mysterious. "It's you."

Her gaze drifted to the pictures.

Oh.

Oh.

CHAPTER
26

This was it. The morning Alice decided the tiptoeing stalemate she and Feenie had entered almost two months ago would end. They would sit down, talk about what happened, and officially move past it.

(. . . and then she'd go to work and deal with Takumi.)

(All she needed was an opening.)

(Where in tarnation was she going to get one of those? It's not like she could say, "We should date. By the way, I'm ace.")

(. . . or could she?)

(No, no, no. That was a bad idea. Terrible.)

(*The deepest of sighs.*)

"Relax, Buttons," Ryan said.

"I'm not scared," she said, pacing back and forth in the kitchen. "It's just she yells. I don't like it when she yells."

"I know. It'll be fine."

"Why won't you just tell me?"

"I told you I can't. Please don't ask. I don't like being stuck between you two."

Oh, how Alice knew that feeling. "Thanks for agreeing to mediate and make a fancy brunch to butter her up."

"You're welcome." He passed her the basket of croissants.

Alice tore into one, shoving more into her mouth between each bite. She leaned on the counter while watching Ryan finish cooking.

Feenie arrived a handful of moments later. "I would have been here sooner, but Don is a sack of shit in human skin who would be late for his own funeral, the bastard." She kissed Ryan on the cheek, who frowned at her.

"Is it really necessary to talk like that?"

"I do what I want." She shrugged out of her jacket, tossing it across the room onto the couch. Glory wound her way around Feenie's legs, meeping to be picked up, which Feenie did for almost exactly two minutes—the time it took to kick off her shoes and plug her phone into the charger. She handed the cat off to Alice.

"Hold her, will you?"

"Sure."

"You look nice," she said, her voice thick with suspicion. "What are you all dressed up for? I know you're not going to work like that."

"I'm not dressed up." Okay, so *maybe* Alice was.

Feenie's eyes narrowed into slits.

"Anyway, Takumi is picking me up in a bit," Alice began, lowering Glory to the ground. Behind Feenie, Ryan had a panicked look in his eyes and started frantically shaking his head. "I was thinking maybe you could finally meet him to make up for the party?"

Ryan covered his face with his hands.

Feenie picked up an apple from the fruit basket, tossed it into the air, and caught it. "No."

"No?" Alice asked. Her eyes flicked to Ryan, who was suddenly interested in the ceiling.

"No. I don't want to meet him." She bit into the apple, waving as she left the kitchen. "I'm going to lie down. Let me know when the food is ready."

"Okay?" Alice let the question hang, waiting for Ryan to answer.

"Yeah." He rubbed the back of his neck. "Okay," he said, lowering his voice. "You did not hear this from me. Don't even mention it. You have to pretend like I never said anything; I really hate doing this, but if you two don't talk soon, I'm going to lose my mind." He paused. "She's mad because she thinks Takumi is taking her place. She doesn't understand why you're treating him like he's your new best friend."

"What?"

"I know, okay? I know. But that's how she feels. Like you don't talk to her anymore and you depend on him for everything now."

"That's ridiculous."

Ryan gave her a funny look. "It isn't. I know it's not true, but I can see why she feels that way. You spend a lot of time with him."

"You two spend a lot of time together without me."

"That's different. We're engaged."

"So I'm just supposed to sit around and wait for you both to remember I exist?"

"Of course not, but you shouldn't edge us out. You're the one making it as if it has to be him *or* us."

"How am I doing that? And why is this all my fault? Why do you two have a Get Out of Ditching Alice pass that I'm supposed to accept because you say so? How is that fair to me?"

"We don't *ditch* you," Ryan said.

"You do. You have for years. I just don't say anything because I don't want us to fight, but the *second* I find an actual friend on my own, you two act like this. Neither of you said anything when I spent time with Margot. Why is Takumi suddenly different?"

"Maybe we minded then and didn't say anything either."

Alice whipped around at the sound of Feenie's voice. Feenie leaned against the refrigerator, arms crossed.

"Maybe," she continued, "we were really hurt, but you were too busy being happy to notice. Just like right now."

An enraged fierceness made the edges of Alice's vision turn red. She balled her hands into fists. "I wouldn't even have met Margot if you hadn't decided to move in with Ryan at the last minute. The millisecond you two started dating, he came first. *You* started to choose him over me every single time." She turned that rage on Ryan. "And you have *always* chosen her over me." Her phone buzzed. "Takumi's outside." She slung her purse strap over her shoulder while marching for the door.

"Buttons, wait."

She paused, fingers tensed around the doorknob. "I don't want to talk about this."

Inside the car, it wasn't hard to pretend to be happy. One look at Takumi's smiling face enabled her to paste a smile on her own. That anger she had felt in the kitchen melted away into a raw, distressing sadness. Alice hated that about herself. She could never stay mad for longer than a few minutes before it morphed into regret. She shouldn't have said those things, she shouldn't have yelled, she shouldn't have she shouldn't have she shouldn't have. . . .

"Alice?" Takumi waved his hand in front of her face. "Where did you go?"

"Sorry," she said. Her lips stretched into a smile she couldn't feel.

"Whoa," he said. "Okay, what's up?"

She clasped her hands together and looked out of the windshield.

A woman and three kids exited the library, each carrying a bag of books. "We're already here?"

He poked her cheek. "What's the matter?"

She didn't want to tell him that it was possible her best friends didn't like him before they even got a chance to get to know him and it was her fault they felt that way. Maybe they had a point—maybe this was all on her.

"Do you think we spend too much time together?"

"I think the opposite actually. I could try to give up sleep to spend more time with you." He cleared his throat and sniffled. His cold hadn't quite gone anywhere yet. "Sure I'd be happier, but I think that would do more harm than good. The consequences of sleep deprivation are terrible."

"I'm serious. Be serious."

"I like how you automatically assumed I wasn't." He laughed, resting his arm on the center console to lean closer to her. "No. I don't think we do. Why?"

Alice took off her seat belt and turned in the seat to face Takumi. "You come to work early to have dinner with me, we hang out every night after work, we spend our weekends together, and when we're not together, we text all the time. Thank God for unlimited messaging. I think our record has to be close to a thousand texts in less than twenty-four hours," she said. "I know that, because my phone is set to save five hundred messages per thread and one night I tried to scroll back to reread something from earlier that day, but half the messages were already gone."

"We're friends," he said, like it was the most obvious thing in the world. "That's what friends do."

"It doesn't seem, I don't know, excessive to you?"

"We like each other. Constant communication is a natural side effect of that."

She sighed. "It doesn't bother you at all? You're not sick of me yet?"

"No," he said. "Does it bother you?"

"No, not exactly."

"Then what's the problem? Does it bother someone else?"

"Maybe." She stared at her shoes.

"Someone else you care about?"

"Possibly." She met his gaze.

"Is this the part where you tell me you've been secretly seeing someone and now they want to fight me?"

"No." She laughed, but then thought of Feenie. "The fighting part might actually be true."

"I guess it's a good thing I have health care, because I cannot fight. If I had to, I'd take a punch for you. Just not in the face."

"I wouldn't let her hurt you." She reached up and rubbed his cheeks. "You have amazing bone structure. I love your beautiful face. These cheekbones are so sharp, they could cut someone."

"You're rubbing my face. This is a little strange, even for you."

She dropped her hands. "I know. I was trying to wait a little longer before I revealed this level of weirdness. Could I perchance convince you not to judge me for it, good sir?"

"I never said I minded." He took her wrists and pressed her hands back onto his cheeks. "If it makes you feel better, go for it."

"No, it's okay." She laughed, pulling away. "I do feel better, though. Thank you."

He kissed her cheek.

"Ah, no kisses! You're still sick."

"No fever, so I'm not contagious. And I think if you were going to catch my cold, you would have by now."

"Speaking of continuous cohabitation—"

"Never said that."

"Can I come over tonight?"

He smiled, eyes crinkling at the corners. "Wherever I am, you are always welcome."

"ARE YOU GOING to make something?" Takumi asked.

Alice peeked around his refrigerator door. "Okay, so you're not expecting me to cook regularly, right? That's your thing. I *like* that that's your thing."

"I'm still sick." He made a feeble cough. "Help?"

"That's pathetic," she said, closing the door, "but how are you feeling?"

"Functional." He tugged her ear gently when she stood in front of him. "Thanks to you."

She raised her hand and placed it on his forehead. His bangs tickled the back of her hand.

"And you've been taking your medicine every four hours?"

"Yes, Nurse Alice. You could have warned me about the alarms you set. I was in a meeting when the first one went off."

She touched his cheeks. A little warm, like he was flushed. It could have been the black turtleneck and red sweater he wore. It had been ungodly hot outside all day, but he worried the library's air-conditioning would send him back to bed. "They didn't appreciate the musical stylings of the *Bob's Burgers* cast?"

"Not really. No."

"I'm sure you smiled your way out of any awkwardness," she said. "Just don't go looking into any ponds."

"You wound me, madam." He clutched his chest, wincing. "Especially since it's your fault. It's hard not to have an ego when you've told me you love my beautiful face."

"Shut it."

"How beautiful are we talking here? What's my code?"

She groaned. "Not this again."

He caught her at the waist, spinning her back around when she tried to walk away. "Tell me and I'll bake you cookies when I'm not sick."

"What kind of cookies?" she asked, leaning back into his arms. "And you have to use real flour. None of that ultra-buckwheat high-fiber stuff."

"Oatmeal chocolate chip?"

"Deal." She stared at the ceiling. "Black. I'd like two dozen cookies, please."

"Black? I thought the Cutie Code was Green to Red."

"It is. Was." The gears and wheels turning inside Alice's head locked into place as realization sank in. Meeting Takumi had challenged everything she thought she knew about herself, made her work to find out who she was on a fundamental level. He challenged her in the best way possible, wholly unaware of the effect he had on her, pushing her so far out of her comfort zone she had to question everything. She had discovered, no, was still discovering, who she was now, who she wanted to be, what she could and could not handle. He had given her a reason to reconnect with herself.

Feenie had been right—this, he, would always be someone she would want to remember.

"You exceeded my Cutie Code," she said. "You're the reason why I retired it. I don't need it anymore."

"I'll make you three dozen cookies." He grinned. "You must be feeling better, yes?"

"As long as I don't think about Them? Yes. Bless you and your powers of distraction."

He lowered his head to her shoulder, and quietly asked, "Did you really fight about me?"

"Stop being so perceptive. And technically, no." Her fingers brushed his hair—a reflex after doing it so many times to comfort him.

"You're like one more straw on an already broken camel, except I thought it was just a few hairline fractures here and there."

Takumi tried to take a deep breath, but it ended in a slight coughing fit. He stood up straight, turning his head into the crook of his arm. She stood beside him to rub his back.

"Would it help if I talked to them?" Takumi asked after he finished coughing.

"It would not. At all."

"Are you sure? I could explain how things are between us. I was hoping to meet them anyway."

(WELL, HELLO THERE, TARNATION.)

Alice nodded and returned to the refrigerator. "So. When you say *how things are* you mean what exactly? Oh, and are sandwiches, okay?"

"That we're friends and yes."

"Yes. Friends." She placed the fixings on the counter. "Friends."

He stood beside her. "Are we something else?"

"No. I mean, I don't know." Sidestepping him, she headed for the utensil drawer. He followed. She could feel him staring at her, trying to catch her eye. "I'm sure it was the cold medicine, but you insisted it wasn't and I was getting a vibe. Actually, I'm not a hundred percent on the concept of vibes, but if I had to put a name to it, I'd say vibe."

Head down, she pulled four slices of bread from the bag.

Takumi leaned over, placing his elbow on the counter. He gazed at her with his fist pressed to his temple.

"Alice?"

"Takumi?" She mimicked his playful tone. "Mustard, right?"

"Look at me, please."

His amused expression made her feel soft and warm and squishy all over. Indecision quivered inside her chest. It terrified her how much she wanted his friendship and the connection they had created. Because it was him and he had turned her whole life upside down and she was so lost, flailing in unfamiliar territory, and if he'd let her, she'd anchor herself to him until she found her way.

And she was about to risk it all.

"I need to tell you something." She took a step back. "Like, whatever you're going to say, don't say it because I need to tell you this first."

"Okay." He hadn't stopped smiling. "You have my full attention."

"Good. Okay." She wanted to stop. "So you know how some people like jogging?"

"I'm one of those people, so yes."

"Ah, yeah, okay. That worked out." Her breathy laugh sounded forced. "So, you see, I am not one of those people. I don't care about jogging."

"Mmm . . ." He squinted at her for a moment. "Somehow, I knew that."

"Oh, great. Good. This is going well." Her hands began to shake. She pressed her fingers to her lips to steel herself before continuing. "Now take the word *jogging* and replace it with *sex*."

"You don't like sex?"

(Wow, he asked that fast.)

"No." She held up her hand. "No, the correct sentence is *I don't care about sex*." She took a deep breath and held it. "Because I'm not sexually attracted to anyone."

Oh shit. Holy shit. Cosmic rainbow-colored unicorn shit.

She said it. She came out *and* she said it. She told him.

Dr. Burris had been wrong. It was not her *job* to be prepared to elucidate or enlighten—it was a kindness. One that she wasn't 100 percent ready to provide. What if Takumi asked questions? What if he made fun of her? What if he said she was lying or regurgitated any of the other knee-jerk responses she had come to fear?

"Huh," he said, face neutral. "I thought you were bisexual."

"I am. Minus the sexual." She waited, watching him process through her answer. She waited for the judgment, the questions, the confusion, the thoughtful concern followed by the inevitable interruptions. Second by second, it dawned on her that she waited in vain because he was waiting for *her*. "My sexuality is nope." She laughed with relief because still, second by second, he continued to wait, to listen. So she laughed again, tiny bubbles of happy that floated out of her. All too soon, she thought better of it. "That's not a joke. I'm being serious."

He frowned and smiled at the same time, a curious look that made her stomach flip. "I can tell the difference between you telling a joke and you being happy about something. How many people have you told?"

"Explicitly? You're number four. Feenie, Ryan, and a counselor I'm seeing."

Takumi started to speak but closed his mouth and stood up straight, focusing on the counter. Each second he didn't look at her made tiny seeds of dread bloom in the depths of her soul. "That's why you're happy," he mumbled. He nodded as if he couldn't stop and sighed before looking at her again. His eyes had taken on a glossy, reddened tint.

"Thank you for trusting me. Realizing that, um," Takumi said, pausing for a moment, "that hit me kind of hard."

"What do you mean?" Alice asked quietly.

"Four. Obviously, you've been keeping this a secret for a reason."

She hadn't been thinking about trust when she told him. Ryan and Feenie had been there when she figured it out (thank God). Dr. Burris had to pry it out of her, didn't he? And she *still* couldn't say the word properly to him. Telling Takumi had been a choice—not by chance or out of necessity. It was *her* decision, completely on her own.

(She trusted him.)

"I have this list," she said. "I got it from Tumblr. It's the things people say when you tell them you're asexual. I only sort of told my ex-girlfriend, but she still said them. Almost verbatim, like she was reading it off the list. My ex-boyfriend before that? Even worse."

(She trusted him not to say those things to her.)

"I'm sorry they did that to you."

"It's okay." She rolled her eyes at herself. "I mean, it's not okay, but I'm okay that it happened now. If I think about it too much it hurts, so I don't. I move on."

"Forgive and forget."

"I didn't say that." Alice eyed him. "Believe it or not, I am capable of holding a grudge."

"I bet it's fearsome to behold."

"It is. I'm like a honeybee hive. Cute, useful, but deadly when provoked. Relatedly," she said, wanting to lighten the mood, "I've always wondered if worker bees ever sting someone and immediately think *I have made a terrible mistake* after."

When he didn't laugh, she rubbed the heel of her hand into her left eye.

"I wasn't trying to have sex with you the other night," he said. "And I am so, so sorry if I made you feel that way."

He was so close and so far away, as if there was an imaginary pane of glass between them. She wanted him to hug her and make the tension go away.

"No, I didn't think that at all. That's not why I told you."

"This should go without saying, but I'm going to say it anyway, partly because I want to, but also because I think you need to hear it. If knowing you're asexual makes someone see you differently, then they don't deserve to be in your life. My feelings for you are exactly the same as they were an hour ago. This doesn't change anything between *us*."

CHAPTER
27

D r. Burris sighed for the third time in five minutes. "I'm afraid I'm still a bit lost. Could you please sit and remember to breathe in between words?"

Alice crossed her arms. She told him the entire Takumi story while pacing from the door to the window. "What's not to get? All I need to know is if he meant it in a good way or a bad way?" Instead of sitting in her usual seat, the armchair, she stomped to the couch, flung her arm over her eyes, and fell backward. "I already know what you're going to say: 'I can't give you the answer you want, Alice,'" she said in a deeply flawed imitation of his voice. "I don't need an answer. I need insight." She sat up. "You are the King of Insight, so get to the reigning."

Dr. Burris chuckled behind his hand. The corners of his smile were too wide to be hidden. "Thank you. I'm honored that you think of me in that way. But, again, I'm still not sure what happened between you and Takumi beyond your confession."

"I said I told him because I thought there was a vibe," she began at a measured pace. "And then he seemed really playful, but then I told him I was ace and he got all serious. I thought maybe he was going to say he liked me, too. No dice. He just said nothing changed between us, *which* is the entire problem and why I'm in this mess. I don't know how he feels!"

"Breathe, Alice." He set his notepad down on the table. "Why don't we try a few breathing exercises to help you get centered before we continue."

"No. It's fine. I'm calm." She breathed in and out. "See? Breathing."

He sat back in his seat, crossing his legs at the knee, and linking his hands together.

"So what should I do? What does it *seem* like he meant? I mean, you know everything. Do you need to check your notes about me?"

"That won't be necessary." Alice thought counselors and thera-pists were required to have professional poker faces, and if they did, Dr. Burris didn't care. He had the greatest smile when he tried not to laugh at her. The thing she loved most? It was never mean laughter— never made her feel small or ashamed. He wasn't her friend—no, there was certainly a professional line between them—but they were friendly. It was almost as if he enjoyed their sessions together almost as much as she did. "The simplest answer is usually the best one. In this case, the best course of action seems to be asking him directly."

Alice stared at him with a blank face. "That is the *worst* advice I have ever heard. This is *me* we're talking about here. Anytime I'm direct, everything falls apart, goes wrong, blows itself to smithereens. I need a backup plan to the backup plan at this point."

"Things don't seem to work when you're indirect either."

"Did you just sass me?" She leaned forward, eyes narrowed. "I knew I liked you. You're like a wizened Feenie."

"May I speak freely?"

"Have at it, Dr. B."

"You are a dynamic and delightful young lady." He removed his glasses. "Any partner you choose would be lucky to have you. You've come a long way in a short amount of time, and quite frankly, I'm impressed."

She grinned at him. He always managed to give her the warm and fuzzies without it being weird and sappy. "Where were you when I was in high school? Do you have any idea how much angst and anguish I had to sort through on my own? I would have started therapy *years* ago."

"I have an idea." He chuckled under his breath, eyes crinkling. "And how are things with Feenie?"

"Seems like we're going to hell in two separate handbaskets, which, honestly? Just sucks all the fun out of living. Thank God I met Takumi when I did because *man*, would this summer have sucked."

"Would you like to talk about it?"

"Not really." She toed the carpet.

"All right," he said. "And your family?"

"Parental convo is a go. T-minus three days and counting. Takumi's been coaching me."

"I see." Dr. Burris sighed. Again. What was with the sighing today? "I'd like to give you some exercises to complete. I would like it if you spent some time alone. Nothing too extreme—maybe a few hours at a time for three days a week without communicating with anyone else if you can manage that. I'd like you to write down your thoughts, how you felt, what you did during that time, and bring them with you to our next session."

"Okay. Sounds easy enough."

"One other thing: I'd like you to think about how you would potentially approach your family to tell them about your orientation. Now, I am not suggesting you carry out the conversation—that is not something I can recommend you go through with unless you feel ready. Mainly, I want you to think about the language and steps you would take as if you were."

"Mmmm." Alice puffed up her cheeks. "Yeah. No. I'm going to respectfully decline that one."

"All right."

"Don't get me wrong. It's because I don't need to," she said. "I'm not telling my mom *anything* right now. But my brother knows I like girls, too, and I'm pretty sure my sister knows. She always said 'that Margot girl,' which could have meant she didn't like Margot in general or she didn't like that I was dating her. I think it was in general, though, because if she had a problem with me dating a girl, she would have said something. Silence is not Aisha's style. Huh"—Alice paused—"I should send her a nice present or something."

"A present?"

"Yeah. Just because. She can be cool when she wants to be."

"Would you be willing to talk about why you don't want to tell your mom?"

"My parents are older. Like close-to-their-seventies older. I don't think she'd be mad or anything, but I don't know if she'd understand immediately, and my dad is the best person to help her get there. It's pretty funny—during sociology last semester, we were discussing the steadily increasing rates of divorce in America and why we thought it was happening. Everyone was referencing their parents' reasons for splitting up and there I was in the corner like, 'My parents love and respect each other. Everything's great in my house.'

"Coming here helped me decide. I made a promise to myself that I'd tell them everything when I turned twenty-one."

"Everything?"

Alice took a deep breath. "All of it."

CHAPTER 28

Takumi in glasses made Alice giggle so hard she snorted diet soda out of her nose.

"It *burns*," she whined, still laughing. "Please take them off. The cute—I can't."

The round frames suited Takumi beautifully. They were academic chic—like he was two seconds away from defending a thesis.

(She always had a thing for super-intelligent people.)

"No." He crossed his arms. "Let's hear it."

He had agreed to listen to her college plans before she went over it with her parents. "Okay, but can you at least stop looking at me like that?"

"This is my *unimpressed dad* face." He glowered for a moment before unleashing what she had christened his *Alice Smile*—full of teeth, victorious, and wide enough to cause a tiny dimple to form on the top of his left cheek. She saw it only when he was looking directly at her. No one else. "I spent the past hour perfecting it so we could do this."

(The little things always snuck up on her.)

"For someone so serious, you are surprisingly ridiculous."

"Only for you. Now stop stalling."

"Okay." She pulled up her bullet-point list on her phone. "Mom. Dad. As you know, I've been struggling with the decision to go to law school. . . . Okay, why is your dad frown intensifying?"

"Stop relying on filler. If you have to say 'as you know,' then they already know. Get to the point. Remember: clear, concise, and with conviction."

"Right." She mumbled the three *c*'s like a mantra before beginning again. "Mom. Dad. I don't want to go to law school. My grades are good now, but I have to fight for them. I'm not the kind of student who would do well in a law school environment and I don't have the desire to carry me through. I'm sure I'll end up dropping out because I won't be able to keep up."

She took a heaving breath. The tension crawling across her shoulders made her back hunch, made her shrink in on herself. Her parents expected academic excellence. Year after year, that's exactly what she gave them, but college had not been easy and she knew law school would kill her.

(If admitting that weakness to her parents didn't get her first.)

"Good," Takumi said. "Keep going."

She nodded. "But I don't want to drop out. I want to graduate. I want to be successful. I want to have a good career that I can be proud of, like both of you. It's just taking me longer to figure out what I want to do, which, you know, isn't a bad thing, because it's super unfair that we're forced to pick something to spend the next fifty years of our life on when we can't even—"

Takumi knocked on the table. "Focus. Come back."

Another deep breath. "Right. Sorry."

"Start with what you want to do."

God, her throat felt dry, and this wasn't even the real thing yet. She'd probably start coughing up sand midway through her speech.

"Right. I've thought about it, really thought about it, and there's one thing I'm good at and I've always been interested in. I made a six-year plan. Mom. Dad. I want to study interior design."

"AND DO WHAT? Decorate rooms for a living?" Her mom had a thick vein that ran down the middle of her forehead. Whenever she got mad, it pulsated. Like now. "That's a *hobby*, Alice."

"It isn't," Alice insisted. "I researched it. My school offers it as a major."

"I'm sure they offer many majors that are a waste of time."

"*Cynthia*," her dad said. Her mom inhaled and pressed her lips together. "Alice, sweetie, you know that's not what she meant. If you like it, it's not a waste of your time. However, I have to agree, it's not something you should pursue professionally."

"Why not?" Alice braced herself for impact.

"Because it's a frivolous *career* choice." Her dad never lost his temper, never disciplined her a day in her life. That stern, unflinching look in his eyes was worse than any switch off a tree.

"As if that's all it is." Her mom had reached the point where she began to talk through her teeth. Alice didn't have much time left. "And what's the salary range for that kind of work? Or do you slave away, interning for free while they pay you in *exposure*? How will you support yourself?"

"Most college grads can't get a job straight out of college anyway, regardless of their major." She stared at her keyboard. Any second now her mom would say, *Look at me when I'm talking to you.*

"Which is why they continue going to school," her dad said. "Is there an advanced degree for this field to make you a more attractive candidate?"

"I don't know," she mumbled. "But I have a plan. Three more years of school, three years to gain work experience. If it doesn't work out then, I'll go to law school."

She hadn't rehearsed that compromise with Takumi. For each millimeter her mom's eyes continued to narrow, the whispered compromise got louder. She didn't want to say it, to make that promise, but now that she had . . . "I just want a chance to do something for me. Please."

Her parents exchanged a look. They had been married nearly twenty years before she was even born—words between them weren't necessary. Her mother raised her eyebrows. Her dad chewed on his cheek. She pursed her lips. He rubbed the lower half of his face. They continued on like that, moving in tandem reactions, until finally, her dad sighed, got up, and left.

It was over.

"Fine," her mom said.

"Fine?" Hope made her voice squeak.

"You want to waste six years of your life? Fine. That's your right. But it will not be on our dime. When you're ready to be serious about your future, your college fund will still be there."

Her mom disconnected the video call.

Alice sat there until her screen turned black. The silence in her room resounded in her ears, her eyes remained dry, and her stomach became a black hole leaching away anything she should have been feeling. Everything was nothing. Her nails tapped against her phone screen as she dialed.

"Hey," Takumi said. "How did it go?"

"I think my parents just disowned me."

She didn't know how much more silence she could take.

"Say something. Please," she said.

"Please tell me you're joking," he said. "Tell me it went fine and you're trying to play a trick on me."

"Nothing feels real right now. I think I might be asleep."

"Do me a favor then? Go to your dream closet and find a bathing suit. Preferably something with polka dots if you can conjure it. I'll be there in ten minutes."

MEGUMI AND MAYUMI squealed as they ran away from the incoming surf. Their matching yellow-and-white-daisy bathing suits sparkled in the sunlight. Every so often they remembered Alice was there and yelled for her to come play with them.

"In a minute," Takumi would call back.

It had been nearly thirty of those already.

Alice hugged her shins, rested her chin on her knees, and watched the horizon, unseeing. Her dad hadn't even looked at her before he walked away. She knew they'd be mad. She had a greater chance of being selected by NASA for the next lunar landing expedition than to have her parents get on board with her decision. But never in a million years did she think they'd actually disown her. Would they pick up if she called? Would they pretend she wasn't there when she went to meet her niece for the first time?

She ached in ways she didn't think possible and it had only been an hour. They were her *family*. Her blood. When she was little her dad told her that she had half of each of them inside her, only the best parts of course, so no matter where she went, no matter how far apart they were, they would always be together. Fused by genetics and love. She had her dad's dark skin and her mom's brown eyes. His hair and her teeth. His kindness and her laugh.

How in the name of heaven was school more important than all that?

Takumi wiped the next few tears away with the pad of his thumb. She hadn't realized they had begun to fall again.

"Sorry," she muttered.

"Don't be." He wrapped his arm around her, tilting their heads together. "I wish I could tell you everything will be okay."

"I hereby give you permission to lie to me. Just this once."

"No," he said, not unkindly. "But I will say it's probably not as bad as you think it is. I don't think they disowned you. Cut off? Yeah, probably. Disowned?" He gazed down at her, thoughtful, measuring again. "No. Never. Not even to teach you a lesson."

"You don't know my parents."

"But I know you. If they love you half as much as I'm sure they do," he said, "you'd be impossible to give up. They'll come around."

"Or not."

Takumi sighed. "No matter how it seems, you're not the only person to go through something like this. My parents are fine now, but, uh, it was rough there for a while."

"It? You mean because of your job?"

"They ignore it mostly. They appreciate that I'm happy, but are positive I'd be happier doing something else with my life."

"But they still talk to you and love you, right?"

"Oh, yeah. Definitely. It's still complicated. I don't like talking about it."

"Okay. Off the table. What should I do, then? I don't want to not call them, but what if I do and I'm right? I'm really scared." An errant hiccup appeared and turned into a sob. "I'll just go to law school. It doesn't matter."

"It does matter. You don't want to go, so you shouldn't have to."

"I told them I would. In six years, but that wasn't good enough."

"Why six years?"

"Because law school isn't going anywhere. I like patterns and prints and organizing and breathing life into spaces because—because why the fuck not? I'm good at it. Why can't I study in order to be *great* at it and get a job that will make me happy? I can always enroll in the school they want later. Why do I have to do the hard things first?"

"It's supposedly harder to go back when you're older."

"Law school is hard now. A six-year delay isn't going to change that. It's my life. Not theirs." She closed her eyes and inhaled. "It's my life," she said, almost a whisper. "And I'm expecting them to pay for it because they always have. Great. On top of everything else, I'm a god-damn spoiled brat of a daughter. No wonder they reacted the way they did."

"That's a pretty big leap you just made, which for the official record, I'm sure you're also wrong about that." He sprinkled sand over her feet. "Side note: I don't think I'm ever going to get used to hearing you swear. Do it again."

"Why?"

"Because you only do it when you're upset and then afterward you start smiling. It's like a stress reliever for you."

"No, it's not." She looked at him. "I swear all the time."

"No. You don't." He laughed. "You know what you need?"

"A time machine?"

"Or an Epic Wallow Session."

"No. Not for this. I'd rather think about anything else other than this. I'm not even hungry."

"That's worrisome." She couldn't tell if that was a joke or not. "What about a weekend away? Forget about everything for a few days and relax. How do you feel about camping?"

"I feel like I'm not going to like it." She rested her head on his shoulder.

He traced the bridge of her nose. "In a cabin, not a tent."

"I feel like I might like it."

"I thought so."

"When would we go?"

"If we call in sick for tomorrow, we can leave tonight. My parents own a cabin about three hours north we can borrow."

"Just the two of us?"

He paused. "Doesn't have to be."

The words were out of her mouth instantly. "I'm okay with just us. I mean, if you are."

The twins ran up the beach in the sand as well as they could. Megumi held out an array of seashells—not a single one was cracked or broken.

"Don't be sad," Mayumi ordered. "Come play with us."

"We want to swim."

Alice placed the shells in a neat pile near the base of the umbrella. "Lead the way, my little mermaids."

After a full afternoon of happy toddler screeches, chasing crabs, running from waves (with Alice fighting fate like hell not to get her hair wet), taking pictures with their seaweed mustaches, and peanut-butter-and-honey sandwiches, the twins finally began to lose steam. Mayumi went down first—she crawled under the shade of the umbrella, lay down, and was asleep in one minute flat. Takumi carried her to the car as Alice and Megumi packed up their beach bag, cooler, and umbrella.

"I want to carry something," Megumi demanded.

Alice handed her the empty cooler just as a volleyball rolled to a stop near her feet. She set the bag down and picked up the ball with the intention of throwing it back, but a white guy with short black hair stood in her way.

"Hey. Sorry about that." His outstretched hands waited for the ball.

"No worries." Alice smiled, handing it to him.

He took it and turned away . . . and then turned right back, grinning at her.

Oh shit. She knew that look—that flirty smile, the hopeful look in his green eyes, the way he suddenly stood up straight yet managed to somehow slouch at the same time. . . .

"Are you from around here?" he asked.

"An hour away actually." She retrieved the bag and started back toward the parking lot.

"Do you need help?" He followed, pointing to the umbrella. "I can carry that for you."

"I got it. Thanks."

"*We* got it," Megumi corrected. "I'm helping."

"My apologies, my dear," she said, affectionately touching the top of Megumi's head.

"Cute kid," he said. "So, I don't usually invite beautiful strangers to hang out with me, but we're having a bonfire later if you want to come."

"Why take the risk? I could be a serial killer."

"Can you sing? Because that sounds like something a siren would say. Warn me before you sing me to my death so your conscience can be clear." His eyes stayed firmly on hers—friendly and open. "You definitely have the right look for it."

"She can sing!" Megumi said.

"Don't talk to strangers," Alice said.

"You are," she challenged.

"I'm trying not to."

"You're not trying very hard," he said. "You haven't told me to go away."

"I already have plans tonight. Sorry."

"What about some other time? An hour's not that far," he said.

"How about this: I give you my number and if you feel like it, call me sometime?"

"Um," Alice said, trying to stall. She wanted to say no, but she didn't want to hurt his feelings. Asking people out was *hard*. It took a lot of confidence (at least it did for her). Maybe he'd take it in stride. Or maybe he wouldn't.

(Maybe he'd call her ugly or fat or something else that didn't seem to matter to him two minutes ago.)

(Maybe *he* was the serial killer.)

(God, *why* did she think that? She wouldn't be able to unthink it now.)

Take his number, she reasoned. *No pressure.*

She set down the bag and umbrella, exchanging them for her phone. "Okay. What's your name?"

"TJ." He recited his number to her. When she looked up to say good-bye, he was staring over her shoulder.

Takumi. He picked up the bag and umbrella. "Ready?" is all he said.

"Yeah." She turned back. "Bye."

"Hold on," TJ said, smiling. "Don't you think you're taking this mermaid thing too far? Are you really not going to tell me your name?"

"I thought I was a siren?"

"Same difference." He shrugged.

"Not really." She shook her head. "If I call you, I'll tell you."

"If." He began to walk backward. "If." He waved once, smiling bright as the sun, and began to jog back down the beach.

In the car, Alice turned her phone over in her hands, thinking. She had three missed calls from Aisha. None from her parents.

The day had been both awful and surprising. For a few hours she was able to forget her parents potentially hated her. The guilt for indulging in those few stolen moments of joy tethered itself to her ankle, dragging her further into sorrow.

Nothing else was supposed to matter except the Call of (Ill-Fated) Destiny.

"Did you just delete his number?" Takumi smiled as if he were happy to see her doing it. A shiver of possibility ran through her.

She winced. More guilt latched on. She wasn't supposed to think about Takumi either.

"Eyes on the road. You're driving precious cargo," she said. "And yes. Why would I keep it?"

"If you weren't interested, why did you take it?"

"It's easier that way. You wouldn't understand."

"Try me."

"I'd rather not." She sighed. Her chest felt heavier than normal. That was always so strange—how her emotions could seemingly change her body chemistry. "Besides, I'm very selective about who I date now. I made a new rule."

"Which is?"

She gazed out the window. "I'm not going to sleep with people to make them happy anymore. It's kind of my thing, but I don't want it to be."

"Wait, he asked to have sex with you?"

"No, but if things went well, he would have. Eventually."

"He might not," he said. "You don't really know what someone will say until you tell them."

That . . . was not what she expected him to say. Her admission should have gotten her a solemn nod, meaningful condolences, and a promise that she'd find someone someday.

Did he really care that she was self-rejecting? Or . . .

Or . . .

Or . . .

No. She wouldn't allow herself to guess. Reading into his responses could get her heart into trouble. Speculation would take her by the hand

and twirl her straight into the fires of Mount Doom. She'd have to be direct.

"It seems easier to just not date," she began, watching for any change in his demeanor. "Sex is too much a part of everything, and I don't think it's reasonable to tell my partner I don't ever want to sleep with them and expect them to stick around. I'm not saying they wouldn't agree. I personally am not okay with asking. And I'm not saying I wouldn't want to try again someday, but I don't want them to have the expectation that I will. It has to be my choice and a lot of people don't respect that."

She stared at his profile so hard she thought her eyes would cross. She prayed he would say the Perfect Thing.

(Not that she knew what that was, but she'd know it if she heard it.)

He said nothing. Alice waited and waited, watched the way his fingers gripped the steering wheel, the way his thumb tapped to the soft music. He looked in the rearview mirror at the sleeping twins in their car seats, out his side mirrors when he changed lanes, but never at her. Not even a glance.

Maybe she shouldn't have told him that.

She always told him everything, but she should not have told him that.

Not yet.

CHAPTER

29

The cabin itself was small, but richly decorated. "Oh, I approve," Alice said, looking around. Dark hardwood floors, plush sofas and armchairs in deep purple, elegant black rugs, a fireplace with a giant flat-screen mounted above it, and a tiny kitchen with granite countertops and black appliances. The walls were bare but wooden, giving it a rustic feel. She couldn't stop herself from touching the curtain fabric.

"Can I take pictures?" Alice asked, phone already in hand. Several texts from Ryan waited for her (and more missed calls from Aisha).

> Text me when you get there please!

> Remember, do not trust the old man in the corner store. He probably eats people.

> DON'T DRINK THE WATER. Flesh-eating bacteria are odorless and tasteless.

> If there's a basement, stay out of it! Don't touch anything!

If an alien comes out of your toilet or tries it while you take a bath, kill it with fire. Or a hot curling iron :)

Pray to Stephen King the film you're about to enter isn't stuffed with racist and sexist tropes. Because you'd be screwed.

She was angry and hurt, not stupid. Flitting off into the middle of nowhere for a weekend? Someone had to know where to send the search party if something went wrong. Ryan seemed the most likely to believe a stranger-than-fiction disappearance.

(And the least likely to hold a grudge in an emergency.)

"What are you smiling at?" Takumi asked when she wandered into the kitchen to find him. They had made a fast-food run on the way there, but Takumi, in usual Takumi fashion, went without and was currently slicing a block of cheese.

She showed him the screen.

"You guys made up?"

"I don't think I was ever really fighting with Ryan. It's Feenie. We're pretty much wrecked. She refuses to talk to me." Alice shrugged. Misery loved a party, apparently. And decided to use Alice's existence to make all its dreams come true. "Do you think I'm being ungrateful?"

"About the school thing?"

"Yeah. Aisha keeps calling. I know that's what she's going to say."

He never told her what he thought she wanted to hear. She cherished that honesty, even if it hurt.

"I think *ungrateful* is the wrong word. I know you and I know you appreciate the gravity of what your parents are offering. You just don't want it. You don't have to accept something solely because it's free."

"I guess I am stupid then."

"I think you're smart enough to know what's best for you right now. Otherwise, why are you fighting so hard against a sure thing?"

"It's possible to be brave and stupid at the same time."

"Stupidity is relative and that's not how I see you. If that's how you feel, I can't make that better. If you want to keep talking about this in circles with me, I'm happy to do it for as long as you need, but I think we've reached the point where it's time for me to say that's really all I can do for you in this situation. Be here and listen."

That was it.

Alice poked him in the ribs, not even trying to hide her smile. He said the Perfect Thing. He didn't have any answers but he would be there until she figured it out. And then long after.

"Have a cracker."

She inhaled it in one smug bite. "You're so good to me. I'm gonna knit you a scarf."

"You can knit?"

"No, but I'd learn for you. You seem like the type to appreciate a good scarf in the dead of winter." Takumi handed her a square of cheddar. "Where are the grapes?"

"Cooler."

Turning around, she spotted the wine rack. Alice wasn't a drinker by nature, but the less-than-nurturing day had tipped her into curious country. She'd been hammered past the point of safety only once and as she clutched the communal dorm-room toilet bowl the morning after, she swore to never do it again.

But that was before. Besides, she only needed enough to get her to that sweet spot between being carefree and memory loss.

"Do you think your parents would mind if we borrowed a bottle?"

"Probably not." He looked over his shoulder at her. "But."

Too late. It was already in her hand. "This one looks good. Not that I know anything about wine."

"I don't know if you should drink."

"Why not? I've been drunk before. I even have a fake ID. Bottle opener?"

Takumi pointed to a drawer. A few twists later, the cork popped out with ease. She brought the bottle to her lips.

"Use a glass, heathen." He handed Alice a wineglass and pinched her cheek. "If you're going to drink a lot, please cut it with water."

She poured and raised her glass. *"Salud!"* The tart aftertaste would take some getting used to. "Takumi?" she asked, already feeling warm.

"No thanks."

"Oh, come on! Drink with me," she pleaded. "It's the next best thing to eating your feelings."

"I thought you didn't want to wallow?"

"We're not. This is," she said, pausing, looking at her glass, "this is prep for embracing the inevitable. See how totally mature I am?"

"Yeah. *Totally.*"

She scrunched her face at him, laughing before going to sit on one of the plush sofas. When Takumi joined her, he set down the tray of food and two bottles of water, and he had a guitar.

"Oh. My. God. Are you *that guy*?" He didn't seem to know what she was talking about. "You know, the guy at parties who pulls out his guitar and plays 'Wonderwall' or Dashboard Confessional songs? My brother told me all about it."

"How old is your brother? I don't think I've ever asked."

"Thirty-five. My sister just turned thirty-seven. I was an accident," Alice said. "That's what they used to call me, Accidental Alice." She snorted—he looked so offended. "Don't worry, it's all love. Anyway, so you're *the guy* who sings his sensitive heart out at parties to pick up girls. And just so you know, a party of two counts."

Takumi's half smile lit up Alice's whole heart. She had his full attention as she so often did.

"Seeing as how I already picked up *the girl*, I don't think that applies here."

It was not lost on Drunk Alice that she was *the girl*.

She was his girl.

The thought made the warm spot idling in her chest combust. She looked at Takumi, who looked at her, and she took a shuddering, steadying breath because she was far too drunk and the irrational thoughts wanted to lead her to that precarious place where *chance* was not synonymous with *worthwhile*.

"I'll play for you," Takumi said. "What do you want to hear?"

A severe case of drunken swoons hit Alice like a battering ram. Heart fluttering, stomach flipping, toes tingling—the works. Sweet Baby Jesus, did she have it bad. If she were two fewer drinks drunk, she would have been afraid, but such was the nature of liquid courage. She curved her hand around her glass, pressing it into her sternum. Eyes brightened by sincerity, she asked, "Do you know any Celine Dion songs?"

Takumi gently tugged on her ear. "Pick something else."

"What about the Backstreet Boys?"

"Let me guess: Your sister was a fan?"

"And me!" Alice said, taking another swig of wine and stretching out her legs. Her calves had begun to fall asleep. Leaning her swimming head on his shoulder seemed like a splendid idea. When she followed through, he didn't make her move. "I love my parents' music, too. Mary J. Blige; Whitney; Prince; Earth, Wind and Fire. Michael and Janet. Babyface—oh my God, 'Whip Appeal' is my jam. Don't even get me started on New Edition. Classics, the lot of them." She wiped her blurry, drunken eyes on Takumi's surprisingly soft cotton shirt and rested her chin on his shoulder. She poked his dimpled cheek. "Hi."

"You're very, very drunk." He was looking at her and she just *loved* it when he did that.

"I am," she admitted, sitting up. "I didn't plan on it. *It just happened.*" She snorted with laughter, nearly falling backward. Alcohol was quick, but he was quicker—his arm gripped her waist, pulling her upright and back toward him.

Takumi turned his head, whispering, "Careful." Once he was sure she wouldn't tip over again, he let her go. She took it upon herself to sit as close to his side as possible—part of the guitar touched her leg.

A familiar melody began to swirl around Alice. She placed her head on his shoulder again. Closing her eyes. Just for a second. To concentrate.

CHAPTER

30

*Y*ou talk in your sleep," Takumi said. "I've been meaning to tell you that."

Alice opened her other eye, groaning the smallest bit. "I do not."

Her tongue felt thick in her sticky mouth. That light-headed feeling persisted, spreading through her body as if cotton had been shoved into her veins. She'd been this drunk before, had fallen asleep and woken up only slightly less intoxicated. She had wobbled to her feet, stood on top of Margot's bed, and shouted, "My blood has been transformed! I'm a stuffed bear! Behold the power of wine!"

(Approximately no one knew what the hell she had meant.)

"You do so," Takumi objected. The guitar had vanished—the only sound in the room came from the crackling wood burning in the fireplace. "Who is Mr. Dimples?" To her mildly horrified look, he said, "That's what I thought."

"Did I say anything else?"

"Maybe." He smiled. "Probably."

"How did I get in the armchair?"

"I carried you so I could make the bed. I thought it'd be better to sleep out here on the sofa bed with the TV instead of in the bedroom."

He helped her stand and her knees buckled as the room spun.

"On the ground, on the ground," she said with urgency, folding herself in half to reach the floor faster. She crawled to her suitcase. "Stop laughing at me, you jerk."

"I'm laughing with you in case you don't hear yourself."

"I need to put on my pajamas."

"Do you want me to take you to the bathroom?"

"Why? I can change here," she said, casting a bleary-eyed glance over her shoulder. "I trust you." Without another thought, she pulled her dress over her head and slipped on her nightgown. She'd actually made an emergency trip to the store to buy a cute enough nightgown, not wanting to be seen in a ratty T-shirt and sweatpants. Her pride wouldn't allow it. Alice had seen plenty of girls who could pull off that *I just rolled out of bed* or the *I'm flawless in rags* look, but she was not one of them by a long shot.

When she turned back around, he stood on the opposite side of the room with his back to her.

"You can look now," she said. She shuffled on her knees toward the bed. He peeked over his shoulder before turning around completely.

"What's with the face?" Even Drunk Alice could tell how relieved he looked. She tried to haul herself onto the bed, stopping halfway and face-planting.

"What's wrong with my face?" He picked up her legs and placed them on the bed.

She rolled onto her back, and said, "Thank you for the boost, good sir. I require all your pillows for maximum comfort."

He leaned in close to her face, squinting. "You're lucky I like you."

She sighed. "I know. You smell all minty."

"Toothpaste."

"Just like Ron and Hermione," she mumbled.

Takumi chuckled, covering her with a blanket before crawling over her to his side of the bed and handing her all the pillows. He propped his head up on his elbow. "You know what else you do in your sleep?"

"Drool?" She lay on her side, holding one of the donated pillows to her chest.

"A little," he admitted, "but that's not what I'm talking about. You mumble-sing. I couldn't figure out what song it was, but when I asked, you told me to shut up because you were serenading me."

"You. Are. Lying." But *oh Jesus*, he might not have been. A fleeting memory of dreaming about singing while on a lake in a rowboat with him rattled in her brain. She buried her face in the empty bit of space between them.

He moved closer. The warmth of his body next to hers made her shiver when it shouldn't have. His words were a soft whisper near her ear. "It was lovely, albeit off-key. I almost recorded you."

"What stopped you?" She peeked up at him.

His fingers trailed over her shoulder. "I didn't want you to get mad."

"I wouldn't have gotten mad. Embarrassed as all get out, yeah, but not mad. I think I was dreaming."

"You dream about me?"

"I dream about everyone," she said. "One time, I was the captain of a spaceship and you were the AI interface that wouldn't stop sassing me in front of my crew."

They stared at each other. Alice blinked first, but her eyes didn't make it back to his. She focused on his smile, his lips, not wanting to kiss them; rather she wanted to touch them to see if they were as soft as they looked. The dangers of drunk-thinking could end in disaster.

Her hand was halfway to his mouth when he asked, "Do you want to watch a movie?"

He didn't wait for an answer, rolling away from her and off the bed. Like a sneaky cat, she usurped his spot and rolled onto her back. She breathed in and out, counting each breath while staring at the wooden beams overhead.

"What are you in the mood for?" he asked, remote in hand, already scrolling through the catalog.

Inhibitions gone, the truth spilled out of her mouth. "Romance."

"I actually don't like those kinds of movies."

"Really?" She gazed up at him, surprised. "Why?"

"Because they try to sell the idea of true love and forever. I think that's a really damaging idea. It doesn't work like that in real life. It's supposed to be fiction, but people rely on it and make it a standard to aspire to."

"People like me," she said without a hint of shame. She sat up, squeezing her eyes shut for a moment to get her bearings.

He gave her a funny look. "You like romance? In real life?"

"Of course I do. How do you not know this about me?"

Takumi laughed, turning away to look out the window for a moment. "I'm trying to figure something out and it's not making sense to me."

"Okay." She willed herself not to be nervous.

"Before, you said 'bisexual minus the sexual' but didn't add in a substitute. So if you don't care about sex, what do you care about?"

"Ah," she said, pleased by the question. She held out her hand—he took it and sat next to her. She interlocked their fingers before laying her head on his shoulder again. This time, he laid his on top of hers, fitting together like puzzle pieces. "Okay, so the way it works for me is I have to like the way someone looks physically, but then that's where it stops. At first. I think lots of people are cute in the same way as baby animals and Lisa Frank notebooks. It's pure aesthetic appreciation. Nothing sexual about it."

"That's a little confusing," he said. "I hear what you're saying, but I have to make an effort to see the disconnect."

"Do you want to have sex with every pretty girl you see? WAIT." Alice held up her hands. "No, don't answer that. I am certain no part of me wants to know the answer to that." She waited for him to finish laughing. She'd come this far, might as well bring it all the way home. "Okay, so, seriously. Say you see a guy and clearly he's good-looking. Like you can't stop yourself from staring at him because he's so beautiful. You just want to look at him until he says he's noticed all the staring and then you start worrying you're creeping him out. And then you feel terrible because he thinks you only like him for his face and really nice body that looks fabulous in clothes."

Takumi stared at her for a long moment before nodding. "Got it. And for the record, continuing with that thinly veiled hypothetical situation, the guy knows you like him for more than his looks now."

"Oh, thank God. I was starting to sweat." She laughed. "So that's how it starts—I'll think they're cute. And sometimes I'll keep thinking about them, about what it would be like to hold their hand or kiss them. And then I start hoping they'll ask me out on a date. That's when I know it's romantic. I get a serious crush on them, there's all of these intense feelings, and stuff."

"Ah, okay." He grinned at her—a lovely and understanding grin.

She wanted Takumi to be hers. Ryan believed that if God closed a door, He opened a window. Her parents had left her lost and reeling. Minutes later, Takumi had been there to lead her back. If that wasn't a sign, she didn't know what was.

"And for the record, I don't believe in true love either, but I think it's possible to feel like it could be real. That it's possible to share something that feels that way with someone."

The skeptical look on his face made her laugh without humor.

"And I think it's possible to feel that way more than once. Sometimes even with more than one person at a time. Feelings are messy and confusing. It takes me a god-awful long time to sort through mine and I don't always completely trust myself. Why not rely on fiction, fantasy, to help steer the way until you figure out what's real and what's not? It's better than being alone all the time."

"How does watching them make you feel less alone? Why would you want to watch something you don't have but want? Wouldn't that make things worse?" he said, sounding genuinely curious.

"I don't know." She laughed quietly to herself.

"Please don't pout." He rubbed her cheek with the backs of his fingers. "I wasn't trying to make you feel bad."

"I don't feel bad." Alice lifted her head, watched him for a moment, and lay back down to resume her watch of the ceiling. "Not really. I've just never gotten to have any of that stuff."

"Stuff like flowers and chocolate and expensive dinner dates?"

"And thoughtful gestures and spending time together and holding hands and slow dancing in the kitchen for no reason," she said, hoping he would catch her hint. "And I don't know, maybe a moonlit carriage ride every once in a while even though those are supposed to be surprisingly smelly."

"They're definitely overhyped."

"You've been on one?"

"Yeah. You're not missing anything."

"Ryan rented a horse-drawn carriage for part of Feenie's promposal. I almost died of jealousy."

"Ah, promposals. They seem ridiculous."

"Yeah," she agreed. "Says the girl who didn't get one."

"You didn't go to prom? That seems like a very un-Alice thing to do."

"No, I went." And spent more than half of it sitting alone. All of her friends had dates. She didn't want to intrude on their moments, so she sat outside on one of the massive balconies and watched the full moon.

"Did you have a good time?"

She nodded.

"Then that's all that matters, right?"

She didn't know how to explain that, yes, her friends had been great, but going alone wasn't in the plan. Every movie and show she had seen portrayed it as this big romantic event and she'd missed out on that because nobody asked her and she had been too afraid to ask anyone else. She wanted to wear her dress, get a corsage, and slow dance. It was stupid and archaic, but that didn't stop her from wanting it like burning. If she thought about it too much, she could still feel that crushing hope that grew each day while she waited to be asked and that pervasive fear stopping her from asking anyone.

So instead, she said, "Yeah. I guess you're right. Hey, where's my phone? I'll show you my dress. I looked *fabulous*."

"I took it from you after it rang and you tried to throw it across the room while half asleep." He leaned over and opened the drawer on the end table. "Aisha kept calling."

She took it from him—and it rang the moment she unlocked the screen. Deep breath, in and out. *Might as well*, she thought.

"Hey, Adam."

"Finally!" he yelled. "Jesus Christ, Alice. When I said figure something out, I didn't say pick something literally impossible for them to accept."

"Please don't yell at me, okay? I'm not exactly coping all that well."

"Have you been drinking?" The judgment in his voice was excruciating to hear. "What are you doing?"

Alice shrank even further. "About to watch a movie with a friend."

"What friend?"

"Why?" She clutched a pillow, pressing it into her torso. Talking to her brother usually made her feel better, not like she wanted to crawl into a hole and quietly wait for death to show up.

"Because you have two friends and you would have just said their names, so where are you?"

"I'm getting too old for the concerned older-brother act."

"I hate to be the one to inform you, but you will always be my baby sister and will never be too old for me to overstep."

"At least you haven't disowned me." Tears pricked at the corners of her eyes. Her parents. *Her parents.*

"You're not disowned." He sighed. "They're just . . . not happy."

"Daddy, too?"

"He's disappointed, for sure. He's been moping all afternoon."

"Alice, what about this one?" Takumi asked, voice lowered. A found-footage movie about a sea monster's first merry jaunt on land that nearly destroyed a city.

"Who the hell is that?" her brother shouted.

She brought the phone back to her ear. "Hmm?"

"You heard me. Who is that?"

"My friend."

"What kind of *friend*? Are you in his house?"

"Oh my God," she whisper-laughed, wiping her face. "Now is really not the time, yeah? Is Mom super murderous right now? If I called her—"

"Oh, yes it is," he said, cutting her off. "Why does he sound like a grown-ass man?"

"Because he is? I guess? I don't—"

"ALICE." Adam sputtered for a few moments. "Put him on the phone. Right now."

She shrugged as if he could see it. It's not like she wanted to keep talking about what happened earlier anyway.

(That's what real life was for.)

(This was a dream.)

(Clearly.)

"Takumi, my brother would like to talk to you."

"About?" He settled onto the bed.

"No clue."

"Okay." She handed Takumi the phone. "Hello?" Takumi paused, listening to Adam. "Yes—no—I don't think so." He glanced at her. "She does—no—I don't see how that's relevant."

"What is he saying?" she whispered. She leaned in closer to hear, but Takumi leaned back, shaking his head with a wry smile. He switched the phone to his other ear.

"At work, actually."

She poked him in the ribs. "Takumi. Tell me."

"We are not—not that I know of. I'm sure she would have mentioned it by now."

"Mentioned what?"

He placed his finger over her lips.

"Yes—I'll keep that in mind. Not that you could stop me if I wanted to, but I hear you."

Her eyebrows slapped her hairline. She grabbed his hand, pulling it to her chest. "Wanted to what?"

Takumi squeezed her hand. Smiling, he looked at Alice and said to her brother, "No. You really couldn't." He hung up the phone. "That was fun."

"What did he say? He didn't want to talk to me again?"

Takumi moved, suddenly, nearly nose to nose with Alice. Her stomach flipped, but she didn't move back. He laughed slightly, eyes brighter than they were a moment before.

"You're not going to tell me, are you?"

He fell to the side, his head landing half on Alice's shoulder, half on the back of the sofa. "Nope." He sat up and back before holding out his arms. "Movie time. Come on."

"No, thank you." She pouted, moving to the opposite side of the bed, their feet in the middle.

"Suit yourself."

She made it fifteen minutes before tapping his ankle with her foot. "Why are you so far away?"

CHAPTER

31

Feenie glowered in Alice's doorway.

"You're alive," Feenie said. Ryan must have told her about the cabin trip. "And here."

At least for another six months, hopefully.

"You didn't tell me to move out. So." Would they want her living with them after they tied the knot? She didn't know any married couples who weren't a part of her familial brood. On TV, newlyweds usually lived on their own, not with friends, or with family if they had a baby. Where would she live? Would her parents let her go home? "I'd appreciate a heads-up if you're planning on doing that."

"You know, I've really fucking had it with you." Feenie stepped into the room, boiling with fury.

Alice shrank back farther onto her bed. She wanted to tell Feenie to leave, to get out (to forgive her and be her best friend again). She wanted to get up, to go see Takumi (to kiss him and ask him to be with her). She wanted to call her dad, to make things right (to make them proud).

(She wanted to be anywhere, anyone else.)

But none of that was possible.

"It doesn't matter what I'm doing or who I'm with. If you need me, I'm there. I *always* make time for you. Always." Feenie loomed over her. "But lately? I'm a fucking afterthought for you. You have a problem? You call him. You want to go out? You call him. You say you're not dating, so that must mean he's your new best friend. I don't matter anymore, just like that." She snapped her fingers.

"That's not true. I always need you," Alice said, head down. Fighting back took energy. She was tapped out.

"To sort out your shit or defend your honor, maybe. That's how it feels—like you're using me."

Alice sucked in a breath like she'd just been punched in the stomach. "How can you say that?" she whispered.

"It is what it is."

"What about you and Ryan?" Her voice got stronger with each word, but she still couldn't meet her best friend's eyes. "You think you're always there for me, but you're not."

"I already told you," Feenie said, "I'm not apologizing for needing alone time with my boyfriend, and yeah, I expect you to understand that. I'm tired of feeling like I'm being replaced as payback for something that doesn't have anything to do with you."

"What about when you told me you wanted to move in with Ryan instead of living with me last year? That *really* hurt."

"Me and Ryan are in a relationship." She placed her hands on her hips. "We're getting married. We needed to start living together and an opportunity came up. Did you expect me to say no? *And* it worked out, didn't it? You live here now."

"That's not the point. *And* I do understand. I try to give you space. I can take a hint when you want to be alone. I'm not stupid. But Family Night is supposed to be for the three of us." Alice rubbed her fingers over her clammy palms, slid her fingernails from the heels of her hands as far up as they would go to calm herself. "Why is it okay for you two to go off on your own on those nights? The costume party was hardly the first time. I've really been thinking about it, and it feels like I was always just your cover story so your mom wouldn't get mad that you two spent so much time together and I've been too dumb to realize it should have ended when we graduated high school. You even changed your wedding date and didn't even tell me." She raised her head. "We're not a family. You two are."

Feenie went completely still—like the eye of a hurricane giving off a false sense of security before you're suddenly hit with 100 mph winds out of nowhere.

It wasn't supposed to be like this. They were both supposed to agree that maybe they were both a little wrong. They were supposed to hug. They were supposed to say they loved each other. Alice was not supposed to speak careless half thoughts. She didn't even *know* she had those feelings until she said them.

Feenie leaned forward, eyes locked on Alice.

"You listen to me, goddamn it," she seethed. "We're family. *You* are *my* family. We won't always get along and sometimes we will fight, but if you think for one goddamn second that means I don't love you, that I wouldn't die for you—" Feenie stopped herself from saying whatever would come next. Her body shook as she took a deep breath. "Jesus fuck, do you infuriate me to no end with that bullshit. How could *you* say that to me? There is nothing in this universe more important to me than you and Ryan." Her face turned bright red, her nostrils flared, her hands were clenched into fists.

Alice was not brave. Her body was hardwired for flight—confrontation made her flee. She had to stay focused, had to resist the urge to run away. She had to face this.

Her soft blanket twisted in her hands as she looked at Feenie. Eye to eye. "Because I'm an asshole," she said.

Feenie's fury flickered for the briefest of moments—her eyebrows drew together and she blinked in confusion. "So am I," she said, slow and thoughtful. "Welcome to the party."

"Yeah, but you own it," Alice said, jaw aching as she tried to force herself not to cry. "I'm an unintentional asshole, which is like the worst kind. I act like I'm a victim, like I'm always innocent, but really I'm a selfish asshole who only thinks about herself and what she wants. Someone always has to rescue me and I only know how to follow someone else's lead or go back to you because it's all I've ever done. I don't know *how* to balance the relationships in my life. I don't know how to show someone I love them. I don't know how to make someone understand me. I don't know how to do anything right.

"And look, here I go again, making everything about me," she sobbed. "Why am I like this?"

Feenie looked away, crossing her arms over her chest. "Stop." She left the room.

Alice's hiccupping gasps for breath were the only sounds left in the room. She swiped at her eyes with trembling hands.

"Here." Feenie held out a towel as she sat on the bed next to Alice. "Everyone makes everything about them. Don't cry about that. And the rest of it—well, yeah. I mean, I *knew* all of that. I choose to love you anyway.

"I'm really not much better, to be honest, but I'm not about to sit here and list all the shit wrong with me. What I will say is that I know I'm not easy to love. I know sometimes I say things that really hurt you because I think they're funny. I know we don't spend enough time together and that it's my fault, too."

Alice leaned over until her head reached Feenie's shoulder and took Feenie's hand in hers. Through everything life and time threw at them, they always had each other to hold on to. How many times had she held Feenie's hand in her life so far? It was a silly thing to wonder about—a hand that had been by her side for almost two decades. A hand she hoped would be there for much, much longer.

Feenie waited for Alice to finish crying before she said, "Being mad at you is too much work, but it's obvious we have . . . *communication* issues." Feenie said the word with a shudder. "I can't read your mind. If you're not okay with something, you need to tell me. It's," she began, face contorting into a grimace, "*important* to me that you trust me to be there for you like I've always been. That's my job. He can't have it. And I need you to be there for me. No one can calm me the way you do. Not even Ryan. You help keep me balanced."

How did Alice get so lucky? Because that's the word that came to her mind—*luck*.

Both Feenie and Takumi found her and wouldn't let go. Feenie gave just as freely as Takumi did, while Alice always took from them.

That's why Dr. B wanted her to spend some time alone. At first those hours had been excruciating. Being alone with her thoughts was not a fun time to be had. She thought about Takumi the most because the memories were fresh, but her lifetime with Feenie refused to be shoved to the side. Alice loved them both and hoped they knew it.

And then she worried they might not.

They did far more for her than she did for them, so she tried to think of all the ways she could repay them for being good to her. Dr. Burris had been surprisingly a bit less than thrilled with her conclusion because it wasn't about *repayment*. It was about balance.

She would be better.

"I've been seeing a counselor," Alice announced.

"Really?" Feenie kissed her forehead. "Good for you."

"Yeah. You kind of sound like him and he's usually right about stuff. So," Alice said, taking a trembling breath. "You know who would be really proud of you right now?"

"Tell Ryan about this and I will end you."

"I won't tell him." She raised her head at the exact moment Feenie looked down at her. "I really want us to grow old together, you know? Go through all the typical life stuff together even if that means we can only e-mail each other once a week because you moved to the middle of nowhere in Nebraska with your ten kids and I'm still in California because it's amazing. Just like in that one movie—we'll never lose touch with each other, ever. Is that weird?"

"No," Feenie said. "It's perfectly fucking normal."

AN HOUR LATER of filling each other in on what they'd missed during their cold war, Feenie's fury had returned.

"Are you fucking kidding me? Even Papa J? He's not talking to you?"

Alice shook her head.

"Okay, like real talk, I'd expect your mom to pull a stunt like this but *never* your dad," she said. "This is bullshit of the highest caliber."

"I have no idea what I'm going to do." Alice rolled onto her side in the small bed.

Feenie remained on her back, staring at the ceiling. "You could switch schools."

"To where?"

"Community college is super cheap compared to Bowen. You could finish your general ed there and when it's time to transfer back to a university, if your grades hold up, you can apply for academic scholarships. You also don't have to take a full course load. If you continue to work full-time, then half-time would be way less stressful on your bank account."

"Okay," Alice said, beginning to smile. "That was a really good on-the-spot answer."

Feenie gave her a half-hearted glare. "I *might* have been thinking about going back to school. *Maybe.*"

"*Maybe* we could take some classes together."

"That'd be nice. You could do my homework for me."

"You promised after graduation you wouldn't ask anymore."

"I know exactly what I said." Her mischievous grin was *everything.* "And that wasn't it."

Alice shook her head before jumping up and going to sit at her desk.

"What are you doing?"

"Research." She opened her laptop and grabbed some paper. "Do you know when classes start there?"

"Soon, I think." She fluffed a pillow. "Tired. Taking a nap. Wake me when you're done."

"Aye, aye, Captain, my Captain."

Alice pulled up the website for Cass Community College. On one side of the paper she listed out all the bills she had to pay (rent, her phone, Internet, bus pass, her share of the electric bill, Dr. Burris's fee, and groceries) and how much each one cost. Then she subtracted that from her average monthly wage.

CCC was cheaper than her university, but it wasn't inexpensive and she'd also have to pay for her books. She was under twenty-five and not legally emancipated, so she didn't qualify for financial aid—her parents made too much money. Tuition fee waivers were also out because they used parental income as well. Why did the government automatically assume parents would help their kids? She knew she had brought this on herself, but what about those who didn't? This was so unfair.

But she could apply for a financial-hardship scholarship that would cover up to six credits. The cutoff was in one week—she'd have to make time to write the essay—but there was no guarantee she would win.

If she lived on nothing but ramen for a month and used her paltry savings, she could afford to pay for nine credits upfront.

If she continued to work the afternoon/evening shift at the library, her mornings would be free for school.

If she took Takumi's sister-in-law up on her offer, she would get paid to babysit the twins every Sunday night.

Alice got up, chewing on her lip, continuing to run numbers and think while pacing from the kitchen to the balcony and back again. It would be hard, but she would make it.

She could do this.

CHAPTER
32

lice and Takumi were set up right in front of the library doors, sitting at a table with a bright blue banner, plenty of pens, key chains, and clipboards. Their task was easy enough: check in the registrants, find out what field interested the job seekers, and either have them a) fill out their info on a clipboard for library sciences or b) promote the upcoming career center the library planned to launch at the beginning of the New Year.

Truthfully, Alice couldn't care less about what she was supposed to do. It wasn't like the library was hiring. They had a maximum of six staff members at any given time. What she wanted was to practice her people skills. Greeting everyone, making eye contact, remembering names; doling out compliments was integral to her success.

She knew how to make a person feel like the universe revolved around them within seconds—her dad called it her charm magic.

In the future, when Alice graduated with the degree that would bring shame upon her family, when she got the job that was a perfect fit for her, this skill would come into play. She knew she was good with people. Knew how to charm them. Her future clients would adore her. And then recommend her to all their (wealthy) friends.

At the end of the day, she didn't even try to hide the proud bounce in her step and the song in her heart. This moment, after the last few weeks she'd had, was everything. She was triumphant. Success incarnated. Finally, she'd not only done something right, but excelled.

It felt *so* good to do something right.

(*Finally.*)

"It's Family Night," Alice told Takumi as they headed to his car. "I have to go home."

"I'm not jealous," he said. "Nope. Not at all."

"I think I'm rubbing off on you." She laughed. "Feenie will come around. Ryan's helping me wear her down. Before you know it, you'll be able to join us."

In the car they sang along to a pop song on the radio—one of the few artists they both liked.

He watched the road.

She watched him.

God, did Alice want to kiss him. She had always liked kisses, small ones here and there. She wanted to kiss his cheeks and temples and the tip of his nose and his jaw and below his ear and every other place he would let her. She wanted to kiss him like he was the darkest night sky and her lips had the power to make stars.

Alice had already sort of, kind of, maybe decided to confess. Tentatively. She had the plan and the words, but the courage had yet to get on board.

When Takumi pulled into her parking lot, Alice clutched the plastic bag she had carried all day.

(What was she doing?)

(Was she really about to do this?)

"I bought you something," she said, taking off her seat belt.

Takumi cut off the car, turning in his seat to face her. Waiting. She slid the bouquet of purple and blue carnations out of the bag and held it out for him.

"You're giving me flowers?" he said, taking them. His smile turned her kneecaps into jelly.

"Yes. Yes, I am."

"Okay." He laughed, seemingly tickled by her gesture. "Thank you, but why?"

"Because it seemed like a good idea at the time. I'd be lying if I said I wasn't seriously doubting Past Alice's judgment."

"They smell nice." He brought the bouquet close to his nose, breathing in. "You're the first person to ever give me flowers."

"Good." She breathed out. "Great." She breathed in. "I like being first. I always want to be first." She focused on the armrest in between them. "With you."

Five beats of silence later, Takumi asked, "Did you just say you want to be first with me?"

"I am really messing this up," she muttered. "So if you could help me help myself that would be amazing."

"Okay," he said. (The dashboard *sure* was interesting to look at.) "Are you trying to ask me out?"

"Yes. Yes, I am."

"On a date?"

"Also yes." She glanced at him. "Or we could skip that part since we hang out so much and jump straight into dating and kissing. If you want. If you're interested. Because I am, obviously."

"Why?"

"Oh, I don't know. I guess I just woke up and thought I should risk total and utter humiliation and potentially be scarred for life and never ask anyone out in the wild ever again because I really want to kiss your face more than I have common sense."

Regret hurt worse than she thought it would. It was a lot like stepping on an errant Lego piece with the instep of her foot. Sharp, brutal, and surprising enough to make you want to swear.

"So now would be a good time to say something," she said when he continued to be silent.

"I'm trying. I'm just"—he paused—"I'm a little floored here."

"I guess that means no." She bit her lip.

"No. I mean, I'm not saying *no*." More pausing. "I think I'm trying to say I need some time to think about this."

"About me?"

"Yeah. And about us being an *us*. How that would work."

"Oh. Okay. That's fair. I don't think it would be much different from how things are now."

Takumi blinked a few times in rapid succession, before exhaling with a tense smile. He ran his hands over the back of his head.

"It's just you've made your stance, I guess, pretty clear on things."

A nervous quiver began to build in the pit of Alice's stomach. "Oh. That." She lowered her head. Her fingers toyed with the collar of her shirt when really they wanted to curl into a fist and press against the pain in her chest. But she didn't want him to see.

"I remember what you said," he said softly. "I don't know if it's something I could give up." He closed his eyes, hands out in front of him as if he were reaching for the perfect combination of words to break her heart. Alice waited—wanting to hear it, wanting to run, wanting, wanting, always waiting and wanting. When he opened his eyes, he said, "I think about you all the time. If I'm not with you, I'm counting the seconds until I get to see you. I want to be with you, too, so I've been reading everything that I could, and I'm sorry, but I don't completely understand. I've been afraid to ask for help."

"It's simple." Alice shrugged. "My liking you doesn't make you an automatic exception to what I said."

"That's not what I'm asking to be. That's not what I'm saying. I want to understand. You like me, but you're not sexually attracted to me, but that doesn't necessarily have to mean you don't want to have sex with me, right? You could, but you don't want to because you don't care, is that right?" Takumi shook his head and exhaled in a huff. "I'm saying this wrong. I'm sorry. I'm sorry."

An eerie calm settled over Alice. Every time this happened, she felt her pain with bone-shattering clarity, but this time—nothing. There was nothing. A numbness, surreal but true, made her heart keep beating at a steady rhythm, kept her breathing even, and allowed her to look at him. She watched him fidget and struggle, unsure where to look, what to do with his hands. Was he shaking from nerves or from worry?

Neither of them believed in forever, but for now wasn't nearly long enough. Until he grew tired, until he moved on, until he left her because of something she had no control over. The thought of pretending, of faking her way through whatever kind of relationship he wanted, made her sick to her stomach. She had to be the one to leave him.

"I like you," she said, voice cold but strong. "A lot. More than I ever thought possible. You snuck into my heart and now you're punching holes in it."

"Alice—"

"It's fine. It's fine." She inhaled, nodding and staring out the windshield at nothing. "It was my mistake. I should've asked and not assumed that you'd be okay with me as is." She turned to him. "Let's just forget the whole thing, okay? Everything."

"I'm sorry."

Alice opened the car door—half in, half out, he touched her elbow. "You know I care about you, right?"

She tried to smile. "Good night, Takumi."

CHAPTER 33

Standing under the shower's healing stream, Alice rolled her neck, tried to massage away the knots forming in her shoulders. She placed her palms flat against the wall and pushed, trying to stretch the muscles in her arms.

Then she did something she never did—she squeezed her eyes shut, held her breath, and plunged her head under the water. She'd regret that tomorrow when the hair shrinkage set in.

But that's what later was for: worry. At that moment, all she wanted to concentrate on was the way her scalp prickled from the sudden heat.

She was not in the business of sadness. Most days, she ignored it like a pebble in her shoe. She resisted giving in to the chip on her shoulder. But when it knocked her backward and sat on her chest like a boulder, she had no choice other than to let it.

(She'd gotten pretty good at not letting people see.)

(Eating her body weight in pizza definitely helped.)

(And running water worked wonders in the soundproofing department.)

By the end of her shower, she had cried so much that she degenerated into a mouth-breathing monster. Her nose was a useless smudge on her face and her lungs ached something fierce. She had to take intermittent deep breaths when her chest quivered from exhaustion.

The TV droned on, Glory slept in her lap, but Alice didn't pay attention to either. Her mind, for the most part, remained blank, looping footage of static. Takumi had crawled into her soul, too, and she had to continue pretending that he hadn't. She was a bubble of raw emotion, a sleeping beast waiting for some dumb knight to come poke her. She didn't want to be rescued from her sorrow. This pain meant it had been genuine.

Her feelings for him were real.

But she wasn't a total masochist. She allowed herself to check her phone once per hour. She held it in her hand, closed her eyes, and took a deep breath. There was always at least one new message (that went unanswered) or a call (that went unreturned) from him.

Because he missed her.

(But one day soon, he would stop trying.)

When she opened her eyes, Takumi was temporarily shocked from her mind. She pressed the Callback button as soon as she saw the name.

"Dad?"

"Hey, baby girl." A tremendous amount of background noise filtered through. Somehow, she heard those three words with stunning clarity. "Let me go outside."

"What are you doing?"

"One of your mom's get-togethers. Your aunts and uncles, the neighbors, the usual," he said. A door closed. The line became quiet. "I left you a voice mail."

"Oh. I didn't listen to it. I just saw that I'd missed your call. You usually text me, so I thought it was urgent."

"Ah," her dad said. "No. I was talking to your aunt Carol and, uh,

I . . . I guess I just wanted to hear your voice. You know you're my heart, right?"

"Yeah," Alice said, voice cracking. Her entire face began to hurt from the effort it took not to cry.

(She cried anyway.)

"I'm sorry, Dad," she hiccupped.

He remained silent until she quieted down.

"I don't want you to apologize. The only thing I want you to do right now is listen." He sat down on their porch swing in the backyard—if her memory of the way it squeaked could be trusted. "We don't want you to be a lawyer because we want you to be like us. We want you to make a *difference*. Everything we have done and fought for has been for our children, to make sure they had every opportunity to succeed. We swore that every success would lead us down that path. No roadblock would permanently stop us because we would find a way around it. We were blessed with two children and God gave us one more much later than what was considered safe. The doctors told us the risks, but your mom was adamant: you would exist. You would be exceptional.

"Living in this world, in this country *is* hard. You don't know much about it because we chose to shelter you as long as we could. Black people have to be perfect, inhumanely good at everything, and even then we can fail, because that's the way the system is set up. It is *rigged* against *us*. The environment, the opportunities we created gave you a leg up so you wouldn't have to fight *as* hard. But we still expected you to fight."

She knew that and wasn't quite as sheltered as they thought.

Twitter, Tumblr, and even Facebook if she was willing to risk blind rage, kept her well-informed of what the world thought of her. She was Black, female, *and* queer. There weren't many spaces left for her to feel safe online, and the real world had just started to get its claws into her.

When she was stronger, braver, when she found her voice, she wouldn't hesitate to use it.

Change the system from the inside out—she knew that plan. Of course she would help, would fight, but law wouldn't be the best option for her to do that. How could she help anyone else if she felt helpless, too?

"Maybe it's our fault. We put too much pressure on Aisha. We know that. And Adam, he chose law on his own. We didn't have to do anything except encourage him. With you"—he paused, sighing—"I knew you didn't want the life we'd chosen for you, and your mom insisted that we give you time."

"Does she hate me?"

"Of course not. She could never," he said. "But she *is* upset. I don't know when she'll come around."

"Dad." Alice sniffled. "I just want to be happy. I'm not trying to be difficult or upset anyone. I love you and Mom and Aisha and Adam and Christy and the baby. I just—"

"—want to be happy. I know. I want that for you, too."

"I already enrolled in school," she said, jaw aching. She fought to keep her voice even. "I had to switch to the community college because it's cheaper, but I'm going to do it. I shouldn't have expected you to pay for me. I'm going to keep working at the library and I'm a babysitter now, too. I'm going to show you I can do this. You're going to be really proud of me again. I promise."

Nothing but silence came through from the other end until he said, "I won't pay for your schooling, but letting you struggle doesn't sit right with me. I can't throw parties to distract myself like your mom. I miss sleeping. And you know how I feel about my sleep."

She wanted to laugh but ended up pressing on her closed eyes before more tears could erupt. "I snore just like you, remember?"

(They were almost there. Almost normal.)

"As long as you're in school and learning and being happy, I will pay your rent and buy your groceries. Okay?"

"Dad, you don't have to."

"I know I don't *have* to. You're my daughter and I'm choosing to. What you don't know is I made the same arrangement with Aisha the first *and* second time she left."

Alice's jaw dropped. "She left *twice*? And she has the *nerve* to lecture me?"

"Don't tell your mom." He laughed.

It was such a *Dad* sound.

CHAPTER

34

"Maybe you should stay home today," Ryan said, leaning against the doorway of the bathroom. He waited for Alice to finish getting ready so he could drive her to work.

"Why?"

"This is fourth time you're reapplying your makeup. You can't even make it out the door."

"I shouldn't wear any, right? But I'm so puffy." She poked at her face. "Everything was good. Great. And then I *ruined* it. It's like I'm standing here and I can see what I want waving at me way over there, but I just can't get to it no matter how hard I try. Something is *always* in the way."

"I think that's called life."

"Don't get all philosophical on me," she said, giving him the stink eye. "I wish it felt like this stupid, small thing I could crush in my hand, but it doesn't. I wish it were some line in the sand that I could hop, skip, and jump over, but it's not. It matters to him enough that the only thing he could say to me was that he cares, which you know, comparatively, wasn't even that bad, but I can't stop crying, because I'm pretty sure my heart's breaking in there.

"A year ago, I would have said whatever. Sure. Yeah. Okay. But not now. Because I really, really like him, he knows everything, and he couldn't answer me, because it matters enough to make him pause. Just that one stupid, small thing."

"I'm calling in for you."

She placed her eyeliner on the sink and turned to him. "It's fine. It's fine. I'll ask Essie to make sure we don't work together today. I can volunteer to dust or something. She'll help me."

"What if he brings dinner?"

"Damn it, Ryan. I *just* fixed my eyeliner. Why would you say that?"

TAKUMI WAS LOOKING at her, but Alice kept her eyes forward.

(Yep.)

(Not today, Satan.)

"Were you going to hide back here all night?"

"I'm not hiding. I'm cleaning." Alice waved her duster at him and then at the neglected shelves in the reference section. "I'm prepping the encyclopedias for recycling and putting out whatever these are." She gestured to the full cart on her left.

(She was also crying.)

(She didn't point to the wastebasket full of tissues.)

"You didn't answer my calls," he said.

"I've been busy."

"Or texts." He put his hands in his pockets. "It only takes like thirty seconds to respond."

"It was the *not a second to spare* kind of busy."

"Fine. What about right now? I would really like to talk to you."

"I don't know. I mean, these dust bunnies are *massive*." She laughed despite the bitter taste in her mouth. "I think they require my full attention."

"I'm sorry about what I said the other night. I'm not perfect, but sometimes it really feels like you're expecting me to be. I know I messed up, but refusing to talk to me isn't fair. I'd never even heard of asexuality before I met you."

Alice turned so fast she got a crick in her neck. "Will you *hush*?" She clamped a hand over his mouth, pushing him back into a corner, and frantically searching the empty space for eavesdroppers. "Don't say that out loud. Ever. I'm a super-private person and I'm still very sensitive about people knowing. I'm working on it, okay?"

"But I didn't say *you* were," he whispered. "I said I'd never heard of it."

(He was right. He didn't.)

(Damn it.)

"Look." Alice face-palmed herself. "I know what you're doing, but I don't think we can be friends anymore. Maybe that makes me a shitty person. I'm coming to terms with the fact that I am indeed an asshole. I'm sorry, but I can't be your friend, because I like you too much and I enjoy not being in pain. So."

"That's what I thought." He nodded, pressing his lips together. "Even though you think you're an asshole, which I disagree with, that doesn't mean you're wrong. I don't think we can be friends either."

Alice could only look at his face in fleeting glances. As soon as their eyes connected, hers became desperate to look elsewhere. "Okay. Well. That's that, then."

"Except it's not." He grasped her wrist, rubbing his thumb gently over her pulse point. "I could say that I knew as soon as I saw you that I was doomed. I could say that I fell in love with you the morning after you fell asleep in my guest room and we got into a pillow fight when I tried to wake you up. I could say that when I was sick and you took care of me, almost asking you to marry me sounded like the greatest idea I'd ever had. I could say that every day I don't talk to you, I feel like I'm dying a slow, melodramatic death."

Alice stared at him, eyes wide, mouth agape. That kind of declaration was the bread and butter of romance movies, and it was for *her*. "Feel free to tell me all that again," she said, dumbstruck. "Slowly. And let me record it."

With his other hand, he held her waist, pulled her close, and kissed her. She forgot to close her eyes—the kiss ended before she had even registered it had happened. His hands slid down to her narrow hips, warming her skin through her clothes. He tilted his head, grazing her nose with his.

Before, her breathing had been shallow but inaudible, but it stopped completely as she watched him move toward her in that impossible moment. And then he stopped.

Inches away, eyes locked onto hers, he stopped moving. Alice pressed her lips together, anxious to get out of that frozen stance, but unsure of what to do. Didn't he want to kiss her again? She wanted him too. What was he waiting for?

Takumi subtly raised his eyebrows.

(A question for her?)

(Oh. *Oh.*)

Now was probably the wrong time to tease him, but . . . "You didn't ask first."

"I realized that. I'm sorry," he whispered back, words tickling her skin. "I'd like to kiss you again."

"I'd like that, too. Yeah."

Alice watched him until her eyelids fluttered, then closed. She kissed him with everything she had and borrowed what she didn't. He exhaled against her cheek. She buried her hands in his hair. He held her face in between his hands.

Blood pumped through her veins and arteries to an unyielding rhythm, chanting his name.

Her heart beat: *TakumiTakumiTakumi*

Her brain skipped: *TakumiTakumiTakumi*

She feared there would be nothing left of her after this kiss.

On the list of things Alice loved about Takumi, touching him was definitely in the top five. Resolutely she added kissing him to that list. Kisses were not supposed to be like this. They were nice and soft and made her feel warm inside, special, when done right, but were overly wet and vomit inducing when they weren't. Kisses had never left her with her chest heaving and desperate for more moments like this. She never wanted to stop. She never wanted this kiss to end.

(Maybe she just wanted it too much.)

(Was this even real?)

She wanted to kiss him, to hold him, to show him, to tell him everything she'd mess up if she tried to explain it in words. She wanted him to feel what she felt. She wanted him to understand that this was different, yes, that it could work, that it could be everything.

Takumi's face revealed nothing when he pulled back to breathe until he placed his forehead on hers, squeezing his eyes shut. It should have been impossible to see him clearly when he was so close, but she did.

"I figured you out pretty early," he said. "I think that's why I liked you so much right away. I never second-guessed myself with you, never got frustrated, never got angry. It's like I instinctively knew what to say, what to do. It was easy. And I don't mean you didn't surprise me or I was bored. It was just . . . everything felt *right*."

"Alice?" Essie called.

Alice leapt out of Takumi's arms, darting back to the shelf where she had left the books and duster. She cleared her throat, pressing her hand to her chest. Her heart thundered under her palm.

"There you are." Essie rounded the corner, coming to a stop with her hands on her hips. "Have you seen Takumi?"

"Ah . . ." Alice looked around—he wasn't behind her. "No. I'm back here by myself."

"Where the hell is he then?"

"Basement, maybe?"

"No. I just came from there. If you see him, tell him to come find me."

"Sure. Will do. Absolutely."

"Are you okay?" Essie asked, narrowing her eyes. "You seem jumpy."

"Too much coffee. My heart is having a field day. Honestly, I'm kinda scared of what's happening in there."

"Hmm. Okay. As soon as you see him," Essie reminded her.

Alice waited until she couldn't see Essie anymore, counted to ten, and then walked back to the corner. "Takumi?" she whispered.

Arms wrapped around her from behind, making her giggle. "Sorry," Alice said, turning around. "Back hugs do things to me."

Takumi's eyes searched her face. He was close enough to kiss her, but a distant look in his eyes had formed in her brief absence.

"So," she began, feeling confused. He hadn't let go of her waist, but that *look*. "You were in the middle of saying some very nice things?"

Takumi's sad smile knocked the wind out of her. Silently, he took her hand and led her to the very back corner of the reference section. He turned, leaning against the wall—she mimicked his body language, conscious of the fact that she was on the outside and he hadn't let go of her hand.

"I already apologized, but I want to do it again, because I truly am sorry that I said what I did. I was too flustered to think properly and instead of taking the time to think like I knew I should have, I tried to answer you right away. I know what I want to say now." His shoulders slumped as he exhaled and he began to tap his thumb against his thigh. "I want to be honest. The last thing I want to do is hurt you again and what I have to say might do that, so if you don't want me to say it, I won't."

"I know I tend to make things about me when maybe they shouldn't be, at least not completely. I'm working on not doing that." Alice emptied her lungs to center herself and stood up straight. "I want to hear what you have to say."

"I'm not asexual," he said immediately.

"I know that." She managed to not roll her eyes.

"Do you? I never said I wasn't and I think I need to because I'm not," he said. "It took me awhile but I think I figured it out. The reason why I hesitated wasn't because of sex itself. You were spot on before. Sex is like jogging. Either you enjoy doing it or you don't. To me, and this is just me, it's the *feeling* that I care about—what sex is supposed to represent."

"And that's what to you?"

"If you felt the same way as I feel about you, you would want to have sex with me."

(Father God . . . did she time-travel and land in a parallel universe?)

Alice kept her eyes stretched wide, because if she blinked it would be all over. She'd feel that tear on her cheek and lose all her control. How many times would she be forced to live through this conversation?

"You would think of me as someone worthy of your passion and desire, and you would show me how you feel physically. Not just with words but with action and urgency," he continued, "but you don't and for the most part, I understand. That's not a part of who you are and I know that doesn't mean that you don't have other feelings for me."

"Because I do! Lots and lots of feelings." She pointed to the spot above her heart. "It's like a volcano in there. I'd put Mount Vesuvius to shame."

Takumi covered his mouth with his fist. "Please don't make me laugh."

"I'm serious!"

"I know you are, but the thing is, that feeling that you can't give me? It's important to me. And I can't apologize for feeling that way or for wanting it."

"Okay. That's fair," she said, voice tight. Her thoughts whirled with certainty. "I don't want you to apologize. That would be like me saying I'm sorry I'm ace when I'm not. We are the way we are and we're just not compatible in that way."

"You know, now that you've mentioned it, you really do assume a lot." He ran his hands through his hair, sighing. "This morning it finally clicked. I was thinking of sex, actually having sex, as the Holy Grail, and when I got frustrated, I tried to look at it from a different point of view and I realized something else.

"No one has ever complimented me as much as you do. Every day. All day. I could show up wearing a burlap sack and a tinfoil hat and you'd probably tell me how avant-garde and handsome I looked. You genuinely listen to what I have to say and value my opinion. You tell me I'm wonderful and talented and amazing—"

Alice didn't mean to laugh—it bubbled out of her before she could stop it. She tilted her head to the side, looked at him, and said, "Because you are."

"When you thought I didn't want you, you started to cry," he said. Alice tried to memorize the gentle look in his eyes as he spoke. "I watched you lower your head, clutch the front of your shirt, and try to smile because you didn't want me to see how much what I was saying hurt you, because you do desire me. You wanted me so much that me saying no caused you actual pain. The thought of me only caring about not being able to have sex with you hurt because you thought I knew how much you wanted me."

"For the record, I didn't cry in the car. I cried in the shower."

"It was still because of me." He raised their joined hands and kissed the backs of hers. "It's the same thing. Whether you're so overwhelmed you can't keep your hands off me or you're crying because you think I don't want you, it's the same thing. It comes from the same place. That's desire. That's passion. You've never held back how you feel about me. "

"Thank you," she whispered, wiping away a rogue tear. She hadn't realized she'd been waiting for someone, anyone, to say that to her. She *knew* it was true, of course, but sometimes hearing it out loud made all the difference in the world. "For saying that. Thank you."

"It's the truth." He wiped away another of her traitorous tears with his thumb. "If we take away everything—there's just you and me, nothing else, I see us together. Stripped down to the core, being with you is what I want because I'm in love with you. If we never had sex, I would still want to be with you because you're in my heart, too. Just laughing, dancing, and twirling in circles, and I know that sounds weird as hell, but you are. And it's important to me that you know that."

Alice made sure she understood every single word and syllable, tried to read between the lines, ensure she wasn't confused in any way. When she reached up and he didn't move, she cradled his face in her hands. "Can I kiss you?"

He nodded and she kissed him in all the places she had wanted to. Featherlight kisses, her lips brushing across his skin. Takumi closed his eyes, letting Alice have her way. She kissed his eyelids, one after the other, the bridge of his nose, the ridge of his forehead, his temples and cheeks and chin, and saved his lips for last.

She became a chaotic mess of wants and needs and desires, both hers and his. Feelings shot through her too fast to grasp. She couldn't sort, couldn't sift through them to analyze what was happening, how she felt as Takumi kissed and touched her. The moment had captured her.

He rubbed his nose against her temple. "Your hair smells nice. Like coconuts."

"I use coconut oil for maximum moisture retention and to make it shiny."

Takumi laughed. He gazed at Alice with a smile that made her heart forget how to beat. "What am I going to do with you?"

"You know, I'm thinking that that was an excellent question. And we should talk about that. I don't want to have sex, but I like other . . . stuff."

He turned his head, pressing kisses into her palm and up the lines of her fingers. "I wasn't talking about that."

"I know. But I'd like to talk about it," she said. "Cuddling, snuggling, hugging, kissing, and touching. All of that is great."

"Like this?" He held her close, nuzzling her skin, tickling her sides, making her giggle and squirm.

(In the library.)

(Because what was shame?)

"Yep, that's the stuff." She buried her face in the crook of his neck, leaving a kiss in the hollow of his throat. "I think I'm overheating from the squee."

"Squee?"

"You know," she said, pulling back and fanning her face, "that feeling you get when you're really happy and it's building in your chest, but you can't find the right words so you just make incoherent noises."

"Ah, that squee. What was I thinking?"

"There's more stuff that I like, but I want to wait to tell you the rest. Okay?"

"Okay."

"Really okay?" She stroked the side of his face, from hairline to chin, taking a moment to *finally* touch his bottom lip. "And, um, what about you? I mean, it's okay?"

Takumi scrunched his face into a frown. "I'm so emotionally drained, all I want to do is take a nap. Preferably with you. It's something that we need to talk about, but not right now." He dropped his head to her shoulder and kissed her neck. "Please." A kiss on her jaw. "Later." A kiss on the corner of her mouth. "Later."

As much as she enjoyed the tiny kisses, she pulled back and shook her head. "Now, please. I'd like to know."

"What do you want me to say?" he said, voice close to an uncomfortable groan. "That, yes, I want to have sex with you? That isn't going to go away."

"So it would make you happy if we had sex?"

"I'm happy now."

"Fine. You'd be happier, then?"

"Alice, we've been dating for five minutes. We have plenty of time to figure out what's best for us."

(DATING.)

"Being in a relationship takes actual effort to be successful," he said. "Not just talking, but listening, being honest, respecting each other, and compromise, you know, those kinds of things. That's why people say make sure to marry your best friend because once the honeymoon is over? Nothing will save you if the foundation is shitty. But us? Me and you? We don't have anything to worry about. We got this."

"Okay." She breathed. "Okay. I think that's it."

"It?"

"Yes. Yeah." She kissed him.

It wasn't the Perfect Thing, but it was real and honest and damn it, she'd take that any day.

EPILOGUE

Surprise!" Alice shouted as Takumi walked through the door.

"How is this a surprise? You're alone. I gave you a key. We agreed we'd meet here."

She twirled around him in a circle with a basket in her hand.

"Please stop throwing rose petals at me." He laughed.

"Well, excuse me for being festive," she said, coming to a stop in front of him with her hands on her hips. "And I am not throwing. I am *showering* you with a stereotypical representation of my affections." She scrunched her nose and stood on her tiptoes. "Happy anniversary."

He kissed her quickly and wrapped her in a hug. "We're still doing this every month? I thought six was the big one for you?"

"Yes, until we hit one year, and then I'll stop being quite so extra. Not a lot though. Just a little. No promises."

It had been seven glorious months.

(SEVEN.)

"Deal. Would you be upset if we had takeout?"

"Takeout?" She clutched her pearls. *"You?"*

"I don't think I'm up for cooking." He kissed one cheek. "Thinking of going to a restaurant makes me want to take a nap." He kissed the other.

She placed a hand on his forehead. "Who are you and what have you done with my Takumi?"

"I worked twelve hours three days in a row. I'm tired."

"The school festival slash play thing was a success?"

"Seemed like it. The parents were . . . interesting." He took a step back, looking at her. "You look nice. Wholesome."

She twirled again. She had chosen a fifties aesthetic.

(Polka-dot dress, fluffy curls in her hair, pearls, and high heels.)

(All the aesthetics of the decade minus the margarine.)

(Because it was disgusting.)

"Were you able to get Friday off?"

"Uh, about that . . ."

"Feenie's going to murder you." She shook her head. "You finally make it into her good graces and now this."

Getting Feenie and Takumi in the same room had taken weeks of machinations and failed attempts. Everything had finally come together on Thanksgiving. Takumi had volunteered to cook, Feenie refused to acknowledge his presence, but right before grabbing a third helping of his macaroni and cheese, she had looked at him, and said, "You hurt Alice, I hurt you. Are we clear? And pass the cranberry sauce. Please."

(Alice had nearly fainted when she got her wedding invitation. It had been addressed to her *and* Takumi.)

"It's just the rehearsal dinner," Takumi said. "Am I really going to miss much? And why is it at noon anyway?"

"Because that night we have plans."

He eyed her. "Plans that don't involve me or Ryan. We're nervous. Extremely so."

"It'll be fine. What's the worst that could happen?"

"You both get arrested and charged with felonies?"

Alice thought about it. "That's actually a solid possibility considering where we're going. But I'm sure everything will be fine. Super fine." She wrapped her arms around his back, tilting her head. "My clean criminal record and I will see you bright and early at the church."

"I'm going to take a shower." Takumi kissed her again before leaving. She could kiss his mouth forever and never get tired.

"I'll order dinner," she told him. "And pick up the rose petals. I guess."

"Leave them!" Takumi called from the room.

After ordering a copious amount of Indian food Alice sat on the couch to wait for him. True to his word, he had let her help decorate his shiny new apartment. They had shopped together over the course of a weekend and through several different stores—he had told her no more than yes—because he waited an excruciatingly long time to tell her he didn't like her idea for dark colors. He had wanted cheery. "Think commercial American Easter minus the hot pink," he had said.

They had lucked out and found a futon in the exact shade he had wanted: a vibrant blue, which became the base color. They spent the following weekend with the twins painting the rest of the wooden furniture to match. He agreed to accent with delicate lavenders, soft yellows, a sweet shade of pale green (to be used *sparingly*), and eggshell white. The best part was the frameless color photos—he wasn't allowed to paint the walls, so they agreed pictures were the next best thing. Some were of family and friends, but the majority were the seemingly hundreds of landscape photos he had taken over the years, but never quite knew what to do with.

She loved being in his apartment. The overall effect was a soothing one—it felt like Takumi.

He had just gotten out of the shower when her phone rang. "Hello," she answered.

"Hi, baby, it's your mom."

"Yes, I know," she said, amused.

"I'm just calling to tell you to check your e-mail. I bought your plane ticket vouchers. The confirmation should be there."

She watched Takumi answer the door and pay for dinner. He stared at her in disbelief when he saw the size of the take-out box, needing both arms to hold it.

(It was cute how the amount of food she could and wanted to eat still surprised him.)

"You bought two, right?" she asked her mom. That was her belated Christmas present—plane tickets. She had asked for two vouchers to use sometime in the future.

"Adam says someone named Takumi is coming with you for the baby's christening?"

ADAM. "That someone is my boyfriend." Takumi glanced at her as he set the box down on the coffee table. "He's looking forward to meeting you."

"And when were you planning to tell me about your little friend?"

"*Boyfriend.* And right now, since Adam can't keep his mouth shut," she joked.

"That's not funny."

"I know. I'm sorry. I'm kind of busy right now. Can I call you tomorrow?"

"You're going to call me? Wow. What an honor."

"Now that's not funny. I love you."

"Love you, too."

"Your dad?" Takumi asked when she hung up.

"Mom."

"Everything okay?"

"Yep. *Takumi Meets the Johnson Family* is officially confirmed." Things still weren't totally back to normal with her parents, but they were getting there. "I picked a movie."

"Start it. I'll get the plates."

Halfway through the movie Alice turned to him, and said, "Fun fact: the only thing the rooms in this spooktastic hotel have in common is the wallpaper. It takes a minute to notice on screen, but it's always the same. If I were the designer, I would have picked something more symbolic than glorified art deco. It becomes super distracting and pulls you right out of the movie."

"You're pretty when you're petty."

"You only said that because it rhymed."

"Just because you're right doesn't mean I'm wrong."

"Look, either write a children's book or cut it out." She laughed. "Here. Happy anniversary. Again."

"We agreed no presents this time," he said, taking her hastily wrapped gift.

"I know, but technically this one is old and overdue. Open it, please?"

He unwrapped the dark green scarf she had struggled to make. Turns out, knitting wasn't as easy as YouTube tutorials made it seem. She thought the color went well with his newly dyed hair—a rich auburn that took some getting used to (she may or may not have screamed when she saw it), but it made his brown eyes even more extraordinary.

"There are a few gaps where I messed up. But if you wear it like this"—she took it from Takumi, looping it around his neck and tucking it into a half bow—"you can't see them."

"You made this? When?"

"In between classes. Sometimes in class if I could get away with it.

I wanted you to be surprised." She showed him the tag she'd made with the date, their names, and the scarf's number. "This was attempt number six."

"What did you do with the other five?"

"Gave them to Glory to play with. I didn't want to feel like I'd wasted the yarn."

"Thank you. I love it." He tucked in his chin and held the scarf up to his nose. "It smells like you." He wrapped his arm around her and she all but jumped into the embrace to hug him.

After they'd eaten dinner and finished their movie, and after they had their moment, when the apartment was quiet and the lights were off, after Takumi told Alice he loved her seven times, and right when Alice had run out of things to tell him to keep him awake, she said, "This was a good anniversary. I mean, sure it wasn't a red-eye flight to Tanzania so we could hike up Mount Kilimanjaro or whatever extreme sporty thing tickles your fancy—"

"You're never going to let me live that down, are you?"

"I'm still trying to figure out what possessed you to take me to an underwater hotel. There were sharks, Takumi."

"It was an amazing deal. How was I supposed to pass it up? And of course I wanted to go with you." He yawned. "I thought it'd be fun."

"Do you even know me?" She snuggled closer to him, trying to absorb some of his sleepiness. She was wide-awake for some reason.

"I know you make me happy," he said, seconds away from falling asleep. "I know you love me."

"I know you love me, too."

ACKNOWLEDGMENTS

If you're like me, this is one of your favorite parts of a book. Nine times out of ten, you flip to the back and read the acknowledgments first. And one time out of ten, the acknowledgments are in the front of the book, so no flipping required. I find it hilarious that even though this is my favorite part, I'm struggling to write it.

I'm a very private person. I'm two sleeps and a panic attack away from becoming a full-on hermit. You won't catch me in the social-media streets for a reason. It's hard for me to express my overwhelming gratitude in such a public place the way that I'd like to—with inside jokes and obscure references and nicknames and copious amounts of swearing, but I'm going to try. Sans swearing.

Thank you—

Jean Feiwel, Lauren Scobell, the entire Swoon Reads team and community: the Swoon Reads website changed my life. My creative birthday is January 1, 2014. That was the day I sat down and began to write my first manuscript. Almost twelve months later, I submitted a different manuscript to Swoon Reads. That one wasn't chosen. Fast forward six months, I submitted another manuscript. That one wasn't chosen either. Turns out, the third time really was the charm. However, by that point, I had learned so much about publishing and craft, had made so many like-minded critique partners/writing friends because of Swoon Reads, that even if my manuscript hadn't been chosen for publication, I knew it would have only been a matter of time (and persistence) before I would have succeeded elsewhere. Your innovative approach to crowdsourced publishing gave, and continues to give, countless writers the tools, support, insight, and resilience needed to make our publishing dreams come true. Long may you reign.

Kat Brzozowski: I was a panicky, indecisive, and ridiculous red panda-like creature the entire editing process. You were always an email *and* phone call away to brainstorm *and* cheer me on with flair *and* awesomeness. I owe you cupcakes. A copious amount of cupcakes. Or cookies. Do you like cookies? Cookies. Because food. Of course.

Anna S: This book wouldn't exist without you. I was flailing around with a song in my heart and a dream in my head, when you said, "LET'S SUBMIT." I said, "YES" and went on to create the bones for *Let's Talk About Love*. It's been an intense ride from start to finish, and no one person was there for me more than you. . . . And remember, we didn't choose the salt life, the salt life chose us.

Sarah: Your boundless optimism and unwavering faith consistently keep me afloat. I will always be your Feenie, from here to the end of time. Also, thanks for checking in on me to make sure I'm not dead!

Macy: My snail-in-arms, my favorite goldfish, my mentor of meaningless inception. One day we will swim in pennies like Scrooge McDuck.

Queen Tuna: It totally helps me concentrate when you drape yourself over my feet while I write for hours and sometimes days at a time. You're my girl, the best cat ever—now stop waking me up at 5 am! I need to sleep!

Melissa, Grace, Kathy, Vera, and Christy: You all were the first friends I made when I joined Swoon Reads. We laughed, we commiserated and had epic gif parties. You made the dark days brighter.

SHINee: I found you while I was suffering through one of the greatest depressions of my life. I've said before that 2016 tried to eat me alive, but you were one of the reasons I made it out. Sometimes holding on to small, precious moments of happiness were all I had while I tried to just make it through life, one day, one hour at a time. I have no shame in admitting you gave me many of those moments.

Authors on YouTube: You might have noticed a serious uptick in views on your videos from 2008 and beyond. That was me. All of them. While editing, I would add your videos to my music playlist to keep me inspired and motivated. I'm so glad you all didn't make those videos private (but I totally understand if you do because I'm about to name drop), Kiera Cass, Susan Dennard, Victoria Schwab, and Temple West.

Tumblr ace community, Wattpad readers, and sensitivity readers: You helped shape this book into its final form, helped me learn more about myself and confront my own internalized biases. It wasn't always fun, but it was 100 percent worth it. 10/10 would do again.

Teasha, Mikee, Dad, Allie, Nikkiee, the Wiggins/Martinez family and my professors in college: I'm a very lucky person. No one has ever laughed at me, told me I couldn't be a writer or that I was wasting my time. I have received nothing but support from you all, which I know is not the norm.

And finally, my mom: I cried when you called me after reading *Exchanged* to tell me how much you loved it and Cinni, gushing about all of your favorite parts, and again when you did the same for FGM. You made me a vision board. You group message all five generations whenever something good happens to me. You pray for me every day. You give me so much even though you have so much less. A cottage with an east and west wing awaits us. I love you.

It's highly likely that I missed someone so let me just throw out a catchall—

Insert your name here: you were the best, the most fantabulous, and inspired me in all the ways that count.

Until next time,

Claire <3

Check out more books chosen for publication by readers like you.

DID YOU KNOW...

this book was picked by readers like you?

Join our book-obsessed community and help us discover awesome new writing talent.

1

Write it.
Share your original YA manuscript.

2

Read it.
Discover bright new bookish talent.

3

Share it.
Discuss, rate, and share your faves.

4

Love it.
Help us publish the books you love.

Share your own manuscript or dive between the pages at **swoonreads.com**